Totally Bound Publishing books by K.E. Turner

The Wolves of Langeais
Wolf's Keep

I0652140

The Wolves of Langeais

WOLF'S KEEP

K.E. TURNER

Wolf's Keep
ISBN # 978-1-80250-551-1
©Copyright K.E. Turner 2023
Cover Art by Erin Dameron-Hill ©Copyright July 2023
Interior text design by Claire Siemaszkiewicz
Totally Bound Publishing

WOLF'S KEEP

Dedication

To Mark.
I crossed the entire country to be with you.
Love you, Babe.

Acknowledgements

Thank you to the wonderful team at Totally Bound Publishing for taking a chance on me and my story. To my editor, Nicki Richards, your patient guidance and encouragement have helped me so much. I promise to do better with my commas, and I'm sorry if you now have a few — or maybe a lot of — gray hairs with my name on them.

To my cover designer, Erin Dameron-Hill, thank you for the amazing cover you created for me. It's better than I imagined it could be, even down to the expression on Gaharet's face. It's perfect.

To my beta readers and fellow authors — Rose de Bruin, Dani Mclean, D.D.Line and Victoria Brown, for your time, your advice and your ongoing support.

And finally, to my family and friends for never not believing that I could get my book published. To Anna and Annette for reading my abominable first draft and assuring me I had something. To my dad, for reading my story and liking it despite 'all the romantic bits' which aren't your thing.

Author's Note

Dear Reader,

When I encounter foreign words I do not know the meaning of in a book, it causes me to pause each time I see them in the text, taking me out of the story. Here is a brief list of foreign words and meanings I have used in this book.

Anglo Saxonne: English
Archeveque: Archbishop
Bretaigne: Britannia/Brittany/Britain
Chevalier: knight
Comte: Count
Comtesse: Countess
Franceis: French
L'enfer: hell
Ma Dame: My Lady
Ma petite pouliche: my little filly
Mademoiselle: Miss
Merde: Fuck/shit
Mon Dieu: My God
Mon Seigneur: My Lord
Mon Seigneur Comte: My Lord Count
Monsieur: Sir
Sacre bleu: Damn it
Votre Grace: Your Grace

Langeais Keep and Langeais are real places. However, they have been used in a fictitious manner. There isn't, and has never been thought to be, an underground cell in the ruins of Langeais Keep. There were many Comtes de Anjou over the centuries (none named Lothair that I am aware of). One of them built Langeais Keep to guard the crossing point of the Loire River. His power base was in Tours, and the keep was just one stronghold for him. My Comte Lothair is a fictitious Comte de Anjou created from a compilation of many counts of that era.

I know always that I am an outsider; a stranger in this century and among those who are still men.
~ HP Lovecraft, The Outsider

Chapter One

Langeais, France
May 2016

Everything about Gaharet d'Louncrais spoke of arrogance, power and sex. The confident tilt of his bearded chin, the hint of a smirk on his lips and those dark, intense eyes making all sorts of heated promises. Not to mention the whole tall, dark and handsome thing he had going on. The man oozed masculinity from every pore.

Erin Richardson gave an exasperated sigh, raking her hair off her face. She'd become obsessed. This job had burrowed under her skin more than any other excavation, working its way deep into her psyche and manifesting in erotic dreams where she awakened in a tangle of sheets, achy and wanting.

Oh, for crying out loud. They were here searching for clues to the man's demise. Hoping for the ultimate discovery of his bones. Fantasizing over the long dead, tenth-century French knight, a chevalier, was the epitome of foolishness.

Erin scowled at the sketch on her clipboard. No longer only in her dreams, she'd succumbed to the urge to draw him. Driven by the need to get him out of her head and onto paper. She'd taken all she'd gleaned about him from documented descriptions, added a touch of her own artistic flair, and rendered him in full Faber-Castell color. Now her creation stared back at her, sword in hand, muscular shoulders covered in chain mail under a blood red surcoat, and a howling black wolf—the d'Louncrais family's crest—emblazoned over his heart. He was magnificent.

I've lost the plot.

Shaking her head, she tucked the clipboard under her arm and headed up the hill to the ruins of Langeais Keep. Below, beyond the rooftops of Langeais, the Loire River snaked through the valley. The smell of baked goods and ground coffee hung over the village as afternoon shadows darkened and the cooler evening air began to seep in. Behind her, the manicured gardens of the fifteenth-century Château de Langeais slowly emptied of tourists who'd streamed through during the day—exploring, taking photos, buying souvenirs. Up here, cordoned off from the public, members of the excavation field team worked undisturbed by lingering sightseers.

She nodded to the security guard and picked her way amongst the crumbling remnants of the tenth-century keep. One full wall of rough, pale stone remained, another partially intact, and a few foundations jutted up out of the ground. Stepping over string grid lines that marked the site, she approached the gaping hole in the ground, pausing on the edge. She shivered. No matter how many times she stood at the entrance, the sight never lost its impact. A narrow, almost vertical, stone stairwell disappeared into the earth, chiseled into rock, lit up by bright lights strung at intervals along the rough stone walls. They could have enough lights in there to outshine the sun, and the sight would still give her the chills.

"Takes your breath away each time, doesn't it?"

Erin started, catching sight of their intern, hunched over, bagging and tagging a heavily corroded piece of iron.

"Yeah, it does. How's it going with the grate?"

"Good, I've found a few pieces so far. Buried deep, but I'm surprised no one found it on the original dig."

Erin shook her head. "Not much of a surprise, really. This is one of the earliest examples of stone keeps. Cells below ground weren't common until the eleventh century, a few years too late for this place." Or so they'd thought.

Taking a deep breath, she began her descent. Two steps down, her phone rang. She puffed out an impatient breath. Juggling her clipboard, her coffee and a bag of chocolate croissants, she pulled her phone from her pocket and glanced at the screen. Her heart sank. Her mother. *Why the hell is she calling now?* They hadn't spoken for over a year. Their last conversation hadn't gone so well.

She let the call go unanswered. Her phone dinged. A text came through and she rolled her eyes.

Call me. I've met someone.

"I bet you have," Erin muttered. Drop-dead gorgeous with bucket loads of charisma and heaps of money, no doubt. Swept her off her feet just like every other man her mother had dated. She grunted. Her mother gravitated to a certain type. Good-looking, confident, suave and usually with either a high-profile job or a high-ranking position, like a media personality or a CEO. Men that had the world at their feet and they knew it. Men that had a never-ending supply of women to choose from, her mother just one of many in a long line of others. That her mother didn't look her age never failed to draw them in.

Ding. Another text.

I think this time it's going to last.

Erin shook her head. Her mother never learned. Erin shoved her phone back into her pocket and descended the steps. She was done being a commiserating shoulder for her mother to cry on. She had work to do.

Reaching the bottom, Erin stepped out into the room — a cramped and airless space, the walls rough, cold and damp. Fluorescent lights cast eerie, elongated shadows across the uneven floor. It couldn't have fit too many prisoners in here. According to their research, it had only ever held one. His bones, partially excavated, lay in the middle of the room.

Greg, lead archaeologist and site supervisor, crouched beside the skeleton, packing away his brushes and tools. Connor worked against the back wall, gathering up labeled airtight bags to be delivered to the lab. They'd spent weeks removing a ton of dirt and rubble from the cell, an arduous task hampered by the narrow steps. They suspected they still had another foot or so to go to reach the original floor.

"Are you sure you want to stay here alone?" Greg stood stretching his spine and rolling his shoulders.

Erin smiled. "I'll be fine. Security patrol the fences. Those kids won't get through again. Besides, I don't plan to stay too long. Just until I have the entire skeleton unearthed." She shook the paper bag. "And I have my snacks."

Greg's eyes brightened at the sight. "Is that what I think it is?"

She grinned. "Chocolate croissants." She turned to Connor. "Any luck finding the shackles to go with those chains you discovered this morning?"

"Yeah. Greg found them not long after you left to get coffee." He, too, held up a bag. "Secure around the ulna and radius bones. And one around the neck vertebrae."

"Around the wrists and neck. Interesting. And the chain had snapped? That would require an awful lot of strength." Erin stepped closer, grasping the bag. "Are they silver?"

"That they are."

"That's strange. Why not use iron? Like the chain. It's stronger. Something to do with the status of the prisoner, maybe?"

"Maybe." Conner's gaze dipped to the bag of croissants. "It seems a bit redundant to lock someone down here and then chain them to the wall as well. Whoever they put in here, they were really afraid of him, or they were making sure he didn't get out. Or both."

Greg reached for Erin's croissants.

Laughing, she tucked them behind her back. "You can buy your own pastries. Both of you. These are mine."

"Wait a minute. What's this?" Greg snatched her clipboard from her and held it up, displaying her drawing.

"Is that a drawing of d'Louncrais?" Connor whistled. "Hot stuff."

Let the ground open up and swallow me now.

"It's good, Erin." Greg gave her a cheeky grin. "He looks just as I imagined him. I think this is the best drawing you've done so far. I liked the one you did of the little girl in front of the château, and that cafe scene, too, but this is so lifelike. Such attention to detail. Right down to the expression in his eyes. You've captured a sense of authority and self-confidence."

"Yeah, he's pretty impressed with himself." Erin snatched the clipboard back. She should have trashed the drawing the minute she'd finished it. What had possessed her to leave it on her clipboard?

Greg chuckled, the sound echoing around the cell. "Well, the man had everything to be arrogant about. Few chevaliers amassed the wealth and influence he did." Greg smirked, amusement twinkling in his eyes. "He's good-looking, too."

Erin blushed. Great. Her fascination with the handsome chevalier was now revealed for all to see.

Connor snorted. "Fat lot of good any of that did him once he ended up down here."

Erin glanced up at Greg's smiling face, catching him studying her. Her gaze dropped back to her clipboard.

"*If* the bones belong to him."

"True," said Greg. "All right, time for a shower and then dinner."

"Sounds good to me. See you, Erin." Connor hefted his backpack over his shoulder and headed up the narrow steps.

"So, Erin." Greg tucked his kit under his arm. "Blue moon tonight. You want to watch it rise over the Loire River with me? I'll have a magnificent view from my balcony. We'll open a bottle of wine…"

"Um, sure." Erin shrugged. The prospect wasn't unappealing. A diversion from her usual routine of going over her notes before bed.

She liked Greg, admired his work ethic and his dedication. His passion for history rivaled hers. They had a lot in common—a good working relationship and an easy camaraderie on site—dare she say they were friends—and he was a genuinely nice guy. As men went, he ticked all the right boxes, and the view from his balcony would be stunning. The illuminated Pont Du Langeais bridging the Loire River made for a postcard-perfect sight on any night, but the added hue of a full moon would make it almost magical.

"Okay then." He smiled.

He had a pleasant smile.

"I'll see you later."

As Greg ascended the steps, brown eyes beckoned from her clipboard, drawing her attention. Erin scowled down at the sexy chevalier. The man was too good-looking for words. According to her drawing.

"Don't forget what I said about blue moons," called Greg over his shoulder.

"I won't."

Blue moons. Pfft! All day Greg had regaled her with the folklore surrounding blue moons. How the superstitious perceived them as a portent of new beginnings. How Wiccans believed they could amplify things. She stared up the stairwell, the shuffle of Greg's footsteps retreating. Was he hoping for a romantic evening?

Her gaze dipped to her clipboard. Greg was no Gaharet d'Louncrais.

She cast a baleful eye over her sketch, and tossed her clipboard to the ground, out of her way. The minute she got back to the hotel, she'd bin that thing. Screw it up and chuck it in the trash. *Promise? Maybe. Okay, probably not.*

She huffed out a breath, knelt beside the skeleton. Opening her kit, she chose a brush, turned her back on that damned drawing and got to work.

From a cursory examination of the skeleton's pelvis and leg bones, they'd established the remains belonged to a tall, over six-feet-tall, male. She'd found some signs of ossification, though the scan would give them a clearer indication of age. D'Louncrais had died around the age of thirty-five, but a lifetime of fighting would've impacted his body. The bones *could* belong to d'Louncrais. They could belong to anyone. She'd need time in a lab and a thorough study of the bones before she could reach any real conclusions.

Her gaze shifted to her sketch. Again. Dark eyes stared back at her, taunting her. Even in death, the man had the power to captivate and intrigue. That's the only explanation she had for the creation on her clipboard — a chevalier in shining armor worthy of a leading role in any blockbuster movie. A flutter started in her belly. Erin groaned, rolling her eyes.

Come on, Erin. He's dead. It's a simple drawing, and you know there's no such thing as a knight in shining armor.

She pulled her gaze back to the bones. Sure, he was good-looking. The women of his time had thought so, if they could believe the written evidence of them swooning in his presence. And he hadn't risen to his position as the count's adviser, or commander of his army, by being dim-witted either. Although, his inherited wealth, title and a level of ruthlessness would've helped there. Bestowing on him qualities of a romantic hero…well…that was ludicrous.

Of its own volition, her gaze strayed to the drawing again, and an unwanted thrill skipped through her veins. She forced the sensation down.

What is wrong with me?

How many men like him had her mother dated? Too many, and none of them had lasted the distance. Erin had always aspired to something more, something stable, a deeper lasting connection with someone who inspired loyalty, conversation and a meeting of minds. A best friend *and* lover. A stayer, not a player. You didn't get that with a man like d'Louncrais, no matter how much you wished it. Not even a modern version of him would deliver. And someone living would be handy.

So why are you so obsessed with him?

Maybe it was genetic—a recessive gene that had remained dormant until now. God, she hoped not.

Puffing out her breath, Erin slammed the door shut on Gaharet d'Louncrais' distracting image. She returned to the last vertebrae, brushing away the remaining dirt. She peered closer.

"What have we here?"

Incised bone trauma. She'd examine it more closely in the lab, but its existence suggested a cause of death. Decapitation. That added credence to Greg's theory of a rift between Count Lothair of Anjou and his most trusted vassal. If the bones belonged to d'Louncrais, what had changed between him and the count? What had he done? Had an affair with the count's wife?

She dug around for the skull and found it not at the apex of the spinal column but off to the side. More evidence to support beheading as the prisoner's demise.

Erin set to work on it, humming along with the rhythmic movement of her hands, her brush sweeping deftly across the cranium. Ridges appeared and orbital arches took shape. The more she revealed, the deeper her frown until her humming dwindled into silence. She sat back on her haunches.

"What the hell?"

Leaning forward, she peered at the alabaster expanse of bone. She pried it loose. This was unexpected. If the silver shackles weren't unusual enough, or an underground cell in a tenth-century keep, this really upped the ante on strange.

She held up the skull, the long muzzle, the flat forehead, curved mandibles and large canines white in the harsh, electric lighting. Definitely not a human skull. Nor that of a dog. No, this belonged to a wolf.

She stared at the cranium crusted in dirt. Had some poor, rabid, half-starved animal been thrown in here to kill the prisoner? They'd already revealed the ribs, humerus, pelvis, clavicle and femurs, and she'd given them a cursory examination. None of them showed any signs of damage pertaining to an animal attack. Or evidence of a wolf having devoured the prisoner after he'd died, gnawing on the bones until it, too, succumbed to death. If she located the wolf's body and the man's skull, would they provide the answers? Or raise more questions.

There was always the possibility the count had removed the prisoner's head, taken it to display on a pike and used it as a warning to others. As one of the more notorious counts of the period, that wasn't out of the equation. What about the wolf, though?

She frowned at the skull, letting the dirt sift out.

Something solid dropped to the ground.

A tooth dislodged when she'd moved the skull? She picked up the loose piece.

"Oh." Erin's eyes widened. Not a tooth. Something far more interesting. She held it in her palm—a small disc of tarnished gold the size of a fifty-cent piece with a hole in the top. A pendant? Flipping it over, she held it up to the light.

"Oh, my."

Stamped into the gold was the d'Louncrais family crest.

Chapter Two

France (Frankia)
August 999

Gaharet d'Louncrais hesitated in the doorway, brow furrowed, studying the men gathered in the hall before him. Flames raged in the large central fire pit, the steel of their mail flickering with shadows and light, the corners of the room hidden in darkness. In the air hung a miasma of smoke and herbs from the oil lamps and the meadowsweet rushes covering the floor — a cloying but not unpleasant smell.

The men divested themselves of their armor and took seats at the large oak table at one end of the hall, awaiting him. Silent, their eyes downcast and expressions bleak. Big men, all of them, by virtue of the armor they bore as much as from what they truly were. Large men, muscular and strong, their faces etched with the concern that also weighed heavily on his mind.

They could not hide their disquiet from him any more than he could conceal his presence from them. As one they turned, regarding him, their keen eyes peering at him through the shadows though he made no sound save for his breathing. They spoke not a word as he crossed the floor to join them.

Once, not so long ago, their numbers were greater, their thoughts less grave and the danger barely a threat. That had all changed. Their days of peace and prosperity were gone, their existence no longer secret. How? Pondering that question gave him nights of restless slumber.

For centuries, their kind had thrived with not a hint of their true nature leaking into the general populace. Over thirty men had once sat in this room, filling the hall with their talk, their laughter and their disputes. Sounds of the past echoed in his ears—of raucous gatherings lasting for days, even weeks. A rumble of male voices, women's gossip and children's laughter. They had once gathered here from across the land, the borders of comtes and kings of no concern to them as they slipped past armies unseen and unheard.

No more. The laughter had gone, the children no longer played and Gaharet now had a significantly reduced band of men to lead. Silence had descended over the keep, the quiet corridors and empty rooms bearing witness to how few remained. It left a hollow emptiness in his chest. He missed the old days. Somehow, someone had exposed them, and one by one, they had fallen. Men, women and children.

Was it the church? Gaharet dismissed the idea. He did not believe so, at least not the church as a whole, for their kind would have been publicly denounced as an abomination. Hunted down, imprisoned, tortured and executed. But perhaps an individual of the church might have used knowledge of their pack to his own advantage, killing them off for his own twisted purpose.

Archeveque Renaud?

The archeveque's name had come up on more than one occasion, and Gaharet had been quick to take action, sending Aimon to investigate. Now the pack met again, all anxious for Aimon's news. Would they finally have their answers?

Gaharet waited for the servants to place their platters of steaming meat, thick, crusty bread and pitchers of wine on the table, ensuring they had left the room before he spoke. His people had served him well, always faithful, loyal and discreet, guarding his family's secret. But these were dangerous times, and one could not be too careful. A tight knot formed in his chest. It pained him to think this way.

He addressed the youngest of the group. "What news, Aimon, of the archeveque?"

Aimon snorted, running his hand through his white-blond hair, blue eyes flashing. "Never have I seen a more ungodly man of God."

Ulrik threw back his head and laughed, a coarse, gravelly sound, revealing vicious scars lacerated across his throat. "Godliness is not a prerequisite for the priesthood." Ulrik leaned back, slouching in his chair, refilling his wine goblet. "Your naivety is showing, Aimon. Grow up young pup, or you will become a liability. Perhaps we should have left you on that battlefield. Not everyone was in favor of Gaharet's decision that day."

Gaharet scowled at Ulrik, a growl rising to his lips, but he held it in check. Ulrik was always wont to provoke him and Gaharet refused to bite.

"I may be young, but do not take me for a fool. I am well aware a calling from God does not motivate all clergymen." Aimon glared at Ulrik. "But Archeveque Renaud has taken corruption to a whole new level. The man has his finger in every dissolute scheme this side of bloody Rome and," he added, "he is busy trying to ingratiate himself with Comte Lothair."

Gaharet snorted. "That is nothing new. I have blocked his access to the comte for years. That alone does not make him responsible for our current woes, Aimon."

Aimon shook his head. "He has petitioned the comte for a private audience specifically excluding you."

"He has been trying that for years, too. He does not like me intervening between him and the comte." Gaharet took a sip of wine, unperturbed by Aimon's revelations. Renaud was a schemer, but did he have the skill, the cunning or the nerve to take them down? Gaharet was not so certain.

"He has petitioned him five times in the last week," Aimon pressed.

Gaharet chuckled. "He is persistent. I will grant him that."

"Well, this time he has convinced the comte. Lothair has approved his final petition."

Gaharet's head snapped up, his knife clattering against the table and his food forgotten.

"What?"

"Word has it Renaud has something he is itching to tell the comte. Something he refuses to disclose to anyone else. Something that will make them allies against an insidious enemy, a great evil."

"When?"

"He is meeting with the comte late tomorrow."

"This is an unexpected development," said Ulrik. "Seems our illustrious leader is not as informed as he would like us to believe. If you were not aware of this meeting, what else do you not know?" Ulrik's brown eyes challenged him, a smug smile turning up the corners of his mouth.

Gaharet scowled, clenching his jaw tight. Picking up his knife, he impaled a piece of meat and glowered at Ulrik. The others remained silent, eyes averted. He stared at Ulrik, lip curled in a snarl, refusing to let this insolence go unchecked, demanding acquiescence. A few moments passed, breaths held. With a grunt, Ulrik dropped his gaze and bowed his head, but his smirk remained. Gaharet forced his shoulders to relax. He would not be drawn into a confrontation. Loud exhalations echoed around the table.

"I was not aware," he said, glancing around at his men. "Lothair has not informed me of this meeting." Leaning back in his chair, he sipped his wine. Lothair, his Seigneur, Comte de Anjou, in collusion with Archeveque Renaud? What an alarming thought. Why was he not privy to this information? Lothair consulted him on everything. Or at least he had.

"It is not beyond Lothair to use Renaud to suit his purposes," he said, picking at his food. "He will often befriend religion before going to war. Perhaps he plans another campaign." Yet Lothair had given no hint in that regard. And why would Lothair exclude him from that?

"But if Renaud *is* the one behind these attacks on us, would Lothair not find such information useful? Would he not try to use it against us?" asked Lance, his dark beard streaked with gray, the only telltale sign of age. The men nodded in agreement.

"It makes our position far more dangerous," said Edmond. "Why has Renaud not denounced us already? From the pulpit or at court? In Rome?"

"We are too powerful for him, and he knows it. Instead of sitting back and doing nothing, we should push our advantage." Ulrik lounged back in his chair and slurped from his goblet, his food untouched.

"Your arrogance will be the death of us, Ulrik," muttered Lance, but Gaharet shook his head, looking around at his men, his vassals.

"Ulrik is right." Gaharet gritted his teeth as he made the admission. "Renaud cannot get to the rest of us. Not yet, not directly. If he could, he would have. Denouncing us publicly would only get him laughed out of the county. He has few friends here and we have good standing with the people, but, while our positions, our titles, our closeness to the comte and our land make us powerful," he said, sending a direct look at Ulrik, "we cannot afford to be complacent. Pushing our advantage would be foolhardy."

With a grunt and a roll of his eyes, Ulrik looked away. He downed the remains of his wine and refilled his goblet.

"We have already lost too many of us. I am not prepared to lose any more over a mistaken belief that we are untouchable," said Gaharet. "No one can lay claim to that."

"Agreed" Lance's gray gaze shifted from man to man before settling on Ulrik. "We are only seven. Let us not become six."

Godfrey rapped his fingers against the table, a thoughtful expression on his face. "So, Renaud has picked us off one by one and now he wants to involve the comte, ally with him, so he can get to the rest of us. Clever."

Godfrey always saw to the heart of things. Though younger than Lance, he had years of experience on

Gaharet. His quiet, thoughtful way often meant people overlooked him.

"Conniving is more like it," growled Aubert.

"We do not yet know if Renaud's true purpose is our extinction. While he has little power in this county, he need only seek the backing of the Pontiff in Rome. Yet he has not done so. One must wonder why." Whatever the reason, Gaharet was grateful. They could do without the full force of the church descending on them.

"And we have no proof it is Archeveque Renaud, only speculation," added Lance. "Focusing on him could close us off from considering the alternatives. Perhaps this threat is from outside the borders. Could this be a plot by the Comte de Blois?"

"Our kind have been murdered, our numbers decimated and now Renaud has an audience with the comte, without Gaharet, to talk about a great evil. In case you have forgotten what we are, it is almost certain that great evil is *us*." Edmond shook his head. "Forget the Comte de Blois."

"We will know soon enough," said Gaharet. "I will be at that meeting, invited or not." He frowned. "Renaud is taking an enormous risk bringing this to the comte. If he plays this wrong... Even I would not care to cross Comte Lothair. Renaud will have to tread with care, or he will end up confined in one of Lothair's towers."

"Or skewered on the end of his sword." Ulrik grinned. "Now *that* is a delightful prospect."

Gaharet had to agree with Ulrik there, too, although having his thoughts align with Ulrik's did not please him at all. If he had the opportunity to drive his sword through Renaud, he would not have hesitated, but killing the archeveque, especially without the comte's permission, would only invite more trouble.

"I would not advise underestimating Renaud," said Lance. "He is a conniving weasel for sure, but he has secured himself the position of archeveque. No simple task. He has survived a long time, despite his nefarious schemes. Lothair would not be the first comte he has crossed, I would wager."

"Why not just kill him and be done with it?" suggested Ulrik. "We can apologize to Lothair later."

"Lothair does not accept apologies." Gaharet pinned Ulrik with his gaze. "You of all people know that, Ulrik."

Ulrik scowled. A deep growl resonated in his throat, and his knuckles turned white around his goblet. "Leave my family out of this."

Gaharet inclined his head, diffusing the situation, but his point had found its mark.

"Perhaps you should pull back from your position so close to the comte," suggested Aimon. "Perhaps we all should."

"No." Gaharet shook his head. "I do not think so. It would only make him wonder more. Lothair is not stupid by any man's measure. We need to know what Archeveque Renaud's plan is so we can stop him. This is our chance. Renaud on his own is concern enough with the rich church coffers financing his schemes. Allying with Comte Lothair is an entirely different matter. Lothair has an army and, while I might have command of it now, that could easily change."

Nodding, they resumed eating in silence, all except Ulrik who sloshed more wine into his goblet. Gaharet's eyes sought Lance, his muscles working in his jaw. His gaze flicked to Ulrik, then back to Lance. Lance grimaced and nodded. Gaharet would have to do something about Ulrik soon. Had he made a mistake in giving Ulrik a second chance? He sighed. He hoped he did not live to regret it.

Gaharet studied his men, glancing at each of them as they ate their meal in silence. Strong men, intelligent, educated, some older than himself, others younger. Aimon, young and bright as a new coin. Lance, whose council he often sought. Ulrik, hot tempered but quick-witted. Godfrey, quiet and studious, and twins Aubert and Edmond, huge, gruff and as wild as the forest, but steadfast assets in battle. All of them seasoned warriors, exceptional chevaliers, fearless in battle and practiced swordsmen.

They looked to him for leadership, and he felt the weight of that responsibility. They were his men, and he would do whatever was necessary to protect them, lead them as best he could, but their situation troubled him. Could they find a way? Would their kind survive?

Gaharet finished his meal, pushed thoughts of Renaud and Lothair aside then rose from the table.

His men followed. Lance held out his hand, halting Gaharet, the others heading for the door, the cool night air and the forest beyond the walls.

Lance put a supportive hand on Gaharet's shoulder. "It is a dark time you have to lead us through, Gaharet, and there is more than myself that is glad this responsibility falls to you. We need your strength, your connections and the stability you provide. None other could give us that."

"Thank you, Lance." He turned to follow his men.

"There is something else we must speak of, Gaharet. You cannot avoid it, you know that."

Lance's words brought Gaharet to a halt. He faced his friend, nodding, suspecting what Lance wished to discuss. It had also been on his mind for several months now.

"The men are getting anxious. They need to know what you plan to do to increase our numbers."

Gaharet grunted. "It is not like we have a lot of choices, Lance. We either turn them or breed them and considering our lack of females…" They had no option either way except to turn others, but Gaharet was hesitant to take that step. He had seen only one turning in his lifetime, a turning he had instigated. He let out a long exhalation. Not an experience he was eager to repeat.

"Aimon is grateful, Gaharet. He does not regret what he has become. You saved his life."

Gaharet nodded. "I know and I am aware I have no choice. We must rebuild our numbers. We are too few and too vulnerable."

"The men have a preference for taking wives, Gaharet, turning women, not soldiers."

"You think I do not wish for that myself? A woman to warm my bed, to confide in, someone to stand by my side, bear me sons? Tell me, Lance, which woman would you choose? Which one woman would you think would accept what she has to become, would put herself through the agony of a turning?"

Lance dropped his gaze.

"What woman in this county would not run screaming from us if she even suspected what we were? If I knew of a woman who would be brave enough to take that on, I would wed tomorrow." Gaharet shrugged. "And I would not care if she were a maid, a peasant or a duchesse, nor where she came from."

No, none of those things mattered to him. She need only accept him, stand by him and keep his secret. He would have liked to find a woman who would love him, need him in equal measure as he would love and need her. He hung his head. That was not to be. Though he longed for it with every fiber of his being, he had given up on that ideal some time ago, their survival taking precedence over his own desires.

To initiate a turning was not a decision made lightly, and he would not sanction the turning of random women in the hopes of finding love. If he expected his men to forsake finding the love of a mate, *he* must be the first to do so. Lead by example. He need find but one woman to accept him, one woman to take as his wife and he had no idea where to find her.

His thoughts troubled, he joined his men beyond the wall as they divested themselves of their tunics and breeches. Concerns or not, the darkness called to them, a sibilant whispering enticing them out into the night. With a melding of bone, their naked, human bodies disappeared, and they slipped into the forest as swift, dark shapes.

Chapter Three

Frankia
999

Gaharet stood surveying the forest, the bulbous orb of the full moon spilling out from behind black clouds, illuminating a patchwork of land. The familiar scent of wood smoke from his farmer's cottages filled his nose and recognizable shapes of trees he had climbed as a child swayed in the breeze. Everything was as it should be. That should have comforted him, but it did not. Right now, Langeais did not feel far enough away.

A storm was brewing, the smell of rain heavy in the air. His keep stood dark behind him, silent for the night. He regarded the moon's fullness, a sense of disquiet brushing against his already troubled mind. A fourth full moon this season was an unusual aberration. What further misfortune did it portend? He banished the thought. He did not need to add to his worries.

His visit to Langeais Keep had not gone well. Detained in Langeais village by an insistent horse trader, the meeting between Archeveque Renaud and Comte Lothair was almost done when he had arrived. Knowing what he knew now, he suspected the man waylaid him on purpose. Their suspicions about the archeveque had proved well-founded.

Gaharet grinned, his large canines extending, pushing at his gums. To have seen Lothair's face when Renaud had used the term werewolf to describe his kind... Gaharet's smile turned to a snarl. Any shock or disbelief on Lothair's part had worn off by the time he had intruded on their meeting, coalescing into something more sinister. A dark and twisted desire to use his kind, force them to do his bidding, to pursue Lothair's more malevolent ambitions.

Gaharet had underestimated Renaud, his cunning, his influence and his reach. The archeveque had got his claws into one of his pack. Betrayal had come from within. How else could Renaud know of things more sacred, more secret than their very existence? Things like the amulets and their inscription. Only one of his kind could have imparted such information. The thought seared his mind, unsettling him in a way the threat of discovery never had.

Gaharet glanced down at his chest, the gold disc of the alpha's amulet resting near his heart. The red stone in its center, the bloodstone, at this very moment, remained dark. He did not wish to see it glow again anytime soon. Too often of late he had awoken to find the body of a friend — half-human, half-wolf — and the bloodstone glowing. In mortal danger they had recited the inscription, the bloodstone acting like a beacon drawing them in, only to have them die at his feet. Would Lothair's desire to use them, to control them, halt the slaughter of his kind? He let out a long, drawn-out sigh. He did not know.

Gaharet returned his attention to the forest, focused in on its sounds and its smells and let its familiarity wash over him, a soothing balm to the brittle edge of his thoughts. It pulsed with life—insects scurrying about, night owls preening on their perches, the scratching of rodents hunting for food. He picked them out one by one. A light breeze touched his face, and he inhaled deeply, catching the scent of damp earth, leaves and pine.

Standing naked, his eyes closed, he listened, he breathed. The worries and cares of the past few months slipping away to a distant part of his mind, he allowed the change to flow through him. His bones shifted beneath his skin, rippling, flowing, melding and realigning. First his hands and feet, then in one fluid movement his spine, pelvis, jaw and limbs, making cracking and grinding noises. The stabbing pain of transformation was brief as he snapped into the shape, his bones contorting and rearranging. Dark, coarse hair sprouted, nails became claws and teeth became fangs until he stood on all fours as a very large black wolf.

If Lothair could only see me now.

Leaving his garments behind, Gaharet trotted off into the forest.

* * * *

2016

Erin squinted at the image on the gold disc again. Had they found him? Gaharet d'Louncrais?

Don't get too excited, Erin. It's a clue, not definitive proof.

She stared at the disc in her hand, running her fingers over it, flipping it over, studying it. She grabbed her brush and cleaned the dirt from the grooves.

She peered closer. *What the – ?* Engraved into the reverse side was writing in small curlicue script. Some type of runic language? Not Latin or Old French. A linguist would know, and they'd consult one for sure, but that didn't help her now.

She chewed on her lip. It may not be very scientific, but... She whipped out her phone, thumbed up her home screen and tried to open Google. *Damn. No service.* She held the phone above her head, searching for a signal. No luck. She was too far underground. With the disc and her phone in hand, she grabbed her clipboard and a pen and headed up the stairs.

Fresh, cool air brushed her face as Erin exited the stairwell. She waited a moment for a signal, then opened Google and typed in runic languages. A whole plethora of options appeared, but none of them matched the symbols on the disc.

Mmm, what else can it be? Some form of forgotten language? She'd never seen this script before, and she'd spent most of her career specializing in medieval Europe.

She tapped her phone, pacing. Why would someone use a language other than the standard Latin? Because they had something to hide. She paused. Could it be a secret code? She typed secret codes into Google. No luck there either. Only a bunch of references to the enigma machine from World War II.

Erin resumed her pacing, running through her mind all she knew of the tenth century – the people, the politics, the religion. Christianity had made great inroads, but some still held to the old ways even though they might have had to hide it from their neighbors. Pagans perhaps? She typed in pagan alphabet and *voila!* There, dancing across her screen, was the curling script on the disc.

Thank you, Wikipedia.

"Theban," she read. "A substitution cipher." Erin peered at the script again. Definitely Theban. She'd never heard of it. She kept reading. "The Theban alphabet was used as a substitution cipher of the Latin alphabet by early occultists. First published in 1518."

Wait, what?

That didn't make any sense. How had it ended up on a disc buried with tenth-century bones? Or were they?

Disappointment tasted thick on her tongue. If the disc belonged with the skeleton, then the bones couldn't belong to Gaharet d'Louncrais. Finding the cell, the shackles and the bones, she'd had high expectations. A sixteenth century script dashed her hopes in one fell swoop. It suggested the cell's use had continued *after* the construction of the larger château, and a much more recent prisoner.

But…could it be too much of a coincidence to find an item stamped with the family crest of the man they were searching for, for it *not* to be him? The d'Louncrais line had died with Gaharet, so it couldn't be a descendant. And they'd found no evidence of another family appropriating the crest. Not in France anyway.

She studied the script again. Could the inscription itself provide any clues to the identity of the pendant's owner? Could she be so lucky? She fingered the disc.

"Ouch!" A sharp edge pierced her finger. Blood formed and dropped onto the disc, sliding into the grooves of the inscription. She pressed her thumb against the spot to stem the flow.

Wonderful.

She'd embedded her DNA on an artifact. Anyone would think she was a newbie. She couldn't clean it. Any chemical used could damage the piece. She'd mention it to the conservator, and should probably look into getting a tetanus shot, but first…

Balancing the phone on her clipboard, she wrote out the script, spacing the lines apart, leaving room for her translation. She hoped her Latin was up to the challenge. If not, she had Google.

She took her time, pausing over the words, scratching out some and replacing them with others. Finishing, she studied her translation. *What. The. Hell?* It made no more sense than the use of the Theban alphabet. Clutching the disc, she read the inscription out loud.

"Vanish from all human sight,
Those who favor moonlit night.
To bloodstone shall they return,
So no man of their secret learns."

Darkness hit like a solid wall, and Erin lost her balance. She screamed, falling, her clipboard and phone slipping from her grip, her pen flying off into the inky blackness. Bracing her arms, she waited an eternity for the impact.

She hit the ground hard, smacking her forehead on something solid—a rock, a piece of the crumbling keep. Pain lanced her head, and she tasted bile at the back of her throat. She raised her hand to her forehead, grimacing. Her palm came away damp. Blood.

"Oh, just great." She'd have a decent egg on her head by morning and, more than likely, a rather nasty headache. She might even need stitches. "Shit."

She looked around, trying to see something, anything, disoriented by the darkness. She took a deep breath… Someone must have turned the lights off. "Idiots."

She scowled at the darkness. They should've checked everyone had left the site. It shouldn't matter.

Security dictated the lights stayed on all night. Maybe a fuse had blown. She groaned.

Well, she couldn't lie here all night. Fumbling around for her phone, she swept her hand around. Nothing. On her knees, she widened her search area. Still nothing.

Crap.

She didn't dare search too far. The last thing she needed was to fall down the steep steps of the underground cell.

Zen breaths, Erin. Breathe in, breathe out.

Inhaling deep diaphragm filling breaths, she steadied herself. She should be able to find her way to the keep wall. From there, she could feel her way around to the chain-link fence. Security guards did the rounds regularly. She'd simply wait for one to turn up. He'd have a torch and he could help her. No big deal.

Erin stood, hesitating. *Damn, it's dark.* Strange. The lights from the château should be visible. A city-wide blackout? And where had that full moon gone when she needed it? Trust this to happen the one night she'd stayed back alone. If she'd gone back to the hotel with Greg, she'd have showered, eaten, been in good company and be two or three glasses into a bottle of red instead of here in the dark. She rubbed her arms against the chill that engulfed her.

Okay, time to make a move. The longer she stayed put, the more she'd freak herself out. She stepped away from the entrance to the cell, lifting her feet a foot off the ground, avoiding the string lines marking out the grid. She'd no plans to take another tumble. She took a few more steps. So far, so good.

Keep going. Keep going. Don't think about the darkness. Don't think about where you are.

Too late. Her mind had already gone there. Gone to the steep steps, down to the macabre underground chamber where a man and a wolf had died horrible deaths. It wouldn't be the first castle, or keep, to sport ghosts. Not that she believed in them, not during the bright light of day when reason and logic held all the power. She shivered. In the inky darkness, her imagination held sway, not logic. She would not think of the skeleton. She would not imagine a ghost of the prisoner climbing those narrow, steep stairs, rattling his chains.

Keep moving, Erin.

She took another step. A low growl cut through the darkness. Close. Erin froze. *What the hell is that?* Her skin prickled.

Silence.

There. Her head snapped to the left, and she winced at the pounding the sudden movement produced in her temple. Staring into the darkness, her ears primed, she waited.

She flinched. There it was again. The oddest sound—a popping, cracking noise. Someone cracking their knuckles? She swiveled to face it, breaking out in a sweat.

"Is someone there?" Her voice, a high squeak, disappeared into the blackness. *Or something.* A faint odor of wet dog reached her nose, and her mind went back to the skull of the wolf. *This cannot be happening.* She shook her head, reining in her wayward imagination.

"Hello?"

* * * *

Gaharet stood preternaturally still, pulled to an abrupt halt at the sight of the woman not two yards in front of him. *Where the hell has she come from?* He had not caught a hint of her scent for leagues, yet here she stood. Close, too close for him to not have sensed her presence until now. Impossible. No human had ever caught him so unawares.

Her heart beat an erratic rhythm loud in his ears, her nostrils flared and her green gaze darted about, but she did not flee. His eyes narrowed in on the gash on her forehead, the scent of her blood sharp on the air. An innocent, injured woman or a trap? Was this how his kind had fallen? Lips curled in a snarl, muscles tensed, he searched his surroundings. Apart from the smells and sounds of the forest, he found nothing unusual. Only her.

The vision before him thrust out her chin, her lips trembling. Long strands of blonde hair escaping from a tie at the back of her head fluttered over her forehead. She gave a huff of breath, blowing them clear of her eyes, and they settled, framing her pale face. Shoulders stiff and hands on her hips, she stood her ground. This little slip of a woman had courage.

How intriguing.

Strange attire clung to her like a second skin, concealing nothing from him — not the soft swell of her breasts, nor the gentle curve of her hips. Clothing that would tempt the most pious of men.

Something stirred within him, something long forgotten, and he licked his lips. He swallowed hard, a fire sparking in his imagination and another, much lower part of his anatomy, his blood flowing south at a rate of knots.

Tantalizing glimpses of creamy bare skin, from her low-cut neckline to rips in the fabric at the knees of her breeches, taunted him. An unexpected longing to touch, to taste, stormed through him unchecked. He bit back a groan as desire pulsed low within his gut and shot straight to his cock.

He sniffed the air again, catching her scent. Citrus and orange blossoms, and a hint of fear, yet still she made no move to retreat. She was either brave, foolish or had ulterior motives. His wolf did not care which. The combination of her assaulting his senses awakened the beast, pushing it to the surface. A growl rose from deep within. He had a sudden need to know this woman — who she was, where she had come from — for reasons beyond the safety of his pack.

La petite séductrice!

Gritting his teeth, he tamped down on his primal instincts. He could not, would not, let his baser urges hold sway over his body or his mind. One look at her, and he had all but forgotten his responsibilities, forgotten what was important. Such as focusing on where she had come from and how she had caught him off guard. A difficult thing to do.

He reined in his lust and searched for clues to her identity, inspecting every inch of her from her well-worn boots and dusty blue breeches to the smudges of dirt on the slender curve of her throat and nose. A farmer's daughter perhaps, helping in the fields? Not one of *his* farmers.

His gaze dipped to her hands, catching sight of something clutched in her slender fingers. His eyes jerked down to his chest. The bloodstone glowed.

"Merde!"

Chapter Four

Taking a shaky breath, Erin peered into the darkness. The spidery tingling on the back of her neck, the low growl, the strange cracking sounds, told her she was not alone. Either that or her imagination had gone into overdrive. Like the time she'd watched *The Conjuring* and didn't sleep for two days.

Her heart pounded and her throat tightened, but she pulled herself together.

There's nothing there.

No apparition of a long dead chevalier, no ghostly wolf, nothing. Tomorrow she'd feel like a complete idiot and have a laugh at her own expense, especially if Connor and Greg got wind of this.

A muttered oath burst out from the darkness. Her body stiffened.

Oh God, there is someone there. Calm down, Erin. Take a breath.

She sucked in air. A security guard? She released her breath on a sigh. Yes, security doing the rounds, checking the site because the lights went out.

Without a torch?

Or more delinquent teenagers intent on mischief, taking advantage of the blackout.

"I know you're there," she called out, hands on her hips. Only kids. She could handle a bunch of kids. Maybe. "Show yourself." She resisted the urge to stamp her foot.

A large shape coalesced, moving toward her. Erin held her ground. As the figure approached, the clouds covering the moon shifted and the darkness ebbed away. Her mouth dropped open. *What the hell?*

A man. A *naked* man.

Her gaze snapped to his face. Her breath whooshed from her lungs.

No, no, no, no.

Her blood turned to icy sludge, and her brain struggled to comprehend what her eyes were seeing. It couldn't be. Ghosts weren't real. No matter how many paranormal shows tried to convince you of their existence, ghosts weren't real. They were a trick of the light, a product of an overactive imagination and a spooky atmosphere. A logical explanation could *always* be found.

Not this time. Nothing else could explain how *he* stood before her. In the flesh. Lots and lots of flesh!

"Gaharet d'Louncrais." The air all but sucked out of her lungs. How was this *possible*? Her drawing was merely a romantic imagining from the most minimal descriptions they had, and yet... Those eyes, the patrician nose...

Erin shook her head. A wave of dizziness swamped her, and she groaned, holding her hand to her forehead. She winced at the tenderness beneath her palm. Erin squeezed her eyes shut, took deep breaths and concentrated on reinstating calm, rational thoughts. The sudden darkness, the disturbing nature of the cell and her fascination with the long dead chevalier had her seeing things that simply weren't there. Ghosts *did not* exist, and they sure as hell *did not* show up naked.

You've got Gaharet d'Louncrais on the brain, Erin. That's all.

She'd had a long day. Fatigue had to be playing a role. Add to that, an unexpected head injury, and she'd conjured him straight off the page and into…whatever this was. She would open her eyes and all she'd see would be the dark silhouette of the keep ruins. Nothing more. Trepidation almost choking her, she slowly prized her lids open.

He's still there! And. Still. Naked!

Erin had worked on medieval grave sites, exhumed bones and worked well into the night many times before. Not once had she ever encountered an apparition. Could this be her first supernatural experience?

A ghost? In the buff?

They squared off, neither making a move toward the other, nor saying a word, and Erin's curiosity spiked, battling it out with her fear for supremacy. Maybe she'd knocked herself out, lay unconscious on the ground and this was all a bad dream. Nope. The pain in her head was real. She narrowed her eyes at the figure before her. Who'd ever heard of a naked ghost?

Erin tried hard, really hard, to contain her gaze to his face, but her eyes refused to take orders from her bruised frontal lobe. The pleasure center of her brain, the part she held responsible for that ridiculous drawing, had control and it steered her gaze lower. Down over his muscular chest, taking in the flash of gold chain and jeweled pendant nestled in dark hair, before moving to his ripped abs. *God, those abs* — sculpted to perfection, except for a raised, jagged scar slicing across them. She itched to run her fingers over that scar.

Her fists clenched to her sides, she continued her exploration downward...for science, for history. She was a professional trained in research and practiced in observation. She licked her lips. She'd study every detail. To document her findings, of course.

Her gaze trailed a path down from those impeccable abs, following twin ropes of muscle leading to... Her mouth went dry, and her gaze did a nervous skip to his muscular thighs with their faint dusting of dark hair, but only for an instant before jerking back up to... *Oh, my*. Well...he'd nothing to be ashamed of in that department. She chewed on her lip. Could ghosts embellish?

The body part in question rose in response to her intense scrutiny, his breath escaping in a hiss. *Oh! Quite the statement*. A sneaky warmth slithered through her body, and her inner thighs clenched. She shook her head, dragging her gaze back up to his face. His dark gaze bored into her with an intensity and heat that was truly unnerving. Fixed on her, it swept over her body like a physical caress. Her knees gave a little wobble, her heart beat a little faster and she wiped a sweaty palm on her jeans.

Was it possible to be turned on by a ghost? Or for a ghost to be turned on? Her eyes slipped back to his groin. *Apparently, yes*. He let out a soft chuckle, and she jerked her head up — the motion sending another wave of wooziness crashing over her. Her vision blurred, and her legs gave way. She would have fallen had he not caught her.

Strong arms enveloped her and pressed her against the length of his hard body. She clung to him, giddy and breathless, desire long held in check stirring, scorching her from head to toe. His breath whispered against her cheek, and she quivered, an involuntary response that resonated through her whole body. He shifted and pulled her closer. Her traitorous body arched against his, and she inhaled the musky scent of him. Pure, hot-blooded male.

He growled, an animal sound deep in his throat that should've frightened her but sent a bolt of heat coursing from the tips of her fingers all the way to her toes. Shocked, her gaze met his, and in that moment she was lost, lost in a haze of longing she never thought could exist. Not for her. Not with a man like him.

For God's sake Erin, he's a ghost!

A very solid, corporeal ghost.

She swallowed hard, blackness darkening the edge of her vision. She squeezed her eyes closed, opened them again, and her vision cleared. The hard reality of his body, muscled, strong and pressed against her remained.

Extending her index finger, she poked his chest. Firm muscle covered bone, resisting pressure. Fingers shaking, she reached up to his face, brushing her fingers through his beard, touching his cheek. His skin was warm against her palm. With a soft moan, he leaned into her hand. She met his hooded gaze, snatching her hand away as though burned.

Not a ghost. A living, breathing man.

Not good. In fact, very, *very* bad.

She struggled against his hold, her heart pounding a thousand beats per minute. She had to get free, but his arms didn't budge one iota. Bigger, stronger, he held her fast. *Who the hell is this guy?* Right now, an exhibitionist ghost would be preferable to any other alternative.

"Let me go."

She meant it as a command, but it came out all breathy and husky. His gaze dipped to her lips, held there, and her breath stalled. So focused on his face, on his mouth only inches from hers, he took her by surprise, plucking the forgotten gold disc from her nerveless fingers, holding it up in front of her face. He spoke foreign words, their meaning dancing beyond her understanding. *Old French? Maybe.* His voice was a deep rumble, smooth with a hint of steel in it, but the words tumbling from his mouth had a gentle, lyrical quality to them, like whisperings of sweet nothings in her ears. Hell, she nearly swooned.

She renewed her efforts to free herself, but he only held her tighter. Whoever this man was, whatever his intentions were, she had to get away from him. And she had to get that disc back. She couldn't let him take something so crucial from the site. She hadn't even photographed it. Too curious, she'd focused on the inscription rather than following protocol.

Shit.

"Give that back to me. You can't take it." She made a grab for it, but he moved it beyond her reach. "It's an artifact. It belongs in a museum."

God, who am I? Indiana Jones?

He snarled at her, a vicious sound, more beast than human, and she stopped reaching for it, her hand frozen in mid-air. Did she really want to risk her life for an artifact?

Hell no.

"Let me go or I'll scream. You won't want to be here when the security guards come running."

His eyes narrowed, but he made no move to relax his hold.

"Where. Did. You. Get. This?" This time he spoke in Latin, the authority in his voice sending a shiver up her spine, his eyes glinting in the moonlight. *Latin now?* Oh, her history loving brain found that really impressive. It also sounded a warning.

"Answer my question and I might consider releasing you."

Would he though? She could only hope. "I found it. It's part of my job," she said, using a garbled mix of Old French, Latin and English. She stared at him, her breath coming in short, sharp pants. "This is crazy. This can't be happening."

He shook his head, frowning at her words. "You are on my land, far from the village and alone. At night. Dressed to seduce a man. Do not tell me this is not what you planned." He growled again, tightening his grip, crushing her against his naked body and lowering his head. "I am more than amenable to your charms."

Dressed to...? She wasn't... The brush of his lips against hers startled her out of her confusion.

Oh, hell no.

Raising her knee, she slammed it into his groin.

"*Merde!*" He released her, doubling over.

Dragging in a gulp of much needed oxygen, Erin turned on her heel and ran. She'd no clue what strange twilight reality she'd stumbled into and right now she didn't care. The disc be damned. She had to escape him before her wobbly legs gave out and the darkness clawing at her mind claimed her. And before she did something really, really stupid—like let him kiss her. She *so* should have gone on that date with Greg.

Recovering faster than she expected, he lunged for her, his hand grasping her wrist and dragging her back against his body. She screamed, her head thumping against his chest, but he didn't release his grip. The thudding in her head intensified and her vision blurred.

"No, no, no, no, no," she whimpered, her words slurring as blackness claimed her.

He caught her as she fell. Nausea roiling in his gut, Gaharet scooped her up, clenching his jaw against the painful throbbing in his injured groin. Laying her gently on the ground next to his clothing, he dressed quickly. She had caught him off guard in more ways than one.

He groaned, adjusting himself in his breeches. It had taken everything he had to remain standing after the blow from her knee. *Merde!* Thank the Lord for his werewolf blood. He was already healing, but the white, hot burst of pain as her knee had connected, he never wanted a repeat of. Slender and unarmed as she appeared to be, he would not be underestimating her again.

He gathered her in his arms, gritting his teeth, and made his way back to his keep. He should not have attempted to kiss her. Held within his arms, her body arching against him, and her lips parted in invitation, temptation had overwhelmed his good sense. Did she have any idea how she affected him? Her nipples puckered, pressing against thin fabric, her curves accentuated by fitted cloth. His naked body had reveled in all her softness pressed against him.

He shivered — the feel of her was still imprinted on his mind if not his body. His beast had stirred, a restlessness taking hold deep within his psyche. His vision had shifted, and his control hanging only by slender threads, threatened to snap at any moment. Not since childhood, as an unpracticed youth, had his darker half pushed for the change, uncalled for, unbidden. She excited him in a way no other woman ever had.

He gathered his wits and ignored the demands of his body, much to its annoyance. There would be time enough for passion as soon as he knew who she was, where she had found the amulet and how she had known how to use it. She was not one of them. That he knew for certain. Even if everything else about her presented a disturbing conundrum. He would find out who she was soon enough. She would remain at his keep until he had his answers.

He looked down at her unconscious form, her lips slightly parted and her breathing soft but steady. His body agreed wholeheartedly with his plan. It would get no satisfaction tonight, but it could live in hope, and with her in his keep, it would have plenty of chances for success.

Even if Renaud has paid her, or Lothair?

A sacrificial lamb sent by his enemies to tempt him, she may be, but Gaharet would not ignore an opportunity, especially not one as compelling as the woman in his arms.

Shifting her weight, he entered his keep via the kitchen, the wide girth of his cook, Anne, standing by the stove stirring the contents of an enormous pot.

"Do you need any help there, lad?" she asked.

"Not tonight, Anne. Perhaps tomorrow. Can you alert Gascon that we have an unexpected visitor, and she is not to leave? Not without my direct orders. Understood?"

Eyeing the woman in his arms, Anne raised an eyebrow. "Whatever you say, lad," she said, returning to her cooking.

Climbing the back stairs to a chamber down the corridor from his own, he kicked the door open, crossed to the bed and laid her down on the cool linens. It took all his willpower not to strip off her dusty clothes. If he did, he would not wish to leave the room, so he contented himself with removing her boots and stockings before pulling the covers over her. Best to hide temptation before he changed his mind and tempt him she did. A lot. But he needed answers first. Then he could better assess the risk.

Leaning over her sleeping form, unable to resist, he gently wiped the smudge of dirt from her nose with his thumb, his fingers lingering in a caress against her cheek. Such soft skin, so beautiful. He brushed her hair from her face, letting the strands glide against his fingers. Could she be a sign their luck was turning? He hoped so. After the hardships of recent months, it was about bloody time.

Leaving the room in darkness, he slipped out of the door, closing it behind him, her boots and socks in one hand, the amulet in the other. She would not get far barefoot. At least not far enough he could not hunt her down. He had her scent now and could track her should she run. He exhaled a long, slow breath. It would also drive him crazy. He palmed himself, trying to ease some of his discomfort.

Perhaps she *would* run. He grinned at the thought, growling low in his throat. Perhaps he should have let her run tonight. The thought of it made him hard, compounding the pain in his poor throbbing groin and he grimaced. With gritted teeth, he moved down the corridor to spend the rest of the night in his bedchamber. Alone.

Chapter Five

"Is it Renaud or not?" asked Edmond, voicing what Gaharet suspected they all wanted to know.

Once again, his men sat at his table, the fire lit, food and wine before them. Outside, a storm raged, but here within the solid walls of his keep his own tumultuous thoughts deafened him. Briefing his men would do little to calm his mind, but perhaps telling them what transpired between him, Archeveque Renaud and Comte Lothair, and observing their reactions, would provide some answers. He would keep to himself Renaud's knowledge of the amulets and Gaharet's belief one of their own had betrayed them.

One of these men, sitting at his table, eating his food and drinking his wine had sold them out and for what? Money? Power? Or did Renaud hold something over them? If so, why had they not come to him? Why had they betrayed them all? God help them when he discovered who. Unlike he had with Ulrik, he would not give them a second chance.

"It is Renaud," said Gaharet. "He was imparting knowledge of our existence to Lothair when I arrived at Langeais Keep. Does Lothair believe him? Unfortunately, yes. He does not trust Renaud, but he knows he would not try to spin him fanciful tales."

A murmur rumbled about the room, a shuffling of weight, and Gaharet eyed each one searching for a hint, a look, an expression, a racing pulse, any indication they were not true, that they were not as disturbed about this as he. He detected nothing.

"So Lothair knows we exist. Did Renaud explain how he fills his spare time killing us off?" Ulrik raised his eyebrows, casting a doubtful glance at him. "I bet not."

"Not surprisingly, Renaud left that part out. Lothair would not be happy if he knew Renaud has killed his chevaliers and their families without sanction, werewolves or not."

Godfrey leaned forward, his elbows on the table. "But does he have names? Can he expose us to Lothair?"

Gaharet sighed. "None of you have been named as far as I am aware."

"But you have?"

At Aimon's question, six shrewd gazes focused on him.

Gaharet shrugged. "Not in so many words, but Renaud gave him enough that he suspects."

"Then you must leave. Protect yourself."

Gaharet understood Aimon's concern, but the wellbeing of the whole pack was his responsibility. They would expect nothing less from him. He would expect nothing less from himself. His own fears, his own desires, were irrelevant.

An image of the woman upstairs strode defiantly into his mind, and he inhaled a slow, steady breath. Now there was a desire he could focus on with enthusiasm. Who was she? Where had she come from? Could he take her as his wife?

He frowned. Now was not the time to be thinking about her. He had already spent many an hour doing just that. Many an uncomfortable hour. His attention needed to be here, in this room, on these men — on determining which one he could no longer trust.

Gaharet regarded his youngest vassal. "I cannot leave, Aimon. To do so would be an admission of guilt. Lothair would hunt me down for his own purposes. I stay, he is certain of my fealty. He believes he owns me, and while that works to his advantage, things will remain as they are."

"What *are* Lothair's plans for us now that he is aware of our existence?" asked Lance.

Gaharet gave a disgusted snort. "He wants to recruit us, use our skills, our innate abilities. He's rather impressed with the idea of a creature that can kill so efficiently yet still be controlled by a human mind."

Lance frowned. "That is very specific information. Being told werewolves exist, surely the myth of a nightmarish half-man, half-beast filled with blood lust would be what first comes to mind. Not us."

Gaharet could only agree.

"If he wants to keep us in his army, he had best stop Renaud killing us off." Aubert thumped his fist on the table.

"He does not need all of us. Just one," said Gaharet, eyeing the men about the table. "He wants to build his own army. An army of werewolves."

Voices broke out louder, punctuated by growls. None seemed any more pleased with the idea than he.

"You are the closest to him, Gaharet. If he suspects you, perhaps he will ask you to turn other chevaliers," said Lance. "Perhaps he will ask it for himself."

A low rumble reverberated in Ulrik's chest. "The last thing we need is for Lothair to be one of us."

Lothair as a werewolf? Gaharet shuddered. "Agreed. He can ask all he likes. I will not turn others for Lothair's benefit and I most certainly will not turn Lothair. But here is what is interesting," he said, leaning forward, his elbows on the table, his fingers steepled. "Renaud has convinced him only the alpha can give him what he wants."

Lance frowned. "But that is not true."

"Precisely. Why, when everything else he knows is accurate, does he have this so wrong?"

"Does he know who the alpha is?" asked Aimon.

"Mayhap he does, and this has as much to do with Lothair as with us." Godfrey stroked his beard, his expression thoughtful. "Perhaps Renaud wants you out of the way, Gaharet, or at least at odds with Lothair. Who is the real target here?"

"So," drawled Ulrik, leaning his elbow on the table. "Can we kill Renaud now?"

"Yes, let us do that." Lance shook his head at Ulrik. "If Renaud turns up dead, or disappears altogether, who do you think Lothair is going to turn on? We would also draw the attention of Rome. Do you really think that is a good idea right now? Do we not have enough enemies?"

Ulrik sighed, dropping his arm. "You spoil all my fun."

They were quiet for a moment, picking at their food, sipping wine.

"And what of the woman?" ventured Godfrey, his eyebrows raised in Gaharet's direction.

The men nodded.

"We sensed her presence," said Lance, and they all looked to him, their eyes reflecting their curiosity, their interest, dark shapes shifting behind their irises.

"Citrus and orange blossoms," said Ulrik, sniffing the air. "And arousal." He slid a sly look in Gaharet's direction.

Lance grinned. "You moved quicker than I expected after our talk the other night."

Gaharet lowered his gaze. He had been a fool to think they would not know. That they would not catch her scent.

"Are you planning to mate her?" asked Godfrey, all eyes fixed on him, watching, waiting, eager for an answer.

Avoiding their stares, Gaharet took a moment to respond. What should he tell them about her? He did not wish to tell them anything. He wanted to keep her all to himself. His reluctance to discuss her was disconcerting. He frowned, fingering the amulet in his palm.

"I found her outside the keep last night... Or more accurately, she found me. She used this."

He tossed the amulet on the table. It spun for a few moments, glittering with reflected light from the fire. *Clink*. It came to rest against the oak surface.

Silence fell, all eyes directed at the small gold disc in the center of the table. Then the room exploded into a cacophony of sound.

"Good God! Where did she get it?"

"Is she one of us?"

"Are there others out there?"

They leaned forward, hungry for answers, and Gaharet's hackles rose. His fists clenching under the table, he stopped the growl in his throat before it even started.

What has gotten into me?

"She is not one of us," said Ulrik, and Gaharet regarded him, mistrust lingering.

Ulrik had reason enough to resent him, but he did not wish to believe it. It hurt to even *think* that one of these men, *his* men, would betray them, especially Ulrik. One of them had.

Ulrik's gaze took in the whole table. "She is not one of us, or she would be here. In this room. At this table. Unless, of course," he said, eyeing Gaharet, "you do not wish to fight for her in case you lose."

Exploding from his seat with a growl, Gaharet drew himself up to his full height, towering over Ulrik. Ulrik sprang up to meet the challenge. Teeth bared, the bones in his face shifting and contorting, Gaharet's jaw elongated, his canines extending.

Ulrik responded, beginning to shift.

Lance jumped to his feet. "That is enough, Ulrik! This time Gaharet might kill you. We are too short on numbers to lose even you."

How dare Ulrik challenge me? Again.

He had found her. She was *his*. Ulrik would not have her. None of them would. Gaharet snarled, teeth snapping at Ulrik's jaw, a strong, musky scent filling the room. He stood over him, ready to pounce, waiting. What would Ulrik choose? To fight him for the woman? Or back down and concede to Gaharet's authority?

An expectant silence filled the room as he stared down the partly shifted, sandy-colored wolf. With a grunt and a slumping of his shoulders, Ulrik averted his gaze, baring his neck in submission. Gaharet snapped his teeth close to Ulrik's neck, close enough for fur to brush against his gums. He growled, berating the wolf for his insolence. Ulrik's shoulders drooped further, and he reversed the change, lowering himself to his seat, his head bowed.

Gaharet snarled, staring down each of his men. With a growl, he forced his wolf to recede, shaking his head as the last vestiges of it disappeared, his face becoming human once more. He sank into his chair.

What have I done?

He had never asserted his dominance like this before. His men stared at him, wary.

"My apologies." Ulrik's eyes remained downcast. "I did not realize you had intentions to claim her."

He frowned. Was that what he wanted? He had met the woman but hours ago. He did not even know her name.

"But if she is not one of us, why is she here? Now? Of all times? Using a sacred amulet? Is it merely a coincidence?" Ulrik looked around the table. "I say bed her, turn her and *then* ask her questions. It will be too late for her then, and we are not in a position to be choosey. If he does not plan to mate her, maybe one of us will."

A chorus of snarls echoed around the table — dark looks sent in Ulrik's direction. Gaharet's nostrils flared and his jaw clenched. The thought of her in the arms, in the bed, of one of his men made his gut recoil. Brushing aside the sensation, he held his hand up for silence.

"Your points are valid, Ulrik. That is why she remains here and will continue to do so until I have answers." His gaze swept around his men. "As for turning her... We will see. It is not entirely off the agenda."

His men grinned. Hope had returned. He should have known he could not hide her from the pack.

Chapter Six

Erin drifted into awareness, the left side of her forehead throbbing and her skin feeling stretched. Warm, cozy, cocooned in thick blankets and a soft mattress, she fought the desire to sink back into oblivion. The last thing she remembered... She scrunched up her face, searching for details. *Ooh, that hurts.* Erin raised her hand to her forehead, feeling the lump and the dried blood. It all came back to her. She groaned. She'd tried to run. He'd stopped her. She'd screamed and...nothing.

Her eyes fluttered open. She lay in a four-poster bed beneath a timber ceiling. A subtle shift of her head confirmed she was alone. Relief washed over her. Almost afraid to look, she lifted the covers.

Oh, thank God.

Fully clothed, although... She wiggled her toes. No shoes or socks, but no bindings or restraints either. That had to be a good sign.

Easing herself onto her elbow, a lead weight lodged in her stomach, she examined her surroundings. Rough stone walls not unlike those of the keep ruins met her searching gaze. A timber floor covered in rushes, a rough handmade candle on a small table beside the bed and a warm, golden glow emanating from hot coals in a brazier in the corner. She sniffed, wrinkling her nose. A sweet, cloying smell saturated the room.

A loud crack of thunder split the air, and she jumped. Where was she? She'd passed out in the clutches of a naked Gaharet d'Louncrais look alike who'd spoken to her in long dead languages. She frowned. What was this? A *Criminal Minds* episode? A history loving serial killer trolling excavation sites for unsuspecting victims?

As bizarre as it seemed, there might be more truth to that than she would've liked. Someone had gone to an awful lot of trouble setting up this room. Everything in keeping with the late tenth century, with a life Gaharet d'Louncrais would've lived. In all likelihood this guy was certifiable.

What was your first clue, Erin? That he ran around tourist sites in the middle of the night starkers?

Whatever his deal, she'd no plans to stick around to find out how truly dedicated he was.

She threw the bedcovers off, swung her bare feet off the bed and rushed to the door. Not locked. Another clap of thunder and she jumped again. Was he in a room on the other side, just waiting for her to regain consciousness? Trying to sneak out through the door might not be the best idea. She needed a better plan.

Searching the room again, she looked for options, a weapon, anything. Her gaze fell on the window, a narrow slit-like aperture, and she strode over to it. The window had no glass, no frame, only external shutters blocking out the light and the weather, a design Erin was acutely familiar with. Early examples of square keeps had windows like this. Keeps that were built in the tenth century.

Had he designed an entire building to tenth-century specs?

A part of her found that impressive. The rest of her, the part more concerned with self-preservation, found it more than a little disturbing. She needed to get out of here before he came to check on her.

Thunder rolled. The noise of the storm would work in her favor. Levering herself up onto the substantial window ledge, her nerveless fingers unlatched the shutters and pushed them open. Dull, gray light spilled across the room. An icy wind gusted in, buffeting the coals in the brazier. She grasped the shutters and thrust her head outside. Rain stung her face as she blinked once, twice.

She gaped at the long drop below her. She was in a tower! A keep tower! Impossible. How far out of Langeais had he taken her? She stared out into the hazy, rain drenched landscape, scanning, searching. Desperate for a recognizable landmark, Erin sought something familiar and came up wanting. Not good. How long had she been unconscious?

She peered through the rain, a flash of lightning revealing rain washed grass and land. From the tower base, the land sloped down a hill. At the bottom, a collection of wooden huts and buildings shuttered up and dark, huddled together in the storm. Beyond them a large stone wall, ramparts lining the top. Tenth-century style ramparts.

Lightning flashed again, and she gasped, her icy fingers clutching the shutters hard. In the courtyard below were men, men wearing hauberks, with swords in scabbards belted to their waists. Rain beat down on them, shields with varying insignia—a boar, a bird, a stag—secured to their saddles, horses held steady by men in tunics and breeches. Surcoats of varying colors, wind whipped and wet, covered their mail.

Her mouth opened, closed, opened, like a fish sucking air.

"Impossible." Thunder peeled out, rolling over the landscape, but she paid it little attention. Chevaliers. *In armor!*

Erin stared at the sight below, trying to make some sense of it. They weren't chevaliers. They couldn't be. She pulled herself back inside and wiped the rain from her face, her thoughts whirling in her brain. She leaned against the cold stone wall. Either her abductor had the astounding foresight to build a replica tower keep, complete with surrounding wall and ramparts, hired some actors to dress up as chevaliers *and* changed his own appearance to fit the description of a legendary chevalier whom she just happened to be excavating…or…or…

She batted the thought away, but the idea persisted. She eyed the room and its contents again. Could she be *in* the tenth century? Could that be a feasible conclusion? If she believed her eyes, it sure looked that way. A low thrum pulsed within her. What if? The potential for exploration, discovery, understanding…

Now just hold on a minute.

She blew out a large breath. She had a PhD for crying out loud. Was she really considering time travel *actually* existed? The idea of exploring living history enthralled her, but... She shook her head. No, time travel didn't exist. Not yet anyway. What were her options, though? Being kidnapped by a naked Gaharet d'Louncrais doppelgänger or being transported back into the tenth century.

She peered out through the window again. She blinked. The same rain swept vista greeted her. There had to be a logical explanation. As an intelligent woman well versed in research and scientific discovery, she could figure this out.

She surveyed the landscape. The entire building, like the windows, appeared to be a part of an early design of a keep, a *donjon* — a square, squat tower sitting atop a hill with a walled courtyard. Beyond the wall, there was only a tree line of dense, darkened forest as far as her eye could see. No sign of the city of Langeais. No evidence of *any* city. Were there other tenth or eleventh century keeps in the French countryside around Langeais? Not still standing. And what about the furniture in the room, the brazier in the corner and the rushes on the floor? What rational explanation could she find for the men below in the courtyard, mounted men, men in mail?

As if simply thinking of them alerted him to her presence, one chevalier looked up. She choked, darting back into the room, slamming the shutters closed. Hell. Her heart pounded and her hands shook. If — God forbid she was even considering it — but if she *had* somehow gone back in time, she would do well to remember the tenth century was no fairy-tale. A woman from the twenty-first century had no place in such a time. That flattened her burgeoning curiosity.

Erin chewed on her bottom lip, pacing. What did she remember?

Think. Think.

Everything had gone dark so abruptly. She ticked her memories off on her fingers. She'd revealed the wolf's skull. Picked it up. The little gold disc had dropped out. She'd read the inscription. Erin paused in her pacing. A Theban inscription. Theban—a substitution cipher used by occultists. Occultists were like witches. Witches wrote spells. A magic spell? She rolled her eyes.

Really?

Was that the best she could come up with? Still, everything happened the instant she'd read the inscription. Out loud.

No, surely not.

Pausing, casting her gaze around the room, the tactile sensation of the linen sheets against her skin still fresh, the heat from the coals in the brazier warming her body, the smell of the rushes on the floor tickling her nose and the evidence of her own eyes... Erin had to concede either the bump on her head had done some serious damage to her cerebral cortex, or... She let out a shaky breath. Or...she no longer stood in twenty-first century France.

She leaned against the wall, letting her hand rest on the rough-hewn stone. Even the stark solidity of it against her back reinforced the idea. Well, that put her confrontation with the naked man in an entirely different light.

"Shit."

Erin shivered at the memory, at the thought of those sculpted abs and that hard body pressed up against hers. She groaned. What would she say to him? Him. Could he really be *the* Gaharet d'Louncrais? How would she be able to look him in the eyes, having seen him naked?

Oh, forget that.

How would she explain her presence? She started pacing again. What would she say?

Hi. My name's Erin Richardson. I found your little gold disc on an excavation in France. In the year 2016.

Yeah, that'd go over well. He'd look at her like she'd grown a second head, or more likely that she'd sprouted a pair of devil's horns. *She* had difficulty with the concept of time travel. Could a tenth-century chevalier fathom such a possibility?

She glanced down at her clothes. She didn't look like she belonged in the tenth century. Would that convince him? Or would it alarm him even more? Superstition reigned supreme here. He would view anything out of the ordinary with suspicion. As the work of evil humors. He'd have her confined as a crazy woman in a heartbeat. Or, even worse, condemned as possessed. The witch trials didn't start for another few centuries, but that didn't mean he, or any other tenth-century person, would welcome her with open arms.

Her mind raced through her options. She could try sneaking out of here — climbing out of the window clearly not an option — and take her chances with whatever the tenth century could throw at her. With her expertise, she'd fare better than most, but where would that get her? Not back to the twenty-first century. Or… She shivered. Or she could brave Gaharet d'Louncrais.

She stopped pacing, rooted to the spot, her heart pounding.

He may not be a kidnapper, but could a tenth-century chevalier be worse? After her reaction to him, that heady flush of desire that had taken her by surprise, avoiding him would be her strategy of choice, but... She frowned. His family crest *was* on the back of that disc. And she'd appeared in front of him, not some other chevalier. That couldn't be random. She could reasonably assume that he would, therefore, have knowledge of the disc and its capabilities. He'd know how to reverse the spell. She cringed. Spell. She'd used the word spell. What was her world coming to?

Get a grip, Erin.

Whatever had brought her here, a bending of the laws of quantum physics, a wormhole, *magic* – ugh – the disc was now in his possession, not hers. If she wanted back home, back to the site and back to her team, she needed that disc.

Erin squared her shoulders. She'd fronted full auditoriums giving lectures to indifferent undergraduates, faced off with government panels over grant funding cuts and stared down belligerent developers resentful of archaeological discoveries that slowed down their building projects. She could do this. She had to do this.

He may be a chevalier, a man with no compunction about killing with a thrust of his sword – his scar attested to battles fought and survived – but he was still a man. She'd no concrete evidence as to the sort of man he was, but with her research as her reference, she could make a fair assessment. Chances were, he'd be as ruthless as the count he served. But she had one thing in her favor. She knew of his impending demise.

Depending on the month and year she now found herself in, he may have six months or five years, but one thing remained certain. His life would end prematurely, unexpectedly and possibly in a way he wouldn't see coming. What would that information be worth to him?

With renewed purpose, Erin strode to the door. She could only pray this time he wouldn't be naked.

Chapter Seven

Following the murmur of muted voices, Erin approached a large open doorway, where light spilled into the corridor. She paused beneath the lintel of the opening. There he sat. Gaharet d'Louncrais. She'd obsessed over finding him, dreamed about him and sketched him, but here, with him in the flesh, touchable, *alive* and barely six feet away, she panicked, wanting to backpedal faster than a prudish puritan in a brothel. She wanted to run.

Dismissing a servant, he turned toward her, beckoning her in, indicating a stool by the fire. She hesitated for a heartbeat before lifting her chin and striding into the room, avoiding his gaze.

She stood in the hall, an impressive room with a double height ceiling and a fire blazing in the central fire pit, giving it warmth and flickering light. Stepping closer to the fire, she rubbed her arms, trying to ward off the chill. On rough, stone walls hung beautiful, embroidered panels in dark reds, greens, browns and yellows. Images of battles and feats of bravery danced across them where they were spaced around the lit oil lamps, little bowls of fat on fire, which smoked up the room. She'd sell her soul to the devil for a chance to examine those wall hangings. Nothing quite like them had survived to the modern era.

At one end of the hall was an enormous table. Twenty people could sit at that table, the room itself large enough to hold a small village. With only the two of them in it, the sheer size and grandeur of the room pressed in on her, doing nothing for her flagging courage. Her plan to confront him now seemed foolhardy. If she'd had her boots, she'd have quaked in them. Stealing herself, she faced him.

He sat by the fire, clothed in a simple, black tunic reaching just above his knees, woolen breeches and soft black boots. Coiled energy radiated from him, an animal alertness as though poised, ready to strike at a moment's notice. Even without armor, without the red surcoat and its black wolf insignia, he looked every inch the tenth-century warrior. He'd a presence about him that dominated the room, all underscored by a sharp intelligence glittering in his eyes. This man would be a formidable enemy on and off the battlefield. She should run while she still could.

He locked eyes with her, staring with an intensity that caused a clenching low in her belly. She squirmed, her skin prickling, as his gaze dropped lower, the weight of his stare burning a path over her body as hot and as heavy as if he'd reached out and touched her. He neither moved nor spoke. His eyes said it all.

She didn't know what scared her more — the way he looked at her or the way her nipples tightened and her core heated in response. She could well believe women of any century swooning at his feet. One more minute and she'd be positively panting for him.

She eyed the doorway, indecision immobilizing her, but as inviting as it looked, turning tail and running wouldn't solve her predicament. Better the devil she knew, and she knew him. As well as anyone from the twenty-first century could know him. Better than she knew anyone else she might encounter. And she knew his type. Pulling a mask of indifference over her face, she met his gaze over the fire and waited.

The silence stretched between them.

"Let us start," he said, his deep voice rumbling, "with how you came by the amulet you had in your possession?"

Caught up in the deep timbre of his voice, it took Erin a few moments to process that his words weren't in Old French, or Latin. Her eyes widened.

"You speak English?" A very old form of English, but understandable all the same.

"I speak your language, yes. Your pronunciations are quite strange," he said, frowning. "So, now that we can...understand one another... Where did you come upon the amulet?"

"The amulet?" The little gold disc. She licked her lips, her nerves getting the better of her, and she floundered beneath his all-consuming stare. The man had the most gorgeous eyes. Bedroom eyes.

Get a hold of yourself, Erin. So he lucked out in the gene pool. Good for him. Imagine him in his underwear. Isn't that what they say? God, no. Don't do that.

"Is it yours? The amulet?" Get him talking.

Yes, a much better idea.

He leaned forward on his stool, elbows resting on his knees, scrutinizing her, and she scuttled back a few steps. Space, she needed space between them. So she could keep her wits about her. To give herself a head start if fleeing into the tenth-century countryside was the better option. So she wouldn't imagine what it would feel like to have him sweep her up in his arms. She slammed a halt to her backward trajectory, and her runaway thoughts, stiffening her spine. Letting him see he intimidated her would only work to his advantage, not hers.

He didn't answer her, tilting his head to the side, his brow furrowing. His gaze raked over her body, absent of its previous heat, taking in every inch of her. Her insides quaked and fired-up nerve endings danced along her skin, but she remained still. What was he searching for?

His attention narrowed partway down the left side of her body. She looked down. Her watch.

Oh hell.

Definitely not from the tenth century. What would he make of that? A piece of witchcraft? His gaze fixed on it, and his eyes narrowed. He couldn't possibly hear its ticking... Could he? She strained, listening for the tick, tick, tick of her watch, but she couldn't hear it over the crackling of the fire and the storm raging outside.

Glancing back at him, she gasped. He was on his feet, striding past the fire, closing the gap between them. Fast. All rational thought vanished, along with her plan and her courage, as six feet, and more, of muscled warrior barreled toward her. Fight had never been an option. That left flight. Erin bolted for the door, swift on bare feet. He gave chase, his long legs giving him the advantage. Two more steps.

Could she make it?

Strong arms snatched her off her feet, pulling her body against his. She squealed, struggling, but he held her tight. Kicking out at him, she tried to slip from his grasp, all too aware of his muscular body pressed firm against every inch of her from behind. A soft groan escaped him, a hint of warm breath on her cheek. She shivered, heat invading her body, her thighs clenching. She bit back a moan, struggling harder.

"Be still," he growled in her ear, his arm a steel band about her waist, her wrists gripped in one large hand. Was that…? Could she feel…? She stiffened, panting. From exertion, fear or in reaction to his arousal? She couldn't be sure.

His chest rose and fell against her back, his breathing as rough as hers. She remained still, uncertain what he'd do, not wishing to provoke him any further. And yet, Lord help her, she wanted to provoke him further.

What has gotten into me?

He loosened his hold, shifting his hips away from hers. She smothered the sting of disappointment, her body trembling. She fought against the desire to press back into him, to rub herself against his thick erection. The inappropriateness of her body's reaction was *unbelievable*.

"Why did you run?" His chest rumbled against her shoulder blades. "I had no reason to hurt you."

"It's the tenth century. Like you need a reason."

"The what?"

He grunted, releasing her from his arms, and Erin pulled away as fast as she could, but he didn't let her go completely. Oh no, that was too much to hope for. He maintained a grip on her wrist, tethering her to him. She didn't want to look him in the eye but keeping her attention on his face restrained her gaze from sliding down. Down to where his intentions would be pointedly obvious.

It didn't comfort her. Heat suffused her cheeks. His gaze hot, lips held in a thin line, his emotions warred across his features.

"You speak," he said, after a few moments, his breathing labored, "as if you are an outsider, a foreigner." He held her wrist up to examine her watch, momentarily distracted by its moving parts.

Erin quivered, conscious of his grip on her arm. "I... I am an outsider."

Shadows flickered in his eyes. A strong, musky scent filled her nostrils. There was a caged energy about him, barely restrained. The chase had excited him, stirred something within him, a darkness, basely sexual. And it hungered for *her*.

Erin thought she'd had a fair chance of making it to the doorway, into the corridor and to a large door she'd pegged as the entrance to the keep. He'd been too fast for her, scarily fast, and the look on his face as he'd come after her had robbed her of her ability to breathe. Stamped onto his face was the exhilaration at having to chase her, and a determination to catch her. He had the eyes of a predator, tested on many a battlefield, and he knew when he had the upper hand. She'd lost the battle before the chase had even begun.

She stood, limbs refusing to respond to her commands to run, to fight as he spent a few moments fascinated by the moving hands of her watch. Turning away from it, he eyed her with a fervency that had her knees buckling and heat storming through her body. Forget running. Right now, she probably couldn't even walk. Oh man, she was in trouble. Big trouble. How had she ever thought she could match wits with him?

"Why did you run from me?"

She jerked her wrist, attempting to pull away, but he wouldn't release her, instead stepping closer. Her heart thumped against her rib cage, threatening to bust out and desert ship. It wouldn't surprise her if he could feel her pulse pounding away at her wrist. She retreated further, but he followed, backing her into the wall.

"It is a simple question."

Erin's breath stalled, the hard stone wall at her back, an equally daunting wall of muscle in front of her. A big, dark chevalier, he loomed over her. Her legs trembled, the consistency of putty rather than flesh and bone.

"Last night, you seemed angry that I had the amulet. And then you came at me so fast... Look, I'm... I'm... I don't follow the old religions. I'm not a witch." Her bottom lip trembled despite her efforts to control it. "Let's clear that up now. I found the amulet. It's not mine. I don't know *who* it belongs to."

Liar, liar, pants on fire.

It belonged to him. It had to.

"And this?" He tugged at her left wrist, her watch a glaring presence not so easily dismissed.

"Jewelry." She gave a small shrug of her shoulders. "It's the new fashion."

"Mmm-hmm."

He smiled, but didn't loosen his grip, nor did he back away. He leaned toward her, his mouth bare inches from hers, dark eyes staring deep into hers, strange shadows flitting behind the irises. She couldn't look away. Any fear of him had fled, replaced by something far more dangerous. It had her quivering inside her skin, superseding everything. It terrified her beyond imagining she'd not only be unable to resist him, but she wouldn't *want* to.

"Never run from me," he said, his breath warm across her lips and they parted in expectation, traitors to her mind's will. "I will *always* catch you."

In one swift move, he captured her other wrist and pinned her against the wall with his body. Her mind screamed a protest. Her body rejoiced. His knee nudged her legs apart, slipping between them, pressing his muscular thigh against the very center of her. And damn if she didn't let him.

Where had her moral outrage gone, her hard-earned determination to never put herself in the arms of such a man? They'd deserted her — overpowered by a rapacious libido she never knew she possessed. It threw common sense to the wind and laughed in the face of her resolution to remain unaffected. Her body burned for him and happily broadcast that fact loud and clear. It couldn't have been more obvious if she'd a neon sign flashing 'all systems are go'.

With a lick of his lips, he captured her mouth. No soft kiss, no gentle seduction. She'd run. He'd caught her. To the victor went the spoils. He was taking what he wanted.

Dredging up some belated form of courage, she tore her mouth from his, refusing to give him what he demanded — an all-access pass to her mouth, her body. Not so easily dissuaded, he leaned into her neck, the tickle of his beard and his lips whisper soft on the sensitive skin of her throat and inhaled deeply.

Her whole body *vibrated* in response, rolling out the welcome mat. Shifting her wrists into one large hand, he ran the other down her cheek to her chin. A gentle press of his fingers and she was facing him, eye to eye, breath to breath.

"You desire this as much as I," he murmured.

She gave a strained shake of her head, denying his words, but when he rubbed his thumb across her bottom lip, she couldn't keep up the pretense. Her eyelids fluttered closed, her lips parted on a sigh, her body providing him all the permission he needed. He recaptured her mouth in his, slipping his tongue between her lips. With delicious hot thrusts, he demanded she respond in kind.

Erin's resistance melted faster than summer hail after a storm. Her body softening against his, she responded with a fierce need of her own. The voice of caution disappeared beneath the roaring of blood through her veins.

He released her, pulling away, ending the kiss as abruptly as he'd started it, leaving Erin dazed and panting. She leaned against the wall, unsure if her legs would hold her if she didn't have support.

"Tell me now you did not want that," he said, his expression triumphant, full of pure male satisfaction.

She scowled, gathering her anger, embarrassed by her easy surrender.

"Of all the arrogance…"

He'd manhandled her, pushed her up against a wall, given her nowhere to go.

"It is not arrogance if I am right."

"You're nothing but an ignorant savage."

Erin clenched her fists, her nails biting into her palms. She *loathed* men like him. Men who had power, wealth and confidence. Men who could turn the charm on when they wanted and turn it off in the blink of an eye. Granted, she'd never met a sword toting chevalier before, but it made little difference. She'd witnessed the damage a man like him could do, over and over again. She'd lived it her entire childhood.

He gave a soft, breathy chuckle. "Savage? Perhaps." A wry smile tilted at the corner of his mouth. "Ignorant? I think not."

So sure of himself, his gaze dipped from her face to her breasts, her nipples still peaked, and he licked his lips, causing her belly to do little flip-flops. She glared at him. If he thought she'd fall for his charm because of one kiss — one heart stopping, amazing kiss — that in future she couldn't, wouldn't, resist his advances, then he really was too arrogant for words. She wasn't some tenth-century virginal maid who'd flutter her eyelashes at him and beg for his attentions. He'd caught her off guard, nothing more.

Lifting her chin and locking her knees, she ignored the heat spreading across her cheeks and the way her body betrayed her. *Little snitch.*

Eyes narrowing, his gaze returning to her face, he placed his hands on the wall on either side of her head, forcing her to look at him, his face inches from hers. Dark, intense eyes pinned her in place, and he thrust out his jaw. Erin wanted to look away but she couldn't.

"Your clothes are of a make I am unfamiliar with. They are of materials I have never seen before and they reveal much more than is acceptable."

She opened her mouth to protest but stilled at a stern look from him. The man liked getting his own way. Why did that not surprise her?

"Your accent is strange, your speech patterns I have not heard before and I have traveled much and met many foreigners," he said. "Your command of my language is poor. You wear on your wrist a device which is not jewelry as you claim, but I believe is a means of marking time. You are not a witch, but you are not from here either. Tell me now you think me ignorant." He raised an eyebrow at her, waiting for her answer.

Erin opened her mouth and closed it again. His insights were unnerving. At her continued silence, a smile tugged at the corner of his mouth.

"I did not think so. Come, sit. You need have no fear I will hurt you, but I will have answers." Dropping his arms, he turned away, walking back to his stool by the fire and sat down. After a few indecisive moments, thoughts of defying him on principle flitting across her mind, Erin followed. For all his arrogance, the man had a shrewd intelligence. No wonder the count relied on him for advice.

Sitting on the stool, Erin folded her arms over her chest, facing him across the fire. His lazy amusement at her capitulation served only to poke at her indignation. Her top lip curled in a snarl. She didn't see she had much of a choice, but she'd keep her distance. Forewarned now, the battle lines were clearly drawn. She'd withstood men like him her entire adult life. She could resist him.

"Where are you from?" he asked, skewering her with that intense stare of his, his gaze flicking to her watch, then back to her face. "Or should I ask…when?"

She gasped. He knew or had at least made an educated guess. No skepticism, no derision. He didn't eye her with suspicion or make the sign of the cross. He crossed his legs in front of him, hands clasped in his lap, watching her. How could he be so calm when she felt like her entire world had turned on its axis? He either had a brilliant poker face or he had a prior knowledge, an understanding of the forces at work here predating her sudden appearance.

"I thought so," he said when she didn't respond. "Tell me how you came by the amulet."

"Not until you tell me what it is?" she fired back, wrapping herself in the shreds of her bravado.

He shrugged. "It is what brought you here."

Her eyes widened. Confirmation. The disc had power. "How?"

"Did you not read the inscription?"

"Well, yes, but... Are you suggesting it's a...*magic spell*?"

"You tell me. You were the one with it in your possession."

"It has your family crest on it."

He tugged on his beard, a thoughtful expression crossing his face. "Tell me where you found it."

Erin hesitated. They could dance around each other all day and get nowhere. He wouldn't simply admit to owning an amulet that could transport a person through time. He already suspected she'd traveled here from another century. Confirming it would change very little.

Taking a deep breath, resisting the urge to squirm on the stool, Erin unfolded her story, outlining her job as an archaeologist, the concept of an excavation site, the location of the dig and her discovery of the gold disc he called an amulet. She made no mention of the underground cell, the skull, the skeleton or his death. Knowledge was power, and she needed that information to tip the scales in her favor.

Finishing her tale, she lapsed into silence. Outside the storm raged, inside the only sound was the crackling of the fireplace. A log shifted, sparks shooting onto the floor, and Erin flinched.

Say something, damn it.

He sat, rubbing his hand over his jaw, tugging at his beard, in no apparent rush to respond. Erin fidgeted. While he appeared the epitome of control, underneath, barely below the surface, lurked something dangerous, ready to burst out at a moment's notice. Had she told him too much? Tested his receptiveness? She didn't want to wake the beast. Not if she could help it.

After what seemed like an age, he spoke. "You found the amulet at Langeais Keep?"

She nodded. "Mmm-hmm."

"Just the amulet?"

She nodded, maintaining eye contact. "So far, but you have to understand the nature of an archaeological dig. These things take time. We sift through dirt and rubble and rocks carefully. Artifacts are often broken, small and scattered. We don't want to miss anything by rushing." Kernels of truth made it easier to lie. Had she convinced him? She couldn't say.

"You mentioned another keep, a newer one."

She came from a time in his future, but did he realize *how far* into his future? Telling him about the fifteenth-century château at Langeais would certainly put things in perspective for him.

"The original keep, the one from the tenth century… I mean now…" She stopped. This was a lot more nerve-racking than she had expected.

"Go on."

He asked for it.

"The original keep is nothing but ruins, destroyed in the Hundred Years War, which took place from 1337 to 1453. All that's left are a few crumbling walls."

She looked up to see how he had digested this information. He'd not moved a muscle.

"Not long after, King Louis XI built a château, more elaborate, still defensive, but not a simple design like the original keep. It still stands, but it's nothing more than a sightseeing attraction now. A place for people to visit, to see what an actual castle looks like."

His eyes widened a little, his Adam's apple jerked up and down. "What year are you from?" he asked, his voice strained.

She bit her lip.

Here goes nothing.

"Two thousand and sixteen."

He gasped, jerking upright on his stool. Erin tensed.

"That is more than a thousand years!"

It took a moment for him to recover his composure, a primitive, almost feral look flashing in his eyes as he stared at her, his warning about running from him and its consequences fresh in her mind. He made no move toward her, save to focus on her mouth. It took all her willpower not to lick her lips again.

"You are telling me you are from over a thousand years in my future?"

Sucking in her courage, she nodded.

"So your language, your accent, it is not foreign at all. It has…evolved over time."

"Basically." Close enough. Now was not the time to introduce him to the, as yet undiscovered, continent of Australia.

His attention shifted to the doorway, and he beckoned a man in. The servant leaned in and whispered something in Gaharet's ear.

"Send them up to see me, Gascon. I will deal with this myself. Old Tumas is a good man, but he can be difficult. We do not need any squabbles between the farmers right now." He turned back to her. "What is your name?"

"Erin. Erin Richardson."

"Erin," he said, nodding. "I think you know I am Gaharet d'Louncrais. I welcome you to my keep. We have much to talk about, but first I have something that needs my attention. I think also," he paused, eyeing her up and down, "I need to procure you something more appropriate to wear, something more suitable for this...century. Gascon will escort you back to your bedchamber. And Gascon," he said, turning to the servant. "Get Anne to see to some clothes for her. I believe my mother's dresses are stored away in chests. They will be most suitable."

"Of course, Mon Seigneur. Anne is currently in the village. I will inform her the moment she returns."

"Very well."

Released from his company, her thoughts in a whirl, Erin followed the servant to the dubious safety of the bedchamber. And so began the battle of wits. What would she have to give to get the answers she needed? Instinct told her she'd need every ounce of her resolve to come out of this unscathed.

Chapter Eight

Gaharet sat waiting for his farmers to arrive, staring into the fire after he let Erin retreat from the room. Watching the play of emotions across her face as they had talked, he had noted every expression, every gesture. The shine of pride in her green eyes when she'd explained her work. The tensing of her muscles and the thinning of her lips as she'd spoken of the inscription, the amulet and its capabilities. Her direct stare as she denied finding anything else. No matter how insignificant, he added it to his compilation of knowledge, storing it away, using it to inform his growing understanding of her.

As an archaeologist, a studier of history and past civilizations, she would require skills in discipline, research and analysis. She was a learned woman, more educated than any woman he had ever known. That such a woman could exist—a foreign woman, really foreign, from another place *and* time—from over a thousand years in the future! He shook his head, his mind shying away from such numbers. How had this happened? The amulet was never meant as a means to transverse time.

He could appreciate the risk she had taken telling him the truth. Had she revealed her story to another, less accepting man, a man who was not his own walking, talking myth… He pinched the bridge of his nose. That consequence did not bear thinking about. She had every right to fear he would label her a witch.

How different would her world be from his? Mayhap she had seen and experienced many things which he, and all in his world, would find astounding. What other things might she readily accept? Things like him. And he desired her like no other woman before her.

He inhaled, taking in her lingering scent. His body heated, and he shifted in his seat, attempting to ease the throbbing in his groin. Could this be what his father experienced when he had first encountered his mother? This heat that burned through his loins, this uncontrollable urge to claim her, imprint himself on her at the earliest possible opportunity? What he wouldn't give to experience a love like his parents had had.

Gaharet eyed the doorway through which Erin had departed. He needed to take a wife. He could take *her* as his wife. His beast roiled beneath the surface. It liked that idea, pushed for it to happen. Now. He tamped the urge down, rubbing his hand over his jaw. Would she take the turning? *Could* he inflict it on another? She looked healthy enough, though slight. *Perhaps.*

She certainly had strength of mind, a boldness tempered with uncertainty, but defiant in the face of it. So unlike the usual insipid women at court who simpered at him, all fluttering eyelashes and coy glances. *She* had called him an ignorant savage. He chuckled. No one had ever dared do that. He glanced at the doorway again. Her swaying hips hugged by that tight fabric were still fresh in his mind. *Mon Dieu*. He tugged on the end of his beard, smiling. For once, the needs of the pack aligned with his own. For once, he would not be forced to choose.

"Mon Seigneur Gaharet." Gascon, his head servant, stood in the doorway. "Farmers Tumas and Brenton are here to see you."

"Show them in, Gascon."

Two men, skin weathered from years of working in the elements, strode into the hall. Tumas, the elder of the two, a man in his fourth decade with graying hair and beard, wore a thunderous expression. It never took much to rile up old Tumas. If his farming skills and knowledge had not been what they were, Gaharet would have moved the old farmer on years ago. Thankfully, Brenton had a more jovial nature. Grizzled and worn, but a good ten years younger than Tumas, he had an easy smile, always ready with a kind word, a laugh and a joke. Brenton fixed a wary glance on Tumas, as though expecting a blow from him at any moment. With Tumas that was always a possibility.

"What seems to be the problem?" asked Gaharet. Tumas scowled at Brenton.

"Mon Seigneur Gaharet," Brenton said, nodding his head in deference. "It appears the fault is all mine. You see —"

"Damn right it is," said Tumas.

"My pigs got out of their yard, Mon Seigneur Gaharet," said Brenton, ignoring Tumas. "Broke straight through. That old sow is a crafty thing, and I swear she has worked on that fence for weeks now, testing for weak spots."

"Got into my cabbages. The stinking lot of them. Filthy animals."

"Now, hold on. My pigs are clean animals. The cleanest animals there are, and they provide good meat for the estate. They are smart, too." He shrugged. "Maybe a little too smart."

"They ate half my damn cabbages and dug up a freshly seeded field."

Gaharet raised an eyebrow at Brenton.

Brenton nodded. "That they did. So I rounded my pigs up and then went to see old Tumas here about compensation and the damn fool chased me around the field with a hoe. Tried to kill me."

"Your pigs destroyed half my crop."

"Which I offered to pay for."

"In small sums over the year."

The two men faced each other, nose to nose.

"I cannot afford the entire sum in one payment," said Brenton. "And half the pigs will not be ready for sale for at least two more months."

"And I cannot afford to lose half my cabbages."

"Enough!" Gaharet brought a halt to the argument before Tumas took a swing at Brenton. Both men lapsed into silence, though Tumas looked like he had more to say. "This is what is going to happen. Brenton." Gaharet pointed a finger at him. "You will repair your yards at your own expense."

"Yes, Mon Seigneur Gaharet."

"Make them stronger this time. We do not want them getting into what is left of Tumas' crop."

"What about my lost cabbages?"

Gaharet glared at the old man and Tumas flinched, taking a step back.

"*I* will reimburse you for your cabbages."

Brenton's eyes went wide. "Mon Seigneur Gaharet?"

Tumas snorted.

"I need both my farmers. Neither of you can bear the loss," said Gaharet, by way of explanation.

"Thank you, Mon Seigneur Gaharet." Brenton bowed his head. "My family is in your debt."

"That will be all," he said, dismissing them both.

Old Tumas turned on his heel. "Keep your damn pigs in your yard from now on," he muttered to Brenton, clomping from the hall.

"Truly, thank you, Mon Seigneur Gaharet."

He waved away the gratitude. "Make sure those pigs do not get out again, Brenton."

"Of course, Mon Seigneur." He bowed again and followed Tumas from the hall.

Gascon appeared at his side.

"Have someone do an inventory on Tumas' lost cabbages. I need to organize payment to him."

"Right away, Mon Seigneur."

"Did old Tumas really chase Brenton around the field with a hoe?"

Gascon nodded. "I am told it was quite the sight."

"Of all the farmer's fields for Brenton's pigs to get into it had to be Tumas'."

Gascon nodded in agreement. "Truly. There is another small matter for you to attend to, Mon Seigneur."

Gaharet sighed, gesturing for Gascon to tell him this new concern.

"Henri from the stables has asked that you come down and look at Crooner when you have a moment. He is lame again. He mentioned you wanted to be informed."

"Of course. I will visit the stables presently. I have a few accounts to settle first."

"Very well, Mon Seigneur." Gascon departed, leaving Gaharet alone in the hall.

Gaharet pinched the bridge of his nose with his fingers. As a boy, the idea of one day being the master of the keep had held great appeal — being in charge, running the estate, the challenge of it all. His father had handled it with such ease. Of course, Gaharet's mother had been by his side, and as Gaharet and D'Artagnon had grown, his father had placed small amounts of responsibility on them, too. Gaharet had no such luxury now, and the day-to-day running of things, of being responsible for so many people, their lives and their livelihoods, weighed heavily on his mind.

Like his father, he had also taken on the leadership of the pack. In this, he at least had the support of his men. Most of them. The one person he had once thought he could count on caused him more trouble than he would have thought possible. Ulrik. Yet another matter that would soon need attention.

He sighed, getting to his feet. He had accounts to deal with and a lame horse to see to. His responsibilities would not wait and in good conscience he could not, would not, shirk them, no matter how much the intriguing woman upstairs drew him. He had obligations — to his men, to his servants, his farmers, his animals, anything and anyone that relied on him for their wellbeing. That duty, as difficult as it might be, always came first.

Chapter Nine

The first thing Erin did upon returning to the bedchamber was to remove her damn watch. Stupid of her to forget it. Look at what it had instigated. She raised her fingers to her lips. The feel of his mouth on hers was forever scorched into her memory. She scowled, scrubbing her hand across her mouth. He'd shaken her resolve, that's all. Knocked her off-kilter. A setback nothing more. Erin wouldn't be making the same mistake again.

She glanced at the time before stuffing her watch into the pocket of her jeans. Four-fifteen. She'd been unconscious all night and most of the day. Using the pitcher and basin to wash, she gently bathed the blood from her face and inspected the gash and the bump with her fingers. The cut wasn't as large as she'd feared, but her forehead was tender. How far the bruise stretched she'd no way of knowing, but it would fade in time.

Assured she'd received no permanent damage, combing her hair back with her fingers and retying her ponytail, she set about exploring every inch of the room, examining every item of furniture and every feature. The mattress made of down, the woolen covers on the bed, the tallow candle, the brazier in the corner, the washbowl on the table—nothing escaped her intense scrutiny. For one, the chance to study artifacts in situ like this might never again present itself, and Erin couldn't let the opportunity slip by. And two, anything she could learn, no matter how insignificant, would only increase her chances of survival.

As the afternoon dragged on and no one came, not a servant to offer her food, or this Anne with more appropriate clothes, Erin's curiosity waned. The coals in the brazier burned down, the room became colder, and as the evening crept in, slowly, but surely, darkness descended. She swaddled herself in the wool blanket and huddled on the bed, considering venturing from the bedchamber.

The fire would be lit in the hall, and Gaharet hadn't said she couldn't leave the room. She'd left it earlier, when she could hold her bladder no longer, to find and use the garderobe and no one raised the alarm. Either Anne had yet to return from the village, or they'd forgotten about her. Sitting here in the cold and dark seemed foolish. At least in the hall, she'd be warm.

Shrugging off the blanket, Erin slid off the bed, strode to the door and ran smack into a solid wall of muscle.

"Erin? What are you doing hiding in the dark? Why has Anne not taken care of you?"

Her breath hitched. Gaharet.

He stepped back out through the doorway and called for a servant, giving a few orders and sending the man hurrying away. He re-entered the room and she tensed. Alone in the dark with him. Not ideal. Not where she wanted to be *at all*.

"Why did you not join me in the hall? It is much warmer down there."

She could only make out his silhouette, but she tilted her face to look up at him. "I was heading in that very direction." Being in the dark had one benefit. He couldn't see her blushing. The lack of control she had over her body's response to him was humiliating.

He reached out, touching her cheek, and she shivered at the gesture, backing away, beyond the reach of his outstretched hand.

"Goodness, you are cold."

A short, prodigiously large, older woman with an enormous bosom that jutted out like the prow of a ship appeared in the doorway sparing her from answering. The woman lumbered into the room, a lit candle in her hand, a food splattered apron tied around her waist and a bundle of clothing over her arm. Her dark hair, streaked with gray, was pinned back from her lined face, and she smiled at Erin, setting the candle on the table. She turned, catching Erin's shivering form, and frowned at Gaharet.

"Good Lord, young man," she said. "Where are your manners? The poor girl must be freezing. It is like the dead of winter in here. And she is injured. Poor child."

Gaharet frowned. "Did I not ask you to arrange clothing for her?"

"I was in the village. Gascon would have told you I was there. I have only just returned. You know I always return late when I visit there, Gaharet." She tsk, tsked at him. "You should have seen to her comfort hours ago, tended to that wound. You disappoint me, Gaharet."

Erin struggled to translate the conversation from Old French, but the tone could not be mistaken. The old woman had *scolded* Gaharet d'Louncrais! Oh dear. Erin's gaze flicked between them, waiting for the reprimand, the outrage.

"Speak slower, Anne. Franceis is not her native tongue," said Gaharet, with no hint of rebuke in his voice.

"Oh. Lovely to have visitors from afar again. The name is Anne, dear," she said, turning her back on Gaharet, speaking slower, enunciating her words clearly, to allow Erin time to translate. "Now love, I will take care of you and I will get you a poultice for this." She touched a gentle hand to Erin's forehead. "Pay no mind to our young Gaharet. He is a good boy." She pursed her lips, shooting him a dark look. "Most of the time."

Erin's gaze settled on d'Louncrais, not really sure what to expect, but his wry smile and resigned expression surprised her.

"I have brought you some clothes, love, and Gascon is organizing a nice hot bath for you down the hall in Gaharet's chambers. Come dear, let us get you warm." She turned to Gaharet. "And you, young man," she said, wagging her finger at him, not at all intimidated by his size and the fact her continued employment rested solely at his discretion, "need to have a think about your behavior." She huffed. "Leaving the poor girl all alone in the cold and dark... I'll not have this keep slipping into disrepute or have the villagers gossip about our poor treatment of guests."

What Anne lacked in height and titles she sure made up for in attitude. Erin liked her. She may prove a useful ally.

Gaharet sighed, rolling his eyes toward the ceiling, but his smile held genuine affection for the old woman. "Yes, Anne." He turned to Erin. "Go with Anne. She will see to your needs, and I will await you both in the hall for the evening meal."

What an intriguing exchange between servant and Lord. Lost in thought, Erin let Anne lead her from the room and down the corridor to another chamber, one with a large tub in the corner.

"Can I help you with your clothes, love?" asked Anne, placing the armful of garments she held onto the bed.

Erin eyed the room. Gaharet's personal chamber. What secrets could it reveal? "Perhaps after I bathe?"

"Of course, dear. I will return in a while to assist you. Then we will adjourn to the hall for the evening meal." With that, Anne left her.

Waiting until the door was firmly closed, Erin stepped farther into the room, moving around it, running her hands over the covers on the bed, fingering the clothes laid out for her and touching the solid wood bed frame. Apart from the deep barrel that served as a bath, steam rising above its lip, this room was much the same as the one she'd come from. The same shutters over the narrow window, a similar brazier sat in the corner full of hot coals and the ever-present meadowsweet rushes covered the floor.

There were some differences, though. In the corner his sword rested in its scabbard. His hauberk lay where he'd thrown it over a chair and above it on a hook, hung his surcoat and his padded gambeson. Reaching out, she ran her fingers over the leather surcoat. Blood red. On the left side his family crest. A bold choice, blood red and black — gules and sable — the colors of a warrior, military might, wisdom and constancy. The motif unmistakable on the battlefield and easily identifiable as the crest on the little gold disc, the amulet, she'd found.

Erin dropped her hand to his sword. The scabbard — deep-red tan leather decorated in wolf motifs and capped with an elaborate, metal tip — rested against the wall. One of her bucket list destinations, the Museum of Medieval Warfare at Château de Castelnaud, she'd planned to visit at the conclusion of the dig. Here, now, she could go one better. She could handle a sword. His sword. Grip the pommel, feel its weight. A well-cared for, still in use sword. Her fingers rested on the grip. An opportunity like this may never present itself again.

Unclipping the leather strap holding the sword in place, she grasped the plain, functional grip and withdrew it, holding it aloft in front of her. Beautiful. And lethal. Just holding it had her pulse racing. Not too heavy and well balanced, it'd still require a decent amount of strength to wield it during a fully fledged battle. To use it to maim and kill. She resisted the urge to wave it around, pretend she was in a skirmish, thrusting it, swinging it, defending herself against an imaginary foe. She'd probably slice her foot off.

She tested its edge, running her finger along the tip of the sword. She winced as it cut her finger. Sharp. Of course. He wouldn't be much of a chevalier if he didn't keep it so. She stuck her finger in her mouth to stem the small drops of blood, sliding the blade carefully back in the scabbard before she cut herself again. Twice now something of his had made her bleed. First the amulet and now the sword.

Careful. These things come in threes.

Turning her attention to the chain mail, she picked it up off the chair. A little on the weighty side. She plunked it back down, but it slithered onto the floor. Rescuing the hauberk, she bunched it up and dropped it on the chair, adjusting it a little, tugging at the edges of it. She couldn't quite get it back into position without risking it falling on the floor again, but a man with the luxury of servants to wait on him shouldn't notice.

Her gaze shifted to a chest beside the bed, a candle and a book perched on top. She flicked the cover of the book open to reveal letters in Greek. He read Greek, spoke Old French, Latin *and* Anglo Saxon. A well-educated man. She thumbed through a few pages. A philosophical treatise? A history? No illuminations suggested so.

She paused. To have such a thing in his possession hinted at an interest in other disciplines like the sciences, rather than relying solely on the religious thought and practices of the time. Unusual, but hardly surprising. Judging from his keep, the man was insanely wealthy and, therefore, powerful. He could probably do almost anything he pleased, be granted any privilege.

Kneeling, she shifted the candle and the book then lifted the lid of the chest. Books — dozens of them, titles in several languages. A well-traveled man. He'd said as much. The variety of tomes suggested he may have journeyed as far as Constantinople. She closed the chest, replacing the candle and the book.

It all begged the question as to why would a man who'd every access to knowledge and advanced scientific thought own something like the amulet? An object more in line with the old religion, a practice more prevalent amongst peasants and illiterate farming folk. Could Gaharet d'Louncrais be a secret pagan at heart? It might explain why she'd encountered him in the middle of the night. Why he'd been naked. Had she caught him returning from a celebration, a ritual of some kind? And where did the Theban script fit in with all this?

She stood, mulling over this new information. She approached the tub and dipped her fingers in. Nice and hot. Scented, too. Stripping off her clothes, she climbed into the barrel-like bath. Immersing herself in the water up to her shoulders, she closed her eyes, letting her head drop back against the rim.

"Oh yes."

Wealth certainly had its advantages. His keep may not have all the mod cons she was used to, but it had this. Unlike her experience with the garderobe, *this* she would enjoy.

Chapter Ten

Erin entered the noisy hall. Dressed as a noblewoman, layers of fine wool with embroidered motifs covered her from neck to toe. Servants and farmers gathered at the enormous table, the hum of their conversation, their muted laughter, filled the hall. Gaharet sat by the fire, his head turned in her direction. He flicked his gaze up and down her body and licked his lips. At his hungry gaze, her steps faltered.

Ignore him.

She turned to the table, taking a step toward an empty seat. She froze, her gaze snapping back to his face. *Did he just…growl?* Her face flushed as they locked gazes. He rose, striding in her direction, the curiosity of his servants in the periphery of her awareness. The urge to flee, to barricade herself in the bedchamber and invent her own version of a chastity belt with flashing, red lights and an air-raid siren surged through her. Quashing the instinct, pretending she had a backbone the consistency of steel rather than of Jell-O, Erin stood her ground, her chin thrust forward.

He stopped in front of her, a smile tugging at the corners of his mouth. Did he really think she'd be stupid enough to run a second time? His eyes told her he hoped she would.

Not his lucky day today.

"You didn't provide me with any shoes." Braving speech, she indicated her bare toes peeking out beneath her gown. All chatter ceased, an expectant silence filling the room. The heat in her face intensified. "My feet will get cold." It took every bit of will she possessed to not take a step back. Didn't the man understand the concept of personal space?

Oh, he understands it all right, and uses it to great effect.

Smiling down at her, he reached out, raising his hand to her hair. She locked her knees and swallowed hard. With a deft twist of his wrist, he removed the tie of her ponytail and her hair tumbled around her shoulders. Her mouth parted on a sharp intake of breath, but she quickly clamped it shut as his eyes zeroed in on her lips. His nostrils flared, and his hand hovered near her face, but he didn't touch her again.

"Come, sit." Withdrawing his hand, he dropped it to his side. "The meal will be soon served and that will warm you."

"I would like some shoes. Or at least my own back. Please."

Lust glimmered in his eyes. Had he heard the husky quality of the word *please*? Did he intuit it to mean more than a simple token of politeness? Had she meant it as more? Hell, she wasn't so sure she hadn't. Standing this close to him had all her intelligent brain cells malfunctioning. The man should come with a warning label, one of those *caution hot* signs.

He pulled back from her, his face taut, jaw clenched.

"No." He moved to take his seat around the other side of the table, amongst his people. "Without shoes, you will not get far."

She glanced at the servants, their faces turned away, whispering. "You're keeping me prisoner here?"

Leaning his elbows on the table, he clasped his fingers together, his chin resting on his hands. "I have no intention of locking you away, but I found you on my lands in the middle of the night. It would be remiss of me to give you the opportunity to wander off. We have yet much to discuss." He indicated the space across from him. "Sit and we can talk. I am curious as to where you would go if you were to leave."

He watched her, waiting for an answer, and Erin fidgeted. "I don't know where I'd go," she finally admitted and caught the hint of a smirk hidden behind his hands. He may not be locking her in a room, but he wasn't going to let her leave either. She opened her mouth to call him on it, but he'd turned away, deep in conversation with a man next to him. Summarily dismissed, all she could do was take the place at the table he'd indicated.

Anne bustled into the hall followed by a trail of women carrying platters of food and jugs of wine, plonking her formidable behind down on the bench seat next to Erin. "Come, love." Anne set a goblet before her and filled it with wine. "Time to eat, dear girl. You must be hungry. Do not be shy."

The heavenly aroma wafting off trays of cooked meat reached her nostrils, and her mouth watered. She eyed large bowls of some sort of vegetable stew and platters of thick cut chunks of dark, crusty bread lathered with butter. Her stomach growled.

Hands reached for food, wine was poured and talk resumed. Erin made herself relax and enjoy the easy camaraderie around the table, listening as conversations flowed, servants mingling with farmers, all seated at the Lord's table.

Someone handed her a platter of bread, and she grabbed a piece before passing the plate along to the man next to her, a farmer by his clothes. He smiled his thanks, and she smiled back. Except for the disturbing presence of the man across the table from her, this wasn't so bad. She caught Gaharet's eye. Deep in conversation with two men on either side of him, he nodded his encouragement at her. Despite herself, she smiled at him.

Following the conversations around her as she ate was difficult, her Old French not practiced enough to keep up. Instead, she watched them, observing their interactions. Most of all, she watched Gaharet through the periphery of her vision, careful not to be caught outright staring. This morning she'd encountered a warrior, an adviser to a ruthless count, master of a keep and a man used to getting his own way with women and with the world. Here, now, across the table from her — deep in conversation with his farmers, his servants — sat an altogether different man.

Affable, relaxed, he listened. He shared bread, poured wine, smiling at a comment here, showing concern over something said there, content to sit amongst them enjoying their company. Not the commanding presence lording it over the table she'd expected. Was it all for her benefit? She didn't think so. She saw no awkwardness from the servants, no obvious curtailing of words lest someone speak out of place. Everything looked…normal.

"Erin," said Anne, pulling her from her thoughts, taking care to slow her speech so Erin could understand. "What is it you do with your spare time? Do you sew? Embroider?"

Erin picked up her goblet, sipping wine, mentally running through the list of acceptable pursuits for noble ladies — sewing, embroidery, weaving, horse riding…nothing remotely close to archaeology, digging in the dirt or restoring artifacts. Reading probably wouldn't make the list either. She did one thing that might fit.

"I like to draw…people, portraits. My mother taught me." Art was her mother's way of coping with the end of her relationships. June came alive under the spotlight of a man's attention. The resulting crash when her lover left her was as equally spectacular. Some days her mother cried, her tears making the paint run. Others she'd slash a pencil across the page in furious strokes. Erin would sit beside her at the kitchen table for hours, never saying a word, watching her mother, patiently waiting for her to remember she was there.

One day, June placed a blank piece of paper in front of her, gave her a pencil and set about teaching her how to draw. Eager to keep her mother's attention for as long as she could, she listened, she learned and she practiced.

She might have had a different career, studied art instead of archaeology, had Thomas Mathiesen not arrived on the scene. The fallout from *that* relationship had destroyed everything. Shared moments amongst pencils, chalk, charcoal and paint, moments all the more precious for their brevity, shattered. Her life had changed that day. So had her relationship with her mother.

She brushed away the bitter edge of old memories, meeting Gaharet's curious gaze across the table. She looked away. Those dark eyes missed nothing.

"We will have to see about getting you some chalks and slate," said Anne. "Or do you prefer parchment and ink? Gaharet, what do you think? The girl needs something to occupy her while she is here."

"Of course. Whatever you need."

She narrowed her eyes at his easy acquiescence. "That's very generous of you, thank you, but I don't plan on staying long."

His mouth twitched in the beginnings of a smirk. "You may find yourself here longer than you anticipated."

She frowned. Not if she could help it. "We'll see." She needed to confront him about the amulet sooner rather than later. He might be a lot more forthcoming with information once he realized how high the stakes were. She resumed eating, returning his smirk with one of her own. His eyes narrowed. He raised an eyebrow at her, his expression wary, but she ignored him. Now was not the time for this discussion. He clearly agreed, for he let it go. For now, she'd concentrate on filling her stomach, listening, observing and learning all that she could.

As platters and bowls emptied and conversations wound down, the servants bid their farewells, retiring for the night, the remains of the meal disappearing from the table. Erin rose to leave.

"Stay," said Gaharet. "We should talk."

Erin sank back down into her seat. He poured her another goblet of wine, and she took a sip, the sweet, fruity liquid sliding down the back of her throat. The fire crackled, oil lamps flickered, a quiet settling as the vast room emptied leaving the two of them alone.

Erin fiddled with the stem of her goblet. "As much as I appreciate the offer, I really don't need you to provide any drawing materials."

He gave a nonchalant shrug of his shoulder. "It is my pleasure to provide you with things to make your stay more pleasant."

"I won't be staying long."

He smiled at her, his amusement at her determination clear.

"You said you weren't keeping me prisoner."

"And I asked you where you would go."

"Home," she said, crossing her arms across her chest. "Back to my world, my own time. Where I belong."

Erin's throat tightened at the thought of home. The team would be frantic. Would they find her phone and clipboard at the top of the stairs? Her kit open beside the bones, her brush abandoned near the wolf's skull? Would they read her translation of the Theban inscription and wonder what the hell?

"Tell me more about this world of yours," he said, relaxing back into his chair.

Erin eyed him across the table. Talking about her world would get her nowhere. She needed answers and letting him control the conversation, extracting information from her, served only to benefit him.

"Perhaps we should talk about your world, being that it's more relevant to my current situation."

He chuckled, then took a leisurely sip of his wine, his smile reaching all the way to his eyes.

Nice.

She frowned, chewing on the inside of her lip.

"Very well." He rested his elbow on the arm of his chair, his chin on his fist. "What is it you would like to know? I assume you have extensive knowledge from your studies. There can be little that I can add to your understanding that you cannot glean from your surroundings." He indicated the room, the wall hangings, the keep itself.

She shrugged. "True. Your keep is very interesting. I would love the chance to see more of it before I go."

"You are welcome to explore as much as you wish."

"Thank you." She would take him up on that offer. Her professional curiosity demanded it, but the moment she found a way to return home, anything she'd yet to discover would remain that way.

"What I don't know" — she paused, placing crossed arms on the table, leaning toward him — "what I'd really like to know…is what soured between you and the Comte de Anjou?"

For an instant, his smile slipped, his eyes widening. *Gotcha!* She knew it. Comte Lothair and Gaharet d'Louncrais had fallen out. As quickly as his smile disappeared, it reappeared.

"I am not sure I understand your meaning."

The hell he doesn't.

"Well, you were the adviser to the comte. He consulted you on almost everything and then —" She held out her hands, palm up.

He sat up straighter in his chair, staring at her across the table, an intensity burning in his eyes. And there he was — the warrior, the dominant male, the aggressor. She'd almost forgotten he existed, lulled by his relaxed manner at dinner, his easy smile and his laugh.

"What *exactly* were you searching for at Langeais Keep?"

Erin stared into her wine, twirling the goblet in her fingers. She raised it to her lips and took a long sip. Placing it carefully on the table in front of her, she looked up, meeting his gaze, thrusting her chin out. "Tell me about the amulet."

"You must have had cause to excavate at Langeais. Tell me why."

The man could command armies with that voice. Did command an army, Lothair's army. Unease fluttered in her stomach. She cradled her goblet as though it contained liquid courage, each sip making her bolder.

"No."

His eyebrows rose, his lips twitched. "No?"

She took another gulp of wine. "Tell me about the amulet. What it is. How it works."

Silence stretched between them. Her foot bounced under the table, her pulse pounding loud in her ears. He cocked his head to the side, regarding her like a curious keepsake whose origins were an intriguing mystery to him.

"Very well," he said, and the tension in her shoulders eased a little. "It belongs to my family. A family crest, if you will. We are given one as we come of age. When we die, they are returned to the family and then passed on, in time, to another."

She waited for him to elaborate further, but he didn't.

"What about the inscription? How could it bring me through time? Why did it bring me to you?" What of the bloodstone and the secret it mentioned? And how did she use it to get home?

He took a deep breath. She may have won a minor victory, but the battle of wits was far from over. She'd no doubt, for every piece of information he gave, he would expect payment in kind.

"The amulets are precious to my family. They have a lot of sentimental and monetary value. More often than not, the men in my family die on the battlefield or in some skirmish. It would be very easy for them to be lost or stolen. Somewhere in the past, a member of my family has invoked a power into them. So, when the wearer recites the inscription, it returns them to the head of the family, bringing them home."

"Uh-huh."

"You read the inscription. I am the head of my family. Here you are."

"Is it a Druidic piece? Something from the old religion? A witch's spell?"

He shook his head. "I have no knowledge of how it came to be imbued with such power, nor the origins of the script. I only know that it works. As do you now. Are you going to answer my question?"

Did he think she was born yesterday? "How could you have something so precious to your family and yet not know anything about it? Where the language comes from, who imbued it with such power and how this power works?"

"Do you know who invented your time piece? How they created it, how it knows to move the pointers at exactly the right moment to mark the passing of time?"

"Well, not exactly no, but—"

"It is the same. I grew up with these in my family. I have had no need to question the whys and wherefores any more than you have with your timepiece."

She didn't buy it. "It seems rather excessive to risk using a runic-style alphabet, potentially putting your whole family at odds with the church, all because of the sentimentality of a few pieces of jewelry."

"They are gold. And very valuable."

His flat tone suggested he would say no more. The man's mind was a steel vault, the information she needed sealed within, and she'd yet to find the entire combination to fully prize open the damn door.

"But anyone with a knowledge of this script, finding an amulet, could read the inscription. You could have all manner of people randomly turning up at your keep." She pointed to her chest. "I did."

His brow furrowed, whether at her persistence here and now, or because she had turned up at his keep unannounced with an amulet in her hand, she couldn't be sure.

"This has never happened before. The script is not in common usage, and the words alone are not enough to make it work."

"But I read it and…"

Wait a minute. Did he just let something slip? Yes, he did.

The script alone didn't make the spell work. So what did? She glanced down at her fingers. She'd cut herself on it. Erin grinned, triumphant.

"It needs blood to work. Blood magic." A single drop of blood, smeared into the inscription, had activated the spell. What were the chances?

His lips tightened into a thin line. "Yes, blood makes it work. Now, tell me, what were you hoping to find at Langeais Keep?"

His tone brooked no more questions. Time to pay up. Time to lay another of her cards on the table.

"All right." Let's see if she could shock him into revealing more. "We were searching for you. Well, your bones, to be precise."

Quiet descended between them. The very air held its breath.

"At Langeais? Why?"

Those few syllables held so much inflection — surprise, curiosity, confusion, determination to have answers. *Join the club, mister.*

"We could find no record of your death." Not uncommon in itself. Records were often lost, destroyed in fires. "There were no details of battles at that time, no written evidence that illness had struck you down. What we do have is a notation in your chaplain's journal."

His gaze never left her face. Oh, she had his attention now.

"Continue."

"The notation speaks of a summons from Comte Lothair, for you to attend him at Langeais Keep."

He shrugged a shoulder. "That is of no consequence. I am summoned often."

"A week later, he added two words." Two simple, yet extraordinary words sending their research into overdrive. *"Numquam rediit* — never returned." Coupled with the other document they'd found, it pointed directly to Gaharet d'Louncrais' bones being in an underground cell at Langeais Keep.

"So I do not return to my keep after this summons from Comte Lothair?" His expression turned thoughtful. "That does not mean with all certainty that I die."

"No, it doesn't. It's merely a theory, one we had yet to find evidence to support."

"And this theory leads you to believe Lothair and I had a disagreement?"

"It does."

He smiled. "Lothair is always disagreeing with people — his wife, the church, the Comte de Blois."

"His wife ended up dead, and he maintained his hold over Langeais despite the efforts of the Comte de Blois. As for the church, he forced them to grant him absolutions for any infractions by taking pilgrimages to the Holy Land. Things don't turn out so well for those who disagree with Lothair of Anjou."

His eyes widened. "Marguerite dies following a dispute with Lothair?"

"Yes." That's what he got out of all that she'd said? "Word supposedly reached Lothair of a treasonous plot instigated by Marguerite. Historians are still divided over whether Marguerite was innocent and Lothair simply used treason as an excuse for getting rid of her. There are hints in recovered documents suggesting Lothair caught Marguerite in a compromising position with another man. A blacksmith, I think. Whatever the case, she ended up dead. There are no records of a trial, or any evidence supporting the charge of treason. There is, however, a record of her being burned at the stake in the public square at Langeais at the order of her husband."

He grimaced. "Not a good way to die." He sighed. Took a sip of wine. "Her fate hardly surprises me, though. She has been less than discreet."

Erin frowned. "I don't condone infidelity, but his reaction is monstrous. And to trump up a charge of treason because his wife cheated... Especially given that *his* extra-marital affairs are legendary. Surely someone could've stopped him, had some influence over his actions."

He raised an eyebrow at her, an amused smile playing across his lips. "He is Comte Lothair. No one in his own county would challenge him. Has your study not taught you the type of man he is? Do your books not tell of his savage temper?"

Oh yeah, Lothair's fondness for killing, burning and pillaging was well documented.

"After he died, they named him *Lothair le Diable*."

"Lothair the Devil? How appropriate."

"My point is, those who disagree with Lothair suffer the consequences."

He grunted in response, rubbing his chin, tugging at his beard, avoiding her eyes. He swirled the last of his wine around and drank it down, placing the goblet on the table with a soft thunk.

He looked up at her. "Do you have any theories on the cause of the disagreement behind Lothair and I?"

"Would I have asked you if I did?"

He grunted again. She hid a smile, taking another sip of her wine. She had him on the back foot now, and he wasn't too pleased about it.

"When is all this due to occur? When does Lothair summon me to Langeais?"

Erin debated whether to tell him more or force him back to the topic she needed to know more about — the amulet. More specifically, how did she reverse the damn spell? He pinned her with his gaze, a look of steely determination flitting across his face. She gulped. Or maybe not.

"A few months before Lothair has Marguerite burned at the stake."

He straightened in his seat, placed his elbows on the table and leaned toward her. "And that is when, exactly?"

Picking up her goblet, Erin took a long drink, focusing her eyes on the wine, her goblet, her hands. "Marguerite dies in January."

"Erin."

A note of warning slid into his voice. Still, she refused to look at him.

"August. The comte's summons comes in August," she mumbled into her wine.

"What year?" he growled, his voice deepening, a guttural sound more beast than human.

She gasped, her chin snapping up. There, shifting in the back of his eyes, was something frightening, raw and predatory. Her heart slammed against her rib cage.

"Nine hundred and ninety-nine," she whispered.

"Next month!" He exploded from his seat. "*Merde!*"

Chapter Eleven

Gaharet paced behind the table. This conversation had not gone in the direction he had expected. *Merde!* Lothair would summon him to Langeais Keep in less than a month and he would not return. Presumably death would claim him, but at whose hands? Lothair's? Renaud's? Or the unknown turncoat in his own pack?

He raked his hand through his hair, placed his hands on his hips and stared at the wall, attempting to get himself under control. When he found some measure of calm, he turned back to Erin. Her white-knuckled hands clasping the table, she stared at him, face pale and eyes agape. He had frightened her, his darker half surfacing to push her into answering. He had never allowed that to happen with a woman before. Strong minded, stubborn and defiant, this woman pushed him in ways no other woman had.

He had been on edge from the moment he had first caught her scent filtering into the room from beyond the doorway, saw her dressed as a woman should be, soft and feminine. He had thought putting her in clothes that covered her would entice him less. It only had him seeking alternatives to look at, and there was no shortage of those. Her soft, pink tongue slipped out to lick her lips. He closed his eyes against temptation. Everything about this woman called to him — her smile, her bright eyes brimming with challenge, her fearlessness, her persistence and her sharp intelligence... *Mon Dieu*, the woman had an incredible mind. He could not remember enjoying a discourse with a woman, with anyone, so much. He could have conversed with her all night and into the morn, traded questions, matched wits, but he had not meant to frighten her.

Gaharet opened his eyes, straightened his chair and eased himself back into his seat. The last thing he wanted was for her to fear him.

"I have but a short time before I am subject to Lothair's summons." He kept his voice soft, banishing his darker half to the depths of his mind and forcing the tension from his body. "I would know if... I would know if my line continued."

She visibly relaxed. Releasing her grip on the table's edge, she grabbed her goblet and took a large gulp of wine. Placing it down, she looked up at him. "No. I'm sorry. There is no mention of the d'Louncrais name beyond you."

He sucked in a breath. It would seem Erin's arrival was most fortuitous. Not only did she come bearing warning of his impending demise, giving him time that he might thwart his fate, she might also be the very thing that would ensure the continuation of his family *and* his pack.

"Why haven't you married? Given how important it is for you to provide an heir to all this?" She gave a sweep of her hand, indicating their surroundings. "It's not like you need a title or money, and by all accounts, you could have your pick of women."

Some of her feistiness had returned. Good.

"I'm sure there is a lovely lady from a noble family who'd be overjoyed to live in this fabulous keep, surrounded by servants and luxury and, in exchange, provide you with many children."

Her facetiousness amused him. Had he not had similar feelings toward the standard view of marriage, he might have found her words offensive, or perhaps naïve. Instead, it intrigued him. "You would not seek an advantageous match, to increase your standing, to secure your financial security?"

"No thank you. Things have changed a lot in the intervening centuries. Arranged marriages have fallen out of favor. People wed for entirely different reasons."

"Such as?"

"Love. It's not about how much money someone has, or their status, or who their family is. At least not for a lot of people. It's about how you feel about someone and whether you want to spend the rest of your life with them."

"You are not married?" He had no thought of how he would respond if she was.

She gave a slight shake of her head. "No."

"Not betrothed?" A betrothal could be broken and was of no consequence to him.

She frowned. "No."

"Why not? You are clearly old enough?"

She laughed, and he delighted in her smile, glad something he had said elicited it and had her fear of him receding.

"As I've said, things have changed a lot over the centuries. Finding a husband isn't the only option for women. Some marry young, some later in life and some choose to not marry at all. I have a job that I love, I am financially independent and I guess I haven't met a man I wish to marry yet. I *was* supposed to meet up with a man to watch the rising of the blue moon but I ended up here instead."

She was supposed to meet a man? His hand curled into a fist. Suppressing a growl, Gaharet slipped his hand beneath the table, hiding the coarse fur sprouting across his knuckles. His hand tightened, his claws cutting into his palms. The thought of another man touching her, kissing her, ignited an unexpected fury within him and had his beast roaring to the surface. He fought it with every ounce of control he had, the struggle to resist the shift, to remain on his side of the table very real.

"This man...he is looking to marry you?" He did his damnedest to keep his voice level. He had already frightened her once this evening.

"I don't know. It's much too soon for that," she protested. "I've only known Greg for a little while. He's an archaeologist, like me. My boss actually, but he asked me to go on a date, to meet him after work for a romantic evening." She gave a weighty sigh. "I should've gone. I probably wouldn't have ended up here if I had."

He released a long, slow breath. There was no flush of arousal when she spoke of this other man and her pulse rate remained steady. Some regret, perhaps, but not for the missed chance of meeting this man. He could not fault this Greg for trying to win her affections — what man wouldn't want to — but he had not succeeded. She had chosen to work over spending time with him, over viewing this blue moon. He unfurled his hand, unblemished by hair or claws — his shift averted.

"A blue moon, you say?" he asked. "I have never seen the moon turn blue."

She chuckled. "The moon doesn't actually turn blue. It's what we call it when there are four full moons in a season. It's not common and we call the fourth one a blue moon."

Gaharet thought back to the night he had found her. There had been this blue moon phenomena here, too. Could that explain how the spell had brought Erin through space *and* time? Brought her here, to his time specifically, not any other? Had the two blue moons across time amplified the spell? Knowing the effect of the moon on his kind, he would never discount its power.

He refilled her wine goblet and his. "What else does your history tell you about Lothair?" Perhaps something she knew, something seemingly insignificant to her, might be the key to unraveling the circumstances around his death.

"Well, history remembers him as a brilliant tactician, despite his atrocities. After Marguerite's death, he remarried. Had five children. He died in 1068 at ninety-eight or nine. Rather long-lived, given the average lifespan of this time period."

Gaharet stilled. Very long-lived. Even for a man with all the luxuries afforded by his status as a comte. Could it be... Had one of his men..."Nothing about his preoccupation with lycanthropes?" An offhand question he did not expect a response to, but her eyes narrowed, and a fleeting look of puzzlement crossed her face, gone in an instant. Had he not been watching her so closely, he would have missed it, thought he had imagined it. A tingle of awareness raced up his spine.

"Werewolves? I thought Lothair was a well-educated man. I didn't think he'd believe in myths and fairy-tales," she said.

But her focus was elsewhere, on something she had read, or something she had discovered, mayhap where she had found the amulet. He waited for her to elaborate, wanting to hear more, not willing to seem too eager lest she retreat into silence. Or push for more information on the amulet. He had told her as much as he dared. He could not risk telling her more. Not yet.

"Science has debunked that myth, well and truly. There are plausible explanations for the things that convinced people such creatures existed. For one," she held up her thumb. "There's a psychological state where a person believes they can turn into a werewolf. And two," she raised her index finger. "There's also a physiological condition called hypertrichosis that produces excess hair growth all over the body. It's rare, but perhaps this is where the legends of werewolves began. The nonsense about eyebrows that meet and long ears and noses being signs of a werewolf is just that—nonsense."

He observed her across the rim of his goblet, gauging her reactions. Werewolves were real. He was one—a walking, talking, living myth. He hid a smile behind his goblet. Her words were confident, even a little derisive, but he sensed a hesitancy in her convictions even as she rattled off the scientific conclusions founded on hundreds of years of research. Research which meant nothing. Gaharet could have told her. He could have *shown* her. He did not. Instead, he amused himself imagining the look on her face had she known sitting across the table from her was the very thing she was trying to convince herself could not possibly exist.

It posed a real problem. If he were to take her as his wife, his mate, she would need to know the truth. His amusement died a quick death. Would she accept him, or would she fear him? Would she be willing to become like him?

His attention shifted to the doorway as Anne lumbered into the room.

"Shall I bring you more wine, Gaharet?"

He looked over at Erin, the large bruise marring her forehead. "No, it is late, Anne. We will retire. Thank you."

"As you wish," she said, bustling around the table collecting the jug and the goblets. "I will take these down to the kitchen and then I will see you in your chamber, Erin. I have a poultice prepared for that wound of yours. It will help it heal much faster."

As she bustled out of the room, Gaharet rose from the table, and Erin followed suit. Reaching the doorway, he stopped. "Please wander my keep and explore as you will. I will inform the servants you have free run of it." He wanted her to relax, to feel comfortable.

"And if I leave the keep?" She stood before him, this diminutive, gutsy woman, barely reaching his shoulder. Such defiance, so beautiful. Did she not know how much she tempted him? Not sense he struggled to keep the beast in check so he would not ravish her right there in the hall? Strip her naked and bend her over the table? His hunger to take up her challenge nearly overwhelmed him.

Glancing down at her bare feet, her toes peeking out from under the linen hem, he caught and held her gaze. Unsaid, but implied, was his exhilaration for the chase and he let all his desire for her show. She swallowed hard, her face flushing a delightful shade of pink. Squaring her shoulders, she pushed past him through the doorway, making her way up the stairs.

"I'll be damned if I'll ever give you *that* satisfaction again." Her grumbled words, barely above a whisper, floated down the stairs.

He let her get around the corner before chuckling loud enough for her to hear. She paused, then on light feet raced up the stairs. It took every ounce of his control to not chase her, his hands gripping the door frame, the effort leaving him breathless. When his breathing calmed, and he was sure she would have reached her chamber, he climbed the stairs to his own room.

Lying stretched out on his bed, dying embers in the brazier giving off a soft glow, Gaharet stared at the ceiling mulling over everything Erin had said. Unsure what to do with this new information, he knew one thing—he would do everything in his power to change his fate. Aside from the problems it would create for the pack, he had no intention of dying. Not now he had found Erin.

Even aware of his impending death, he could not stop his mind from wandering back to her, sleeping down the hall. In another four hours, he must face her again. He groaned at the thought. Her presence in his keep he found difficult enough but lying in his chamber trying to banish her from his mind was a special kind of torture.

Her scent clung to everything, especially the clothes she had left behind. Citrus and orange blossoms and an erotic scent lingering in her breeches — the sweet aroma of her arousal. It drove him almost wild.

He could smell her on everything — in the barrel he bathed in, on the covers of his bed, on his armor and surcoat, even on his sword. She'd cut herself on it, the heady fragrance of her blood lingering in the air. On first noticing his hauberk bunched up on the chair, he had smiled. Now, after inhaling her scent for an hour, he cursed her inquisitiveness. She had embedded her damn scent in its steel links. Should he have to wear it in the next few days, the smell of her warm flesh would hang about his body, driving him to distraction. *As if I am not already there!*

Had she been aware, by touching things, that she had given away her every movement she may not have felt comfortable being in his chamber. Had he known the effect her overpowering scent would have on him, Gaharet would never have allowed her within ten feet of his chamber. Bathing would now be a testament to his endurance.

Several times he found himself heading for her room before he stopped, forcing himself to return to his chamber to await the morn. With a frustrated growl, he compelled himself to leave his bed, to leave the keep and step out into the night, stripping and shifting to his wolf the moment he stepped beyond the walls. A run would expend some of his pent-up energy, and the cool night air would take the heat out of his relentless lust. Maybe.

Out in the forest, he stayed away from where he had found her, avoiding any lingering signs of her presence, inhaling only the smells of pine needles and damp earth. Patrolling his lands, a hint of breeze ruffling his fur, he searched for hints of unannounced visitors. He found nothing amiss. No one had come for her. He had not expected someone would, but he had not survived by taking unnecessary risks. Caution had kept him alive, safe.

Stretching himself out in a long, loping gait, he relished the freedom, the darkness of the forest and the cool night air. Pushing himself until his body and mind tired, he turned and headed for home. His run having taken the edge of his restlessness, he slipped through the gatehouse, pausing within the confines of the walls. He stared up at her window.

What should he do with this woman from another time? He knew what he wanted to do. He wanted to fling open the door to her chamber, take her in his arms, take her beneath him, before him, anyway she would have him. A vision of her bare skin flushed, pressed against the length of his body, flashed through his mind. He shook his big, furry head.

When he had given in, in part, to his desire and kissed her, pressed his body against hers, the change had come unbidden, unasked for. Could he be with this woman and not reveal himself? Reveal who, what, he really was?

He had stayed too long staring up at the window. The shutters opened, and she appeared, backlit by the light of the room, hair loose and drifting about her face. He froze. Had she, too, struggled to find sleep? Had she paced the room, her thoughts of him, of their kiss, of the passion that flared between them?

Sitting on his haunches, he contemplated her for a moment before slinking into the cover of darkness. She was not yet ready to meet his wolf. He had trained horses less skittish in his presence than her. Horses that could scent his true nature. Feared it. With calm, with patience, with *time*, he had won them over. According to Erin, time he did not have.

From his camouflaged position, he stared up at her, arms clasped about her body, warding off the chill. Leaning forward, she grasped the shutters, banging them closed, vanishing from view. Gaharet called forth the change, pulling on his clothes, and made his way back to his bedchamber, uncertain if he wanted to encounter her in the corridor or not.

Chapter Twelve

Grumbling, her old knees creaking and groaning, Anne mounted the stairs to Erin's bedchamber to wake the girl. Truth be known, it did not dissatisfy her that Gaharet had put the young woman in her charge, but the way Gaharet was treating the girl really had her mad. No shoes indeed. What had gotten into that young man?

He had come into the kitchen that very morning, tasking her with ensuring the girl's comfort, making no mention of her strange clothes, the foreign tongue she spoke or where she had come from. Anne did not bother asking. She had been part of the d'Louncrais household for too long to ask questions. She knew what he was, what all the d'Louncrais family had been, and his vassals' families, God rest their souls, and his vassals. All of her family who served here did, and she had learned to turn a blind eye to the strange goings on in this keep. This, however, was different. This young woman was not one of their kind. Anne would stake her life on it.

Nigh on thirty-five years had passed since a human woman, other than a servant, had entered this keep — when Jacques d'Louncrais, Gaharet's father, had chosen a mate outside the pack. A stark contrast to these circumstances, Elise Beauchene had entered the keep of her own volition and stayed by choice. Gaharet had carried this woman in unconscious and now, he informed her, the girl, Erin, was not to leave. He had given Erin free rein to explore as long as she stayed within the confines of the outer wall. If she wanted to leave the keep, he forbade it.

"Should I find some shoes for her?" Anne had asked, for she had noticed Erin's bare feet. As if the girl would run out into the forest with no shoes on.

"No. No shoes. I do not want her leaving here," he had said, his tone firm, brooking no disagreement. That had never stopped Anne.

"The girl will catch a chill, bare feet on these floors," she had protested, "what with the days cooling and autumn on its way."

Gaharet had shaken his head. "No shoes, Anne."

Anne had frowned, leaving off cleaning the dishes to stare at Gaharet, hands on her ample hips. "Next, you will be wanting me to confine her in the training room on the top floor. Your mother brought you up better than that, lad."

Gaharet had stood his ground. "Do not cross me on this one, Anne." He had given her a stern look.

"Very well," she had agreed, "but do not forget, I warned you. It is not good for the girl to be running around barefoot on these cold floors. When she falls ill, do not think for one moment I will not hold you responsible."

Growling, he had stalked out of the kitchen only to return a few moments later with a pair of ankle length stockings, slapping them down on the bench in front of her.

"These are hers. It is as far as I am willing to go right now."

Smiling to herself, Anne reached the top of the stairs, stockings in one hand and fresh clothes slung over the other. She knew that boy too well.

Mayhap things were not so different from Jacques and Elise, after all. She had caught the heated glances between Gaharet and Erin, though Erin tried her best to hide them. Nothing escaped old Anne's sharp eyes. Suppressing a chuckle, Anne entered the bedchamber. Young men. They were so transparent sometimes.

* * * *

Erin stirred, a slow rousing from sleep, warm and cozy in the bed. She smiled, a sleepy smile, until it filtered into her mind it'd be another five more centuries before Europe discovered coffee. Groaning, she pulled the covers over her head. No coffee. How would she ever survive without caffeine? And no breakfast either. It'd be like going on one of those fad fasting diets. *Ugh.*

"Morning, child."

A cheery female voice greeted her, as shutters banged open and light streamed into the room.

Erin peered out from beneath the covers at Anne. Sitting up, she rubbed her face with her hands. Coffee. She *so* needed coffee. She rubbed the sleep from her eyes, slipped out from under the covers and padded across to the table to where a jug of water and a washbowl stood. She sponged down her body with the cold water, drying it on a linen provided as Anne straightened bed covers, fluffed pillows, and laid out a fresh dress for her. She paused, damp linen in her hands. Beside the dress lay a pair of socks.

"My socks? Where did you find them?"

"I told that young man you needed something on your feet. He gave me these. Said they were yours. I will work on getting you some shoes," Anne said, busying herself stoking the coals in the brazier.

Young man? "You mean, Gaharet?" she asked, slipping on her bra and knickers, ignoring the strange look Anne gave her underwear. She refused to ditch them no matter what the custom. Facing Gaharet while going commando, didn't bear thinking about.

"Of course, love. Gaharet is the master of this house. What he says goes." Anne smiled at her, a twinkle in her eye. "Most of the time."

Erin grinned. "You're the cook, right?"

"Yes, love. How do you think I got so round?" She chuckled, patting her enormous hips. "Comes from tasting all the food. My place is normally in the kitchen, but Gaharet asked me to take care of you while you are here. Not so many people to care for these days. All the young maids were let go."

"Doesn't he expect you to, you know, treat him like the master of the keep?"

"Oh, I probably should call him Mon Seigneur. All the other servants do, but" — she gave a little shrug — "I helped raise him from a babe. He is like a son to me. When his mother passed and then his father, someone needed to keep that boy in line. Seemed like I was the best person to do that. Now, if you have finished washing, I will help you dress." She held up a simple linen chemise.

Erin shimmied into it, then slipped on an underdress of cream linen, the hem falling to her feet, large voluminous sleeves finishing past her wrists. Anne pulled the laces firm, tying them at the nape of her neck. Erin lifted her arms and Anne slid an outer garment of deep green over her head. Short cuff sleeves accentuated the linen ones, the embroidered hem of the skirt falling just below her knees. Once more, she resembled a noblewoman of the tenth century. Curious that Gaharet had chosen such clothes and not those of a peasant.

"Let me help you with the headscarf, love."

Anne ushered her to a seat, running a comb through Erin's hair, fixing the material in place. Long and a little restrictive, it fell past her waist.

"Now, Gaharet tells me you have a keen interest in keeps and the like. There is much to explore here. Beautiful hangings in the hall, the view of the forest from the ramparts is wonderful — you can access that from the top floor — and you can always visit me in the kitchen if you are looking for some company. Gaharet spends most mornings in the library of late, should you require him. Once I get you some shoes, you might wish to go for a wander beyond these walls, visit the stables, get some fresh air."

Erin slipped her socks on her feet.

"Off you go now. Go on and explore. No sense hiding away here in this room all day." Anne handed her a lit candle, ushering her toward the door.

Erin paused in the corridor, her socks a barrier against the cold floor, debating which way to go. Anne was right. Staying in the bedchamber served no purpose. She'd learn nothing more here, though Gaharet may come to regret giving her free rein in his home. She'd explore his keep from top to bottom, leave no room un-entered, no corner unexplored and no door unopened. As an archaeologist, she could dream of no greater opportunity. She'd be crazy not to take it, and perhaps she'd stumble onto something useful.

Erin made her way down the darkened corridor, passing Gaharet's bedchamber, pausing at a set of stairs disappearing up into darkness. The flickering candle held in front of her, she ascended, one step at a time, slow, cautious, but resolute, a clutch of fabric in her hand lifting the hem of her dress as she went. A little darkness would not stop her. Anne said she could access the ramparts from up there, and her own knowledge of keeps and castles suggested the armory would also be on the top floor. The armory — now that's a sight she'd like to see.

Reaching the top step, she paused, holding the candle first one way, then the other. To the right lay a long corridor, its end barely visible in the candlelight. She took a few steps that way, holding her candle aloft. Beyond the row of doors, down the very end of the darkened corridor, stood a solid door. A beam across its width barricaded it against the outside. It would open onto the ramparts for sure.

She turned around, moving in the opposite direction, back past the stairwell and around the corner. One doorway. She kept walking until she was halfway down the corridor. Another doorway, this one with a door. There were only two doorways, suggesting two large rooms. One would be the armory, but what of the other? Storage? No, the larder and pantry would be on the lowest floor, down near the kitchen.

She turned back down the corridor and stood before the first doorway. The ramparts could wait. The puzzle of the two large rooms presented a much more curious prospect. She thrust the candle in front of her and stepped into the first room. Light glinted off steel. She grinned. The armory.

Her gaze flickered along the walls, taking in the sheer volume of weapons.

Wow! Chateau de Castlenaud has nothing on this place.

If she'd ever doubted Gaharet's ability to defend his keep, a single glance around this room quashed it. Racks of spears, bows and arrows lined one wall — twenty, forty of each, maybe more. She swung the candle around, holding it aloft. Along the opposite wall, shields of varying shapes and sizes, all with the howling wolf insignia. She took a few more steps into the room, pushing the candlelight further. Hanging along the back wall, hauberks glimmered. In the middle, a dozen benches covered in oil-cloth wrapped bundles. Swords, axes, daggers?

The money that had gone into making and procuring so much weaponry could feed a small village for a year, maybe longer. They'd known Gaharet d'Louncrais had means, but the true magnitude of his wealth took her breath away. How many generations had it taken to amass such a collection? Two, maybe three, at least. Where had all this gone when he'd died?

Erin could easily spend a day or two in here exploring, examining every single piece in this room, perhaps avail herself of a weapon just in case, but... Her mind skittered away, down the corridor. What of the other room? More weapons? Her curiosity burning far brighter than her candle, she left the armory and continued down the corridor, stopping in front of the entrance to the second room.

This one had a door, a substantial door. She held the candle up, her hand against it, ready to push it open. She paused. This door differed from any other door she'd seen in the keep. Fastened to it were two iron locking bolts. *Huge* bolts. Strong. The door itself looked very solid, thicker than the others, and had a slot cut out of it at eye height. What did he keep in this room? Or who? The nape of her neck tingled and foreboding slithered down her spine, settling like a lead weight in her stomach.

The door was unlocked. She hesitated. The feeling in her gut told her to leave this room alone. To not go inside. To not even look.

What sort of archaeologist would I be if I did that?

Gaharet had said nothing about not entering any rooms. Given no warning. Put no limits on her exploration other than she couldn't leave. Surely, he'd have forbidden her to enter it if this room posed a threat, a danger.

It's just a room.

Still, she hesitated. Perhaps she should leave this door unopened.

Oh, for crying out loud. You're an archaeologist in a tenth-century keep, not some hapless teenager in a B-grade horror movie.

She pushed the door open. The candle thrust out, its meager light creating disconcerting shadows, she crossed the threshold. She swung the candle from one darkened corner to another, forcing light into every inch of darkness. Empty but for a few pieces of furniture. She let out a pent-up breath. Too little light, an atmospheric building and way too many spooky movies had her expecting…what…a monster? She laughed, the sound echoing off the walls, sending chills up her spine.

She swung the candle around again. A simple table, a chair and a single cot bed with a few blankets. And no windows. She moved closer, inspecting the cot, examining the thick leather straps attached to the frame. Straps to bind someone. A tower prison. History told many tales of people being confined in towers — family members gone mad, wives who'd been unfaithful and two young princes in the fifteen hundreds never seen again. Who'd Gaharet confined in here? And how long ago? To think *she* could've ended up in here. She shivered. A timely reminder not to get too comfortable, not to underestimate Gaharet. Nor let him lull her with any generosity he might show her.

She fingered the leather straps. The buckles remained fastened. Something had snapped them in two. That would require an awful lot of strength. She thought back to the shackles in the underground cell, the iron chain broken. What did it all mean?

Dropping the straps, she turned to leave, pulling up short as something else caught her eye. There were iron bolts on the *inside* of the door and on the outside. Why? Erin pushed the door closed to have a better look. Yes, two heavy bolts, the same as those on the outside. What on earth for? Locks on the inside were to keep people out, not in. If the room was used to confine someone, why give them bolts on the inside? It made no sense. She'd never seen anything like it.

Leaning forward, she held the candle closer to the door. Claw marks. Deep gouges in the timber. Reaching out, she slid her fingers down the grooves. What had driven someone to do this? Fear, madness, hunger? Trying to claw their way out? Had someone bolted the door from the outside?

She doubted Gaharet had this room in mind when he'd urged her to look around. Or maybe he did. Maybe he wanted her to see what fate awaited her if she crossed him. Gaharet d'Louncrais was likely no less barbaric than any other lord in the tenth century. She'd do well to keep that in mind.

Stepping back, knees a little less steady, she exited the room without a backward glance, seeking refuge in the armory, the simplicity of its instruments of death far more preferable than the grim confusion of the room next door.

Chapter Thirteen

Gaharet tossed the scroll on the table. He had found no new information in that one either. Ensconced in the library, a cozy room he usually found soothing, today it only added to his frustrations. Books, scrolls, tomes on every topic he could think of, yet nothing of what he looked for, what he needed to find. This task he had set himself a far more difficult exercise than he had anticipated. How many months had he been at it? Too many, and the answers to his questions still eluded him.

Last night, Erin had rightly questioned his lack of knowledge regarding the amulet. Not knowing anything of its origins had proven a mistake. Until recently, he never had cause to question it, but their complacency regarding their lore was inexcusable and something he planned to rectify. Now they were under threat, their numbers dwindling, they needed all the knowledge they could get.

It had occurred to him, late one night, that those who had created the amulet, had imbued it with its power, may very well be able to assist them now. If only he knew who they were. After months of searching, he was still no closer to knowing.

He leaned back in the chair, rubbing his face with his hands. This morning, his task proved more challenging than usual, his attention distracted by thoughts of Erin. The determined way she thrust out her chin when evading his questions. How her green eyes sparkled when she laughed. The two little lines that appeared between her eyebrows when his answers did not please her. The way she chewed on her bottom lip when she was unsure of herself. He leaned his elbows on the desk, his chin on his hands. It all played havoc with his concentration. That and knowing he most likely had only weeks to live.

Not if I can prevent it.

His first inclination upon waking was to seek Erin out and continue their conversation — to elicit more information about his death, about this excavation site of hers, about the location of the amulet she had found — but after such a restless night, he needed time to cool his own ardor. So he had kept to his routine of spending the morning in the library researching the pack origins, the amulet, their history, leaving her to her own devices. Anne would see to it she did not remain in her bedchamber all day.

He eyed the two piles of books and scrolls before him. One stack he had already skimmed through and found nothing of use. The other he had yet to start on. He scowled at the second, larger pile, forcing himself to pick up a smooth, leather-bound book. Stained and marked with age, its pages worn, its cover stamped with the d'Louncrais wax seal. A journal. This one showed some promise. Obscured beneath a stack of scrolls at the bottom of a chest, he had come across it this morning. Could it hold the information he searched for? He opened it to the first page, the date in the top right-hand corner — December 565. The name: Robert d'Louncrais.

Writing flowed across the page. Latin. So his forebears were of the nobility even back then. He read the first line.

I hereby commit thine thoughts to page to guide thy progeny with wisdom and true knowledge, for we are cast divergent from mortal men, and so our paths shall always differ.

Finally. Some mention of his kind. He flicked through the journal. Page after page of daily entries, a chronicle of Robert's life, his sons, their sons, generation after generation. He found the last entry, recognizing his father's bold, concise writing. His father had known of this journal? He checked the date.

The twentieth day of the month of October, year 988.

Barely one week before his father had died.

Gaharet skimmed the page, searching for a hint of despair his father must have been feeling, his overwhelming grief at the loss of his wife, his mate. Nothing else could explain his lackluster form during the battle that had cost him his life the following week. He found hints of sorrow when he made mention of Gaharet and D'Artagnon, but nothing more. Mostly his father detailed issues cropping up on the estate, issues amongst the pack.

Gaharet turned back a few more pages and found the same. He went further back looking for the day his mother had died, but he couldn't find an entry for that day, nor the next month. Then the entries started again.

He read through a few of the pages, skipping ahead. He could see changes over the months, less bitter ramblings of love lost and more day-to-day business. Yes, his father had been grieving, but if this journal revealed anything, by the last entry Jacques had begun the slow process of healing. What the hell had happened during that battle?

A knock on the door interrupted his thoughts.

"Enter."

Anne poked her head around the door. "Shall I bring your meal to you here, Gaharet?"

"Where is Erin? Has she eaten?"

"She ate in the kitchen with me earlier. She is in the hall now, admiring the wall hangings." Anne chuckled. "Curious one, that one. Asking all sorts of questions about the keep."

Gaharet nodded at Anne. "Good. I will eat in the hall presently."

"Very well." She disappeared out through the door.

Curious indeed. Smiling, he tossed the leather-bound book on the table. He would spend more time with it tomorrow, reading it in more depth, especially his father's entries. Leaving the library, crossing the corridor to the hall, he paused in the doorway, watching Erin unobserved.

"Must've cost a fortune," she muttered, tracing her fingers across an embroidered figure, her fascination with the piece keeping her engrossed and oblivious to his presence. The sway of fabric as she moved betrayed a hint of her body, the gentle touch of her hand across the fabric... Would that she touch him with such reverence. *Mon Dieu.* Just looking at her affected him, his darker half a throb of lust and raw emotion. He gritted his teeth and ran his hands through his hair. Midnight runs for the foreseeable future, it seemed.

Moving across the room, he came to stand beside her. "I trust you slept well?"

She spun to face him, her hand clasped to her chest. "Gaharet! You startled me. I didn't hear you come in. A bit of warning next time." She inhaled deeply. "Yes. To answer your question, I slept well. Thank you."

Liar. He could sense the untruth as it spilled from her mouth, saw the dark circles under her eyes. Had she, too, laid awake thinking of him, of his mouth on hers? The pupils dilated in those lovely eyes of hers. Yes, she had. He allowed himself a small smile.

He motioned to the wall hanging of figures on horseback galloping across its surface. "It interests you, this one?" Of all the pieces to captivate her, it had to be this one. An old, familiar sadness welled up inside him. How long had it been now? Eleven, twelve years? Time had blunted the pain, yet not removed it. Would one day his sense of loss lessen and fade?

"Yes, I like it very much. Is there a story to it?"

Her voice snagged him away from his memories. She leaned closer to the piece, two little lines appearing between her eyebrows. For the first time in a very long time, Gaharet *wanted* to talk about his parents.

"Yes. My father had it commissioned after he married my mother."

"Pardon?" She glanced up at him, raised her eyebrows, then turned back to the piece again. Stepping back a few steps, she took the whole of it in. "I see no marriage motif, no images of dowries exchanged, no merging of families. From what I can tell, it depicts a hunt of some sort, then here," she said, pointing to the far right, "at the end there's a battle. How can it have anything to do with your parents getting married?"

He chuckled, some of the ache easing, fonder memories overwhelming the bad ones. "Most people see only that. Those who did not know my parents well. You have to understand my mother and her relationship with my father to fully comprehend this piece. Here"—he pointed to a figure on horseback dressed in deep green, flame-red hair streaming behind her—"this is my mother. Her temper was as fiery as her hair. All of us, my father, my brother and I, were on the receiving end of her wrath at one time or another. My brother and I would escape to the forest whenever we could." He grinned. "As boys, we spent *a lot* of time in the forest. I confess we gave her much to be angry about—stealing food from the larder, salting the boiled fruit and creating havoc for the servants."

In truth, they had terrorized the servants, and his mother had had every right to lose her temper with them. They were incorrigible. He had fond memories of laughing as he fled the pantry, his brother in tow, Anne not far behind brandishing whatever kitchen implement came to hand—a rolling pin, a large pot, a carving knife.

"My father"—he pointed to another figure with black hair and beard several horse lengths behind his mother—"thrived on her temper. D'Artagnon, my brother, and I believed my father deliberately provoked her at times, delighting in her reactions." Given that his parent's disputes had often ended in the bedchamber, Gaharet could well understand why. "From the first time he met my mother, my father was besotted, so taken with her strong will and defiant spirit he determined right in that moment she would be his wife. Their courtship was…unconventional. She led him on a merry hunt and would not concede to marry my father without a fight, or so the story goes."

"Huh." She studied the figures, moving back and forth along the wall hanging. "The way you tell it makes it sound like they were in love."

"They were." He smiled. "Their arguments were legendary, but their marriage was strong and passionate."

"Isn't that unusual?"

"I suppose. My father loved my mother very much, and she him, until the day she…" He sighed. "My father was never the same after she died." Her death had changed them all, three men adrift in the world without her, but his father the most. He had retreated from life, from his sons, from his responsibilities to the pack and all had suffered because of it. Before today, Gaharet would have sworn his father had died of a broken heart, aided by a sharpened sword wielded in battle. Now he was not so sure.

Those two little lines appeared between her eyebrows again.

She studied him for a moment. "Your parents were very lucky, then. Love in a tenth-century marriage is a rare thing."

"Yes." Not rare amongst his kind. Not when they found their mates. "What of your parents? Do they have wall hangings to celebrate such things in your time?"

She snorted. "My mother's relationships wouldn't make for a good piece of art."

He raised his eyebrows. *Relationships? Plural?*

"She was married. Once. My father died when I was a baby. I think she would like to be married again, but…" She blew out a breath. "She just doesn't seem to choose the right kind of man. None of her relationships, other than with my father, have ever gotten to the point of a proposal." She frowned. "She used to talk about my father a lot. About how he was this wonderful, caring, gentle man who used to buy her flowers, bring her breakfast in bed on Sundays and massage her swollen feet when she was pregnant with me. I sometimes wonder if she chooses the men she does because they are *nothing* like him. Perhaps she just can't bear the thought of replacing him, but she doesn't want to be alone. I'd rather be alone than put myself through all that heartache."

"She is not alone. She has you."

"You would think so, wouldn't you? She doesn't see it that way." Pain flashed across her face then smoothed away, replaced with resigned acceptance.

She stepped back from the embroidered story of his parent's marriage, moving in front of a different wall hanging. His little filly was not merely skittish. She was wounded. She would require a gentle hand and patience if he were to get close to her, gain her trust. Letting the conversation drop, he followed her.

"What about this one? What's its story?"

"Ah, this is an actual battle. At Montsoreau. Here you see the two opposing sides." He indicated the rival forces.

"Is that you? With the black beard and the red surcoat?" She pointed to a figure, standing in the stirrups, bloodstained sword raised, preparing to strike another chevalier.

"You have keen eyes. Yes, it is me with my men." He gestured to several other figures on horseback. "That man there on the ground, with the white hair, is Aimon, seriously injured."

"Did he survive?"

"Thankfully, yes. He became one of my vassals after this very battle."

"You have six vassals?"

He nodded. "I do."

"That's a lot of vassals."

He smiled. "I suppose so. They are all good men." Well, until recently, he had believed them all to be good men.

"You've been injured, too. I saw —" She chewed on her bottom lip, blushing.

Their gazes locked. He knew exactly what she referred to. She'd taken in every bare-skinned inch of him the night they had first met. His groin twitched at the memory. It really did not need any encouragement.

"I saw your scars." She turned back to the embroidered battle.

"I have suffered a few injuries. Nothing as serious as Aimon."

She turned to look at him, her gaze sliding down his body and across his stomach. His groin tightened further. *Merde.* In a heartbeat, he had gone from wanting to gain her trust to wanting to... As a grown man, he should have more control over his body.

"But the one on your abdomen..." She reached out, almost touching him.

He eyed her outstretched fingers. Could he control himself if she touched him? She snatched her hand back, clenching her fingers into a fist by her side.

"That one looked pretty serious. Without the benefit of advanced medical practices, antibiotics, anesthetics… It's surprising you're still alive."

He knew naught of these antibiotics or anesthetics, but he could not elaborate on his scar. The ax blow responsible for it would have killed an ordinary man, a human, and while it had laid him up for a week, he had survived. Not something he wished to disclose to her. Not yet.

Leaning in closer, shutting down further talk about his injuries, he bridged the space between them. He needed to prove to her, and himself, that he could touch her and not drag her into his arms and ravish her. Reaching out, he plucked one of the stays holding her headscarf in place. Her lips parted on a gasp.

From the moment he had laid eyes on her, engrossed in the wall hanging, he had wanted nothing more than to remove this scarf, to see her blonde hair spilling over her shoulders. What had Anne been thinking when she had helped secure it to her head? He suspected Anne of goading him. The old cook saw too much. She always had.

"No need to stand on ceremony here." He pulled another of the stays free. "I much prefer you without this, anyway." He slipped the last clip out, brushing the headscarf to the floor.

"Oh." She looked down at the scarf now bunched at her feet, color rising from the neck of her gown to her cheeks. He leaned in, reached up and threaded his fingers through her hair.

"Beautiful." He closed his eyes, inhaling a deep breath through his nose. "Your hair smells like citrus and orange blossoms." His fingers brushed her scalp as he ran them through the long strands. She shivered, and as much as he longed for more, he forced himself to be satisfied with that simple touch. If he wanted to win her over, and he did, he must give her space. Let her come to him. Right now, flustered by his presence, he sensed her need to flee. He let his hand drop to his side, backing away.

Scooping up the headscarf, she scuttled away from him, toward the door. Pausing, she looked back at him. "Thank you for telling me the stories behind these wall hangings."

He smiled, watching her leave the hall, her pace swift, yet not a run. She was learning. He growled low in his throat, his body strung taut like a bow and his wolf held in check. Barely.

Chapter Fourteen

Power walking from the hall, running not an option, Erin headed straight down the back stairs to the kitchen, counting on Anne as an effective barrier against Gaharet. The man had her so damn confused. For a few moments there in the hall the warrior with the coiled energy and sharp intelligence, the arrogant in-your-face-seducer who'd kissed her, lip locking her into responding, had disappeared. In his place, had been a congenial host revealing gems of family history, baring a little of his soul.

She'd not missed the sorrow he'd tried to hide when he talked about his parents. In that moment he'd dropped his guard, a deep melancholy visible in his eyes. His mother's death had affected him greatly. His father's too. Listening to him talk, she'd perceived a depth in him she'd not counted on, and that had been her undoing. Why else would she have told him so much about her mother?

Her shoulders slumped against the kitchen wall, Erin took a moment to gather her wits. What had she been thinking? She'd never shared so much about her childhood before, not even to her flat mates from her university days. Lord, if she'd stood any longer in front of that damn beautiful testament to his parents' marriage and their grand, passionate love, she probably would've shared more. Detailed a list of her mother's lovers—John, the hedge fund manager, Patrick, the high-profile rugby league player. Neil, the Maserati-driving billionaire whose job she never did figure out. Mark, the CEO of some Fortune 500 company. And worst of all, Thomas Mathiesen, the prominent politician, married with three kids.

She closed her eyes, the memory of his face as vivid today as it was then. Thomas Mathiesen. The shit storm she'd faced at school when the news broke, on national television, no less. The ultimate betrayal by her mother. How the whispers, the stares, the pointing fingers and the snarky comments about her mother being a home-wrecker followed her everywhere. On the quad, in the classroom, in the toilets. At fifteen, being the single focus of the entire school for all the wrong reasons had been a brutal humiliation. That her mother had given no thought to the consequences for her own daughter had been a revelation. Erin had never spoken of that day to a single person. Today she'd come close.

"You are looking a little flustered there, love. Are you well?"

Anne's voice snapped her from her memories.

Opening her eyes, she gave Anne a tremulous smile. "I'm fine thanks, Anne. I thought I would give you a hand this afternoon. I've seen enough of the keep today."

At Anne's welcoming smile, Erin relaxed, letting the kitchen envelop her in its warmth. An enormous pot hung over a large cooking fire and the smells of baking bread hung in the air. Anne, motherly, at home here amongst the shelves of large pots, pans, ladles, platters and drying herbs, stood at a large workbench. With her food splattered apron on and dustings of flour on her hands, she kneaded a ball of dough.

"Mmm-hmm." Anne looked her up and down. "If you say so. I could always use an extra pair of hands and it is nice to have company."

Erin moved to the bench and dropped the headscarf on it, catching Anne's sharp gaze as she did so.

"Gaharet says I don't have to wear this here." She didn't want the old cook to think she flouted social norms. That she was a woman of loose morals inviting the approaches of men.

"Does he, now? Very well," she said, her response loaded with all sorts of meaning that Erin didn't care to pursue.

"We're making bread?" She donned an apron and stepped up to the bench to knead a ball of dough Anne placed in front of her.

"There is bread to be made every day, love. It is always best fresh."

Placing her hands on the dough, she mimicked Anne's practiced kneading.

"You said you've worked here since Gaharet was a baby. You must've seen a lot in all those years."

"Oh love, I have worked here since I was a young girl, well before Gaharet was born."

"Wow. That's a long time. You'd probably know more about Gaharet than anyone else."

"The stories I could tell you about Gaharet and his brother D'Artagnon." She chuckled. "They could get themselves into all manner of strife as young lads."

"He told me they used to steal food and salt the boiled fruit."

"That and much more. There was this one time Jacques, Gaharet's father, had organized delivery of a very particular, very expensive barrel of wine. You see, we were to have visitors that week from Bretaigne and the visiting vicomte had developed a taste for this wine grown only in one region. Jacques had purchased a barrel and stored it beneath the keep."

Anne paused and handed her another ball of dough, taking the kneaded one and placing it in a bowl covered with a cloth for it to rise. Erin went back to kneading.

"Gaharet would have been...oh...a decade and six years or so, and D'Artagnon was two years younger. This time they included Gaharet's friend, Ulrik, in their little scheme. They were inseparable, those three and trouble followed wherever they went."

Erin grinned. She could imagine where the story was going. Teenage boys, a barrel of wine...

"Jacques, of course, was well aware of his boy's propensity for getting into trouble, so he had ordered two barrels. One of the expensive wine and one of the cheapest, nastiest, local gut rot wine he could find. The boys' plan was to buy their own barrel of cheap wine and swap it for Jacques' barrel."

"Let me guess. Jacques put the barrel of cheap wine out and hid the good stuff."

Anne nodded, chuckling as she continued to knead her dough. "You should have seen how sick those boys were. So convinced they were drinking something special, none of them wanted to admit to the others it tasted awful. They drank so much of that damn wine they didn't get out of bed for days. I have never seen those boys look so sick, turning away food, heads over buckets for hours. D'Artagnon swore off drinking wine altogether, and Gaharet could not bear the smell of it for nearly a month."

Erin laughed. It sounded like the hangover from hell. "And the visiting vicomte?"

"He got to enjoy his wine, as Jacques planned. I think the boys left the barrels of wine alone after that for a good number of years. They learned their lesson that day — to never underestimate their father. Oh, those were happier times, so carefree, full of fun and laughter."

Anne swapped out Erin's dough again. "How many more of these are there to do?"

"Only another two."

Erin massaged her hands and cracked her knuckles. "Oh good. My hands are getting sore. So, things changed after Gaharet's mother died?"

Anne's eyebrows shot up. "He talked to you about his parents?"

Erin nodded. "A little. He told me the story behind the wall hanging in the hall."

"He has not spoken of them in years. Not to anyone." She regarded Erin, a knowing glint in her eyes.

Erin dropped her gaze to her ball of dough. Did it make her feel better that he, too, had opened up about something he normally wouldn't? Yeah, it did. Just a bit.

"Elise was the center of those boys' world, the center of Jacques' world. When she died, Jacques became a shell of the man he was. He retreated from life for a while and left those two boys grieving for their mother, facing the world alone. Oh, they had each other, and Gaharet tried to be so strong for D'Artagnon, but it was a hard time for them all."

"What about Ulrik? Their friend?"

Anne shook her head. "His parents had sent him to Bretaigne over some trouble with Comte Lothair."

"Oh."

"When Jacques died less than a year after Elise, Gaharet had to step into his role as master of the keep. A lot of responsibility on top of his grief. He managed it, though. Takes his responsibilities very seriously, he does. He saw the way things had deteriorated while his father wallowed in his grief, and he refused to allow that to continue. I thought Jacques had strength, but Gaharet…" She sighed. "Well, he put his father to shame. And at that time he still had D'Artagnon."

"He lost him, too?"

"Yes. Not two years later."

Erin's hands stilled, resting on the ball of dough. He'd lost his entire family in the space of a few years? What would that do to a man? And his childhood friend gone, living in another country.

"Did Ulrik ever return?"

"Oh, yes." Anne shook her head. "But by then Ulrik had his own pain, and his own way of dealing with things. Gaharet did not approve. Their friendship paid the price. Things were never the same between those two again." Anne passed her another ball of dough. "This is the last one," she promised. "For Gaharet, rattling around alone in this keep, all that loss, the solitude, bearing the responsibility of it all on his own, it changed him. Stole all the laughter, all the joy from him. Breaks my heart to see it," she said. "What he needs is a good woman by his side." Anne looked directly at Erin, her meaning clear.

Erin nearly choked.

Hell no.

Erin started kneading again with renewed vigor. Was the universe plotting against her? She'd thought Anne would be on her side, not trying to get her into Gaharet's bed. As his wife!

"I'm sure there are plenty of women vying to be Dame d'Louncrais. He's wealthy, has a title. He's got a lot going for him. Many a family would consider him a good marriage prospect."

Not Erin. The whole idea was moot, anyway. She'd be gone soon, back home in her own century, and he'd be dead or dying in the cell beneath Langeais Keep. With or without her, history would plow on to its inexorable conclusion. As sad as that might be, she couldn't allow herself to get involved. As soon as she could wring out of him the secrets of the amulet, she'd be gone.

"He is handsome, too." Anne's eyes twinkled and Erin's ears flushed with heat.

"Well, I suppose so." Erin shrugged, keeping her attention on the dough, pounding at it much harder than it warranted. "The women of the court might think so."

Anne snorted. "One of those women would never catch his eye. The ladies of the comte's court are all caught up in the traditions and expectations of society, of creating a match for their own advancement. They would play the role of dutiful wife well enough, but Gaharet wants more than that. He *needs* more than that. Do not forget he has his parent's marriage as an example, and he wants what his father had with his mother. You saw the wall hanging, heard the story."

"I guess we all need something to aspire to," muttered Erin, wishing Anne would let this go.

"He wants a woman to set his blood on fire. A woman who can hold her own with him, who is passionate about what she believes in. Someone that will love *him* and not all of this." She swept her hand around, indicating the keep and all it encompassed.

Great. Just what Erin needed to hear — that Gaharet was a man searching for the love of his life.

"I think he needs someone with a bit of personality," continued Anne, oblivious to Erin's discomfort. "A woman with ideas of her own, who will challenge him, keep him on his toes, at least a little. It is not good to let the boy have his way all the time."

Anne as her ally would be formidable. Against her, Erin didn't stand a chance. No wonder Gaharet humored her. Anne used her will like a bulldozer. She needed to put a stop to this conversation. Right now.

"Anne, what's the room on the top floor for?" She rushed the words out before she thought too much about the consequences of asking and changed her mind. "The one beside the armory with locks on both sides of the door?"

"Ah." Anne smiled. "Now *that* is what I am talking about. Not afraid to speak your mind, are you, child?"

Erin gritted her teeth. "Who did he confine in there?" she persisted. "And for how long? I saw the marks gouged out of the back of the door."

Anne nodded. "That, my dear, is something you need to raise with Gaharet. Do not be afraid to ask him. It is something you will need to know when you decide to stay."

"I'm not staying."

Anne chuckled, her eyes full of mirth.

Why did everyone think she would want to stay?

"I think I'll take this dough now." Anne eased Erin's hands away. "It is well and truly kneaded. Why don't you run along to your chamber? Gaharet had me place some drawing materials there for you." A knowing smile tugged at her lips. "Unless you plan to be here when Gaharet comes looking for the meal I promised him earlier."

Erin relinquished the ball of dough, removed her apron, snatched up her headscarf and quickly vacated the room. She'd come to the kitchen to escape Gaharet, not to be handed over to him on a platter.

Climbing the narrow stairs, she cast a puzzled look back at Anne. That room on the top floor held secrets. Secrets Anne wanted her to know, wanted Gaharet to tell her. Did it have something to do with the amulet, the Theban inscription? Could it be the clue to why he ended up in an underground cell, chained to a wall? The more she learned about that damned man, the more he intrigued her. *Bloody hell.* Next thing she knew, she'd be trying to save him.

Chapter Fifteen

Erin stared at the image on the parchment, her index finger and thumb stained with ink. When Anne had told her materials to draw with awaited her in her chamber almost a week ago, she'd expected to find chalk and slate. Ink, pounce, and parchment were expensive, and she didn't for a minute expect they'd waste them on her. Yet when she'd entered the chamber, there on the table beside the water pitcher were sheets of parchment, a pot of ink, a small container of powdery pounce, a goose quill and a paring knife to shape it.

After a few false starts, a poorly angled cut on the end of the quill, thick blobs of ink soaking into the parchment and ink-stained fingers, she'd adapted to using the unfamiliar implements. By mealtime, she'd half a portrait done. That first afternoon she'd chosen to draw Anne, the wrinkled lines on the cook's face full of laughter, love and the attitude she gave to everyone, including Gaharet. Anne's delight when Erin gave her the portrait told Erin she'd chosen her first subject well.

Each evening since, by candlelight, she'd taken up the quill and drawn a portrait — the burly, ruddy faced blacksmith who often sat beside Gaharet at mealtimes, Gascon, Gaharet's tall, thin, balding head servant. Last night she'd drawn Brenton, the grizzled farmer, after he regaled her with the tale of his escape artist pigs and the mess they made of old Tumas' cabbages. She'd laughed so hard she'd almost cried at Brenton, his face scrunched in a mimicry of a furious Tumas chasing him around the field with his hoe, cursing him and his pigs. The night before she'd sketched Eleonore, a heavily pregnant woman whose husband, Henri, worked in the stables. The baby was due any day now and Erin wanted to gift them the drawing.

Dipping her quill in the inkpot, the scratch of its tip against parchment the only sound as the keep settled in to sleep, she drew faces, listening for footsteps passing her door. They came every night, a soft tread, barely discernible even in the stillness of the keep. They paused outside her door every single night, and Erin would hold her breath.

Would this be the night he entered?

The image of Gaharet hesitating on the other side of the door flushed goosebumps over her skin. Her hand would pause over her drawing, her breath held in anticipation until he moved on and she'd release a long sigh of...relief? Disappointment? A combination of the two?

She'd peeked once, after the footsteps receded, nudging the door ajar enough so she could see down the corridor, catching sight of him descending the stairs. Where did he go so late at night? To the hall? She didn't think so. On a hunch, the portrait of Eleonore almost complete, she'd opened the shutters and waited, watching the courtyard. She'd spied him leaving the keep, heading for the forest.

What did he do out there every night? Did he shed his clothes and enter the forest naked? Did he still follow the old religions, celebrating rituals with other like-minded individuals in the dark of night, in the depths of the forest? Could that have been what he was doing when she'd first encountered him?

She paused, staring down at her current work in progress, Gaharet's eyes staring back at her. She'd drawn him again, outlining the shape of his jaw, his nose, his brow line before giving it a second thought. And once she'd started, she couldn't stop. The differences between this drawing and her first were obvious, and they had nothing to do with the materials. He stared out at her, no hint of arrogance visible, the burning intensity of his eyes softened, a look of affection and admiration shining through, and a hint of a smile curling on his lips.

Nowhere in the drawing could she see the man who advised the brutal Comte de Anjou, the mounted chevalier from the wall hanging, wielding a bloody sword. Or the man with alarming sexual hunger who'd chased her like a predator chases prey because she ran from him. She grunted, dissatisfied with her effort. This would be the first drawing she'd have to scrap and start again. How could she have got it so wrong?

A knock interrupted her, and Anne bustled in, a bundle of clothing over her arm. She placed the items on the bed and moved to Erin's side, looking over her shoulder at her newest creation.

"I haven't quite finished yet," said Erin, chewing on her thumbnail. "I think I may have to start again. His expression isn't quite right."

"It looks right to me. I saw him with that exact look only the other day."

Erin looked at the drawing again. "You think so?" She held the parchment away from her, studying it. "Maybe." She couldn't deny it was Gaharet, but that expression, the gentleness of it, surprised her. Who would he have been looking at with that expression? Anne, perhaps? "I don't think I've ever seen him with that expression."

"Then perhaps, when you next see him, you need to look a little closer."

Erin screwed up her nose, pushing the drawing aside and setting down the quill. She didn't need to be staring at Gaharet any more than she already did. It was embarrassing enough. He'd caught her in the act more than a few times.

"What are you afraid of, child? That you will see something you do not like, or something that you do?"

Erin stared at Anne for a moment, startled by the old woman's perception, then dropped her gaze. Both. She feared both, but the latter more than anything.

She dipped her hands in the bowl of water, washing off the ink as best she could. "It's best I don't forget who he really is, what he stands for."

"And what does he stand for?"

"You said it yourself, Anne. He's a man who's used to getting what he wants. He'll use charm, wealth, or power, whatever it takes. And men like that never appreciate what they have." Gaharet's smiling eyes stared back at her and her conviction wavered. Could she have him all wrong?

"Whatever gave you that impression, child?"

Everything. His looks, his confidence, the way he stared at her, his gaze hot, his intentions clear. "He advises the Comte de Anjou. I know what Lothair is capable of, and he does it all with Gaharet at his side," she said instead.

"Our comte is ruthless, I will grant you that, but Gaharet is a good man. There is none better in my opinion. Without Gaharet's influence, we would see much worse from the Comte de Anjou."

Of course Anne would believe that. She'd known Gaharet since he was born, helped raise him. Besides, if he was such a good man, as Anne professed, why hadn't he helped her to get home? Why did he avoid talking about the amulet? Every time she raised the topic, he suddenly found somewhere else to be, something that needed his attention — accounts to be seen to, a sick farmer to visit, a new acquisition in the stables to appraise. Gaharet's recalcitrance to discuss it was a never-ending source of frustration for her. The man was locked up tighter than Fort bloody Knox. No matter how hard she pressed, he would reveal nothing more.

"I've known men like him, Anne. Only heartache comes from pinning your hopes on them."

Anne frowned, shaking out the clothes she'd brought, folding them neatly and placing them in the chests that now lined the wall.

"Anne." Erin swiveled around to watch the old cook. "Did you know Gaharet goes for a walk alone in the forest every night?"

"Oh yes, love." Anne shuffled across the room with a chemise.

"That's where I first met him, you know, in the forest."

"Mmm-hmm."

"He was naked."

"You have seen him naked?" Anne straightened out an under-dress before placing it in the chest on top of the chemise.

Erin studied the embroidered hem of her dress with avid interest. She'd seen him naked all right. More than seen him. A memory she wouldn't soon forget.

"Did you like what you saw? Cannot say I would mind such a sight myself, even at my age." Anne chuckled. "He is a fine-looking boy is our Gaharet."

"Looks aren't everything."

"No, but there is more to him than being handsome, mark my words." Anne picked up a burgundy overdress, holding it up for Erin to see. "This one would look lovely on you."

"But don't you think it odd him running around in the woods at night not wearing any clothes?" said Erin, barely giving the dress a second glance.

Anne raised her eyebrows at her. "Says the girl who turned up in the middle of the night in strange clothes, at the keep of a man she had never met before, with only a passing knowledge of the common tongue?"

Erin stared at Anne, eyes wide. "I did, and you never said a word. Nobody said a word. Why is that?"

"Not my place." Anne shrugged. "And I have seen far stranger things in my years." Erin opened her mouth to respond, but Anne continued, "It is nice having a young woman here. These halls have been quiet for far too long. Gaharet's been so dour with all the recent trouble, and yet yesterday I heard him laugh for the first time in a long time. Something *you* said had him laughing. You being here is good for him." She sent a sly look in Erin's direction. "Maybe good for you, too." She picked up the last dress, revealing Erin's jeans, her T-shirt and boots. Erin stared. How did Anne get those out from under Gaharet's nose?

"It is obvious, if you do not mind my saying, some man has hurt you, not treated you right. I do not know what he did to you. It is not my business to be poking my nose in, but Gaharet is not that man. Judge him if you must, but do it on his own merit, not by comparing him to someone else."

Erin flushed and looked away, her gaze falling to her drawing. Was it that obvious? Even before she'd met Gaharet, she'd judged him, pegged him as arrogant and a womanizer. Had she done him a disservice? She'd always prided herself on her ability to see past the surface veneer of men. To see them for who they truly were, ignoring their charm, their good physiques, their position in society, their fancy cars and expensive suits. Had she, though? Seen the real Gaharet? Was she so blinded by her own bias, by her experience with her mother's lovers, she'd judged him *because* of those things?

Erin looked up at Anne, chewing on her bottom lip. Could she, dare she, get to know Gaharet? See him as Anne saw him?

Anne placed the dress in the chest and shut the lid. "Take a closer look, my dear. If you do, I believe you *will* find a man worth pinning your hopes on."

Erin didn't answer.

"You want to know what he gets up to at night?" Anne scooped up the jeans, T-shirt and boots, depositing them in Erin's arms. "Go see for yourself." She gave Erin a steady stare, turned and waddled toward the door. "And that expression on his face," she said, turning back to Erin. "The one in your drawing. I see that when he looks at you."

Chapter Sixteen

"I hope you know what you are doing, Anne." Gascon scowled at Anne as she pottered about the kitchen, busy cleaning dishes, ignoring the dark looks her brother sent her way. "Seigneur Gaharet gave explicit instructions the girl could not have her shoes back, and under no circumstances could she leave."

"I know."

"You have given her back her shoes *and* her original clothes. Now you are asking me to ensure the gates are unmanned."

"Yes."

"You have encouraged her to follow Seigneur Gaharet into the forest. What were you thinking? You know what happens when he goes out into the forest. What if she sees him? What if she finds out what he is?"

Sighing, Anne put down the plate and turned to face her brother, her hands on her hips. "She could not sneak up behind him no matter how hard she tried, you know that. And what if she does see him in his other form? She will need to know anyway when he takes her as his mate."

"You do not know that is his plan."

Anne stared at Gascon. "Have you gone blind, brother? Do you not see the way he looks at her? The way she looks at him?"

"Of course I have. But I know my place. It is not for us to interfere."

Smiling at her brother, Anne handed him a cloth and waved him over to a stack of wet platters. "I am not interfering. I have given the girl a little nudge in the right direction, nothing more. Gaharet deserves some happiness after all he has been through. All I have done is help things along a bit."

Gascon picked up a platter and began drying it. "What if the girl makes a run for it, tries to leave?"

Anne chuckled. "That girl is not going anywhere, at least not anywhere too far away from Gaharet. Trust me, Gascon."

"What if she gets lost in the forest?"

"Gaharet will know she is following him long before he leaves the keep. He will not allow anything to happen to her."

Gascon sighed, slapping his cloth down on the bench and running a hand through his thinning, gray hair. "Have a care, Anne. The d'Louncrais have been very good to our family over the years, in more ways than you could ever know. If you meddle too much, you might find yourself looking for another family to work for."

"Oh, Gascon," said Anne. "You think I do not know what Jacques did for me? You think you kept secret from me what really happened all those years ago? You think I believed you and Jacques when you told me that reckless young man I made the mistake of falling in love with died in a freak riding accident?"

Gascon's face drained of color.

"I knew, even back then, he had betrayed me. Tried blackmailing Jacques with the d'Louncrais' secret I so stupidly confided to him."

"Oh, Anne." Gascon stared at her, his face crestfallen. "We never meant for you to know."

"Gascon." Anne stared him down. "I have known since the day he died, when Jacques killed him. Got what he deserved, if you ask me. I know my place, Gascon. It is here, looking after that boy. I owe Jacques that much. And what that boy needs right now is the young woman upstairs, and I aim to see he gets her. Are you going to help me or not? Do I need to go speak to the men manning the gates myself?"

Taking a deep breath, Gascon raised his gaze to the ceiling. "Very well, Anne. We will do this your way. I will talk to the gate guards, but please, no more meddling. I'm sure Seigneur Gaharet is more than capable of securing his own mate."

* * * *

As the keep settled into taciturn darkness, oil lamps tamped down and the bustle of servants declining, Erin leaned against the door of her room listening for the sound of footsteps telling her Gaharet was on the move. Dressed in the clothes she'd arrived in, a dagger she'd filched from the armory tucked into her belt, she waited. Her plan was simple. Goaded by Anne's provocation, she would follow Gaharet into the forest.

A meeting in the forest could precipitate the amulet's use. If others had used it, transporting themselves to Gaharet, they could use it to leave. If he wouldn't tell her about the amulet, she'd find out for herself. She also had a burning desire to know where he went every night. Could it go some way to explaining how and why he'd ended up in Lothair's underground cell? Would he be naked? She puffed out a breath.

Focus on the big picture, Erin.

Measured footsteps padded down the corridor, and she tensed, stealing herself to follow him. The footsteps paused right outside her bedchamber, as they did every night. She held her breath, every nerve ending attuned to the presence on the other side of the door. Would he come in? This one time she didn't want him to. Needed him not to. A shiver ran up her spine. The man could affect her without even being in the same room. Her eyes sought her drawing on the table. Had Anne really seen him looking at her like that?

Closing her eyes, she placed her palm flat against the door, imagined his hand on the other side, his palm to her palm. She swallowed. If he knocked, would she invite him in? Would she take him to her bed? Her nipples pebbled at the image of them entwined, skin to skin, Gaharet touching her body the way his eyes told her he longed to. Erin leaned her flushed face against the smooth timber. She could almost feel the heat of him seeping through the door. She held her breath, her heart pounding. An interminable moment passed.

Footsteps moved away from the door, and Erin let out her breath, not sure if she was relieved or disappointed. She waited another few minutes before opening the door. The hinge squeaked. She cringed, peering into the darkened hall, light spilling out from her chamber. Had he heard it? Her eyes adjusted to the absence of light. No sign of him.

Erin stepped into the corridor, taking extra care to make as little sound as possible. She scurried to the head of the stairs and peered down, glimpsing a dark shape disappearing around the bend. She waited a few tense seconds before following. Plunging after him into darkness, her hands followed the wall, her steps tentative. He had the benefit of familiarity with this keep. Not so Erin. Blind in the darkness, and with a lack of fluorescent lighting, the last thing she needed was to break her neck falling down the stairs.

At the base of the stairwell, his footsteps receded, soft, barely above a whisper, down the second stairway to the kitchen. Erin followed, clinging to the wall. She paused at the door of the now empty kitchen, coals still glowing hot in the fireplace giving Erin blessed light, Anne's words echoing in her mind.

"Judge him if you must but do it on his own merit."

All right. What could she make of these strange nightly walks? What conclusion about his character would she draw from his actions this evening?

Opening the door to the courtyard, he turned, and she ducked back into the corridor. Had he seen her? Did she really think she could match the skill of a trained warrior? What would he do if he caught her following him? Would he be angry? She risked a peek around the corner. Stopped in the doorway, he surveyed the kitchen, his gaze sliding past her. Evidently satisfied, he turned away, disappearing out through the door. It took a few moments to rein in her galloping pulse. She gave him enough time to get across the grounds, before pushing off from the wall, slipping through the kitchen and following him out into the cool, night air.

Erin eyed the heavy-hung moon and its generous glow with ambivalence. On the one hand, light was helpful. On the other, a hindrance, spotlighting her against the landscape. Somehow she must cross the courtyard, get through two gates, at least one of which would have a guard, and into the forest. All without being seen by the sharp eyes of the master of the keep.

She raced down the hill to the inner wooden wall, slinking low, and plastered herself against it like a Band-Aid to a scraped knee. Inching along, she racked her brain for a strategy. She hadn't planned this far ahead, not truly believing she'd make it beyond the keep.

The first gate had no guard. Strange. She continued on through the bailey, weaving from building to building—the stables, the storehouses, the worker's cottages. With them as cover, she advanced on the main gate and the outer wall, keeping Gaharet at the very edge of her vision. She became a veritable ninja, stealthy and furtive. She grinned at Gaharet's retreating back, her enjoyment at outwitting him, at this adventure, a little discombobulating.

As he passed through the main gate, Erin scuttled across to the outer wall. She didn't want to lose him before he reached the forest. A glance inside the gatehouse told her this one also lacked a guard. The man either had confidence that no one would dare attack his keep, or he'd arranged for their absence to conceal his departure. Whatever the case, Erin wasn't about to register a complaint. She slipped through the gate unnoticed.

Between her and the trees lay a manmade ditch, a bridge over it and another large open area leading up to the tree line. To follow Gaharet, she'd have to cross both. Should Gaharet look back, he couldn't fail to see her. If there ever was a point of no return, this was it. The cold night air raised goosebumps on her arms. The expectant forest held its breath waiting for her, and the threat of discovery jangled her nerves.

Suck it up, Erin. You've come this far.

Keeping low, she raced across the bridge and out onto open ground.

Please don't let me stumble. Please don't let me fall. Please don't let him see me.

Erin reached the tree line and plunged into the forest. The trees greeted her, enveloping her in their darkened green-brown foliage. She skidded to a halt, the safety of the moonlit keep behind her beckoning her to turn back, the forest's gloom menacing. And empty. No sign of Gaharet anywhere.

Beneath the canopy of interlocking limbs, darkness reigned, patches of filtered moonlight the only reprieve. Scanning her surroundings, heart beating a little faster, she chose a path and moved forward, hesitant but determined. She flinched as a branch unseen scratched her face, pulling at her hair, but she plowed on. Her shoelace caught on the bark of a rotting log, and she stumbled. Cursing in a violent whisper, she wrenched it free. Dappled light from the moon making it easier to see, Erin chose a path and increased her pace.

Still no sign of Gaharet. Had he changed direction once he'd entered the forest? Worse still, did she still head in a straight line? She stopped. What if she got lost? Not implausible. A tremble started at her knees and worked its way through her body. She swiveled her head, her gaze darting about, searching. Every direction looked identical. What *had* she been thinking? Urged on by Anne, in the safety of the keep, with its warming brazier and soft bed, her plan had seemed brilliant, inspired. Not so much now.

She took a few more steps and paused again, indecision paralyzing her. How could Gaharet have vanished so fast? She hadn't been *that* far behind him. Maybe she should turn back and chalk this up to a bad idea and an overestimation of her own abilities.

Face it, Erin, you're not Bear Grylls. You weren't even a girl scout.

An unnatural and sudden silence descended over the forest. The sounds of buzzing night insects cut off, scurrying rodents stilled, and an owl ceased its hooting. A deep knot coiled in her stomach. She searched her surroundings, looking for a cause. Nothing. There could be several reasons for the unnatural silence. Things she should be afraid of. Things like wild pigs, armed bandits and wolves.

Her heart pounded, a bass drum, rhythmic and loud. Thump, thump, thump. She slipped her hand to the hilt of the dagger, drawing it out, keeping her focus on the trees, her gaze darting left, then right, then left again. This had been a really *stupid* idea. Time to admit she was no tracker, forget about following Gaharet through the forest and return herself to where she should've been. Tucked up in bed, sleeping.

Her restless eyes widened, fixing on a spot, a shadow. A head turned toward her, ears pricked forward. Her fingers tightened on the dagger and she raised it before her. The animal stalked its way through the trees, moving closer. Her breath hitched. A wolf, black, big-boned and muscled, the breeze ruffling its fur, halted not five feet away. Oh, dear God. What had she done?

Stupid, stupid, stupid idea.

She should never have left the safety of the keep. Her hands shook so hard she almost lost her grip on the dagger. Seconds ticked by—her breath sharp and shallow, sweat trickling down her back. She faced off with the wolf. It had teeth, *large* teeth. It could eat her. And it was big, really big. She hadn't known wolves could be this size. Obviously, they could. The proof stood right in front of her.

"Shoo!" She waved the dagger at it. As if that would scare it away. Dear God, she hoped it wasn't hungry.

The wolf tilted its head sideways, ears pricked forward but it made no move toward her. It didn't growl, snarl or bare its canines. It merely stood there, watching her and waiting. Erin stared at it, afraid to take her eyes off it, her weapon raised. Should she strike it first? Or would that antagonize it, force it into attacking her? She inched away. The wolf followed. Okay, now what?

The wolf stalked forward. The urge to void her bladder was almost overwhelming. Erin stood her ground. Running would only put her back to the wolf. It moved to the left, circling around her. Its dark eyes, shadows dancing in their depths, never left her face. Following its movements, Erin turned her body in a tight circle, keeping them face to face.

She looked closer. Was that...? A gold chain hung around its neck, almost buried in the black fur. A collar? Someone's pet? A cross breed? A bit hound, a bit wolf? Hope filled her. Gaharet's *pet*? Could this be the wolf she'd spotted one night within the walls of the keep? She was willing to believe almost anything right now.

It sniffed the air, tilting its big head in her direction. Did she smell tasty? Edible? It most likely could smell her fear, sense her vulnerability. With shaking hands, she waited for the moment it launched itself at her.

It never came.

With a shake of its head, the big black wolf turned and trotted off. With a moan, Erin sank to her knees. She'd almost peed her pants.

"You are way out of your depth here, Erin." Her voice shook, but the threat of the wolf returning got her to her feet. "Time to leave before it comes back to eat you. With friends."

With the dagger clutched in her white-knuckled hand and keeping an apprehensive eye on the forest behind her, she beat a hasty retreat. After minutes of frantic, stumbling steps, Erin stopped. Shit. She hadn't gone that deep into the forest. The edge of the trees should be visible by now, the bailey's outer wall within sight. Was she going in the wrong direction? She didn't think so. Bloody hell, she hoped not. She wanted to sob, sink back to her knees, scream her frustration and fear, but she didn't dare. She continued on, stopped again, her breathing harsh and shallow. Was she lost? In a forest containing at least one wolf?

Don't panic, don't panic. That'll only make things worse.

What she wouldn't give to spot Gaharet, naked or otherwise, wandering through the trees. She'd brave his anger, his suspicion, anything to see his familiar face right now.

"Going for a midnight stroll, or making a break for it?"

She screamed and spun around, weapon raised, and came face to face with a fully clothed Gaharet. Unwanted tears pricked her eyes. He was here. She wouldn't die tonight. She was safe. Everything would be okay now. The dagger slipped from her nerveless fingers, and she resisted the impulse to throw herself at him and hug him. Barely. She took in deep, calming breaths.

"Thank God you're here. There are wolves in this forest. Did you know that? I had a close encounter with a huge black one. I thought—" She brushed the back of her hand over her eyes, wiping away unshed tears. "It scared the hell out of me."

In two steps, he'd pulled her against his chest and wrapped her in his arms. "You are safe, Erin. I will let nothing harm you. I will protect you." His words were a soft murmur against her forehead as his hand stroked her head. She melted into him, succumbing to his protective embrace.

God, he feels so good.

Warm, strong, and with her face pressed against his chest, his musky scent surrounded her. Safe. She could stay like this forever.

She pulled away, taking a few steps back, self-conscious at the ease with which she sought him out for comfort. "Sorry… I… I was just a little freaked out." She flushed.

His arms dropped to his side, sizing up her clothing, her shoes, his gaze raking her from head to toe. Would Anne get into trouble for giving them back to her?

"You should know Langeais is that way," he said, pointing behind her. "If that is where you were heading."

"What?"

"If you were making a run for it."

"Oh...um... I—" She looked in the direction he pointed, shaking her head. "No, I'm... I think I'll head back to the...to the um...the keep."

Gaharet nodded, moving a few steps closer, reaching up to brush a strand of hair off her face, tucking it behind her ear. It took all her will to not lean into his touch. Tilting her head up, she met his gaze. Those eyes. Dark shadows flitted across their depths. She blinked. Blinked again, tearing her gaze away. Just a trick of the moonlight, nothing more. She risked another glimpse. Bad idea. His gaze zeroed in on her lips.

"I think I'll head back now," she whispered, but she didn't budge an inch, letting him slip his hand behind her neck and draw her to him. Her mouth parted, his lips bare millimeters from hers, his warm breath dancing across her skin. They stood there, almost touching, as the moment stretched, the anticipation almost painful, his hooded eyes fixed on hers. A strangled moan slipped from her lips, and she gave in, closed the gap and pressed her mouth to his.

His arm snaked around her waist, easing her into his embrace, letting her take the lead. The hunger she knew him capable of, controlled. Erin swore she could hear her defenses, that had once stood as strong as Hadrian's Wall, crumble. Her hands, obeying commands she no longer issued, reached up to clasp behind his neck to tangle her fingers in his hair, crushing her body against his and willing him to deepen the kiss. He groaned against her mouth, tightening his hold on her. His tongue dove between her parted lips accepting her invitation.

He ground his hips against hers, the unmistakable evidence of his arousal pressing against her belly. She clung to him, sliding her leg up and crooking her ankle around his knee. She wanted him closer, to feel his thick length pressed against her heated core. He grabbed her thigh, lifting her leg higher, notching himself against the v of her thighs. She moaned against his mouth, and he released her neck. He moved his hand to her waist and slid his fingers beneath her T-shirt, caressing up her spine.

God, I can't get enough of him.

He tugged at the hem of her top, pulling it up. Cold night air brushed against her heated skin.

What was she doing? She wrested herself out of his arms and pushed him away, gasping for air. She wrenched her T-shirt back into place, ignoring the growl he released deep in the back of his throat. Turning on her heel, she stalked off through the trees, her emotions raging out of control.

She scowled at the moon.

You're not helping.

"Erin," he called after her.

Coming to an abrupt halt, her shoulders tensing, Erin spun to face him, eyes downcast and fists clenched at her side. She would not go to him. Under no circumstances would she let him draw her back into his arms. Oh, how she wanted to. Wanted nothing more than to get buck naked with him right here on the forest floor. She dug her heels in.

"What?" She refused to meet his gaze. If she looked into his eyes and saw the same lust that gripped her own body, she'd be lost.

"The keep's that way."

She looked up, his arm outstretched, pointing in the opposite direction.

"Oh."

The man didn't look the least bit flustered. She scowled at him. He suppressed a grin.

"After you then," she said, composing herself, waving him ahead. No way would she walk ahead of him, knowing his eyes would be on her, watching her all the way back to the keep.

Nodding, he scooped up the discarded dagger, running his hands over it. She shifted from foot to foot. He must know it came from his armory.

"You never know when you might need this." He handed it to her, hilt first, then turned and walked ahead of her.

Surprised he'd let her keep it, she had to hurry to catch up to his long stride, her body screaming at her to jump him. Right now. While she had the chance. She gritted her teeth and let him lead her out of the forest and back to the safety of the keep.

Chapter Seventeen

Erin pushed open the door to the room across from the hall. After last night's debacle in the forest and a restless sleep, she had risen more determined than ever to unearth Gaharet's secrets. Only, she wouldn't be following him into the forest again to do it. And since he wasn't at all forthcoming with answers to her questions, that left exploring the rest of his keep.

She'd relinquished her jeans and T-shirt once more, in favor of tenth-century clothes, and this morning, Anne had presented her with a beautiful pair of soft, fur lined leather ankle boots. Her inability to navigate the forest, and her fear of its inhabitants, must have allayed any concerns Gaharet had about her running off.

Erin closed the door behind her and scanned the room. Her eyes widened. Chests upon chests hugged the walls. Some lay propped open, filled with scrolls, books, and tomes of all kinds. Some remained closed, books scattered on their lids. She'd found the library.

She approached a chest, skimming her fingers across a heavy book, flicking it open. Greek. She closed it, opening another. Latin.

"*Praecepta Militaria*." Rules of Military. Some light reading there. She opened another book. Arabic? Continuing around the room, she moved from chest to chest, examining books, unfurling scrolls, handling them all with great care. The extent of knowledge stored in this room astounded her. Like the armory with its weapons, the d'Louncrais collection of literature was extensive. Some of these works she'd heard of, others not. Others still she'd no idea what they contained or who wrote them because they were written in languages she couldn't read.

Erin eyed the two haphazard stacks of books and scrolls on the desk. Out of all these books in this room, what had Gaharet chosen to read? One drew her eye, belonging to neither pile. She eased herself into the chair and slid the book toward her. Leather-bound, with the d'Louncrais crest stamped on the front in thick, red wax, its cover was smooth and worn. Well used.

Erin glanced at the closed door. She fingered the wax seal. What if it contained the reverse spell for the amulet?

She opened the book.

The first thing that caught her attention was the date. December 565. Handwritten Latin words flowed across the page beneath it. She rubbed her hands together. A journal. What secrets would it reveal about the d'Louncrais? She ran her finger along the neat script, her hands shaking in her eagerness.

"I hereby commit thine thoughts to page to guide thy... Children?" She squinted at the word, trying to remember her Latin. No, not children. *"Respice prolem, respice problem."* Not descendants. Descendants was *et semini.* "Mmm, what else could it be?" She tapped her finger against her chin. Progeny? Yes, progeny.

"I hereby commit thine thoughts to page to guide thy *progeny* with wisdom and true knowledge, for we are…cast divergent from mortal men and so our paths shall always differ."

Erin frowned and paused in her reading, her finger poised above the passage. "Cast divergent from mortal men?" What the hell did that mean?

The door swung open, and Erin slammed the book shut as Gaharet entered the room. His gaze went straight to the journal resting beneath her hand.

"Morning, Gaharet." She smiled, dropping her hands into her lap.

He lifted his eyes to her face, raised a single eyebrow. "Find anything interesting?"

"You have an amazing collection here. Where does one start? Unfortunately, I can't read Greek or Arabic, so at least half of them are beyond me."

"But you can read Latin."

It took all of Erin's willpower to not drop her gaze to the journal. "Reasonably well," she said, "but even restricting myself to only those written in Latin, it would take me months to get through the sheer volume of works you have here."

His gaze shifted down to the journal again, a slight frown his only reaction.

"Eleonore gave birth yesterday morning. A baby boy," he said, changing the subject. "I am going to visit her. I thought you might like to join me."

Erin smiled. "I'd love to see Eleonore and her new baby." Not now, though. Now she wanted to read more of the journal.

He inclined his head to the door. "Shall we go?"

Damn it.

Erin stepped out from behind the desk, giving the journal one last look. In all probability, she'd never see it again, and she'd been so close to uncovering...something.

With a smile plastered on her face, hiding her disappointment, she followed Gaharet from the keep, past the stables and storehouses to a small cottage, wisps of smoke curling from the chimney hole in the roof. At Gaharet's knock, the door opened and Henri welcomed them inside. Warmed by a fire pit in the center of the floor, the room was small, but cozy. A pot hung over the flames, and the ever-present rushes lay scattered over the earthen floor.

"Congratulations, Henri." Gaharet clasped the young man's hand.

Henri beamed. "*Merci*, Mon Seigneur."

"Anne tells me you have a healthy baby boy."

"Come." Henri beckoned them over to a heavy curtain of material, pushing it aside to reveal a small alcove. A tired-looking Eleonore lay on a cot, a baby swaddled in blankets in her arms.

"Congratulations, Eleonore."

"Thank you, Mon Seigneur Gaharet."

"How are you feeling?" asked Erin, perching on the edge of the cot.

"Tired, and a little sore." Eleonore smiled down at her baby. "But happy, too."

"I will leave you women to talk." Gaharet stepped back, letting the curtain drop.

"He's beautiful." Erin leaned forward, peering at the tiny, pink face. She brushed her finger across the baby's check. "Have you thought of a name yet?"

"Georges, after Henri's father."

"Oh, that's lovely. Now, how are you really feeling?"

Eleonore smiled. "According to Anne, my labor was quick. Once he decided to be born, Georges was eager to get out into the world."

"I bet it didn't feel so quick for you?" Erin grinned, and Eleonore shook her head.

"No, it did not." She looked down at her son, her face full of adoration. "But I have Georges, and that makes it worth every moment. Could you hold him for a moment?" Eleonore handed the baby to her.

Erin cuddled Georges close against her chest. He fussed a little then settled.

"Take him into the main room. I will freshen up and I will join you."

"Don't fuss on my account, Eleonore. You've just given birth to a baby. Lie in bed and relax. I doubt you'll get much of a chance over the next couple of months, so take this opportunity."

"Mon Seigneur Gaharet is here. I cannot lie in bed while he sits at our table."

Erin scowled. "He can't expect a new mother to get out of bed all because he stops by for a visit."

The poor woman had been in labor not twenty-four hours ago. No happy gas, no epidural, just the help of midwives, hot water, prayers and a primal urge to push. She'd like to see him go through that and be happy to get out of bed for guests the next day.

"I'll talk to him if you like. Tell him you need your rest."

Eleonore's gaze darted to voices of the men muffled beyond the curtain. "No, Mademoiselle Erin," she hissed, with a vigorous shake of her head. "Please do not do that. Monsieur Gaharet has been so good to us."

Erin sighed. "Well, all right then. I don't agree that it's necessary, but if you feel you have to…"

Eleonore touched her arm. "Mademoiselle Erin, you do not understand." Her soft voice, almost a whisper, forced Erin to lean closer to hear. "I have no family, only Henri. We had arranged for Anne and a few other women to come and help me a little as soon as the baby was born. But Seigneur Gaharet insisted Henri take a week from his work in the stables so he can be with me and the baby. Family, he told us, is the most important thing, and Henri should be here for the first week with our baby."

"Oh. That's…very kind." And highly unusual.

"Yes. Edith, my friend from the village, married a man from the Vautour estate and her husband could take only a day away from work, the day of the birthing. When I first met Henri, he told me how wonderful Seigneur Gaharet was, how well he treated his people, like family. I confess I did not imagine he would be any different from any other Seigneur, but Henri was right. It *is* different living here on the d'Louncrais estate. It is not Seigneur Gaharet demanding my presence, Mademoiselle Erin, but I who wish to do this for him."

Erin didn't quite know what to say. "Right. I'll give you privacy to freshen up." Erin edged off the cot and slipped past the curtain with baby Georges in her arms.

Gaharet and Henri ceased talking and turned in her direction.

"Eleonore will be out in a moment."

She glanced in Gaharet's direction as she took a seat beside him at the table. He stared back at her, an unfathomable look in his eyes. Had he heard their whispered conversation? She turned her attention to baby Georges, who gave a big yawn, his eyes popping open. "Oh, look. He's awake. Congratulations Henri. You have a beautiful baby boy."

Henri grinned from ear to ear. "I have a son." A look of bewildered happiness crossed his face.

"Anne has ensured you have all the supplies you need, Henri?" asked Gaharet.

"Yes, Mon Seigneur. Thank you." He stood, retrieved the boiling pot from over the fire, and filled a mug with its contents. "She brought many things on her last visit, including the leaves for this brew for Eleonore." He made a face. "It is raspberry leaves. Anne says it is good for new mothers." Henri shrugged. He placed three more mugs on the table. "Mead for us," he explained, filling the mugs from another jug. "That tea may be good for Eleonore, but it tastes horrible."

Gaharet chuckled, handing a mug of mead to Erin and taking one himself. "Anne's brews often do, but in my experience, they always work."

"Even if it does nothing, I am not about to cross Anne." Henri shuddered.

"Wise choice, Henri," said Gaharet.

"Look at these two grown men, Georges." Erin smiled down at baby Georges, tickling his chin. "Afraid of a little old woman. You'll need to grow up braver than these two."

Gaharet snorted. "You wait until Anne bullies you into something. You might see things a little differently then."

"She already has," admitted Erin.

Gaharet raised his eyebrows at her. "Last night?"

She gave him a rueful smile, nodding. "And the other day in the kitchen when she..." Erin flushed. She'd said too much.

"When she what?" pressed Gaharet, curiosity lighting up his eyes.

"When she tried convincing me you needed a wife." Erin rushed the words out, keeping her eyes on baby Georges. She risked a peek at the two men. Henri darted glances between her and Gaharet, while Gaharet grinned, amusement twinkling in his eyes.

"Well, Erin," said Gaharet. "Are *you* brave enough to defy Anne?"

The curtain to the bedroom alcove moved aside, and Eleonore entered the room.

"Mon Seigneur Gaharet. Thank you for coming to visit us."

Erin could have hugged her new friend for the timely interruption.

"Congratulations on your beautiful son, Eleonore, but should you not be in bed? You have just had a baby."

Erin stared at Gaharet's profile. Just a kind and caring Seigneur or a man making a point? He turned and locked gazes with her, and her heart thudded to attention. Could the man be both? Erin tore her gaze away.

Eleonore took a seat at the table, sipping from the mug of tea, her nose wrinkling at the taste. "It is nice to have company, and Henri has been so eager to show you our son."

Erin glanced at the baby, then at Gaharet. She hid a smirk. "I've been selfish. I'm sorry. Gaharet, here." She pushed baby Georges in his direction. To her surprise,

Gaharet took him from her without hesitation, snuggling him against his chest. Georges' face scrunched, his mouth opened, and Erin prepared for an ear-piercing cry. This would test him. He'd shove the baby back any minute now. She'd stake her life on it.

"Shh, Georges," Gaharet crooned, starting up a gentle rocking motion with his arms, and Georges settled.

Erin chewed on her lip, watching him, frowning. Large, strong, he cradled tiny Georges with such tenderness. A fleeting look of yearning so poignant flickered across his face and something within her stirred, softening toward him, while other parts of her heated in response. She shifted in her seat.

He'd have made beautiful babies.

An image of a little boy with Gaharet's black hair and her green eyes popped into her brain. She nearly choked. See a man hold a baby and she took leave of her common sense.

Gaharet shifted his focus to her. Their eyes met and held. He raised an eyebrow, the hint of a smile tugging at the corner of his mouth.

Erin turned away, grabbing her cup of mead and taking a long sip, catching a shared look between Henri and Eleonore. She closed her eyes, blocking them all out. She needed to get out of this cottage, away from Gaharet doing a great impression of fatherhood, and out of this century. If she didn't act soon and get herself home, it wouldn't be too long before the entire d'Louncrais estate would have her lined up to be the new Dame d'Louncrais. Her included.

Chapter Eighteen

The smell of hay and horse greeted Gaharet as he strode into the stables, overwhelming the lingering scent of Erin embedded in the steel links of his hauberk.

"Henri, good to see you back," he greeted the young stable master. "How are Eleonore and baby Georges?"

"They are well, thank you, Mon Seigneur. Are you riding today?" he asked, running his gaze over Gaharet's armor, surcoat and sword.

"Erin and I will ride today," he said, pulling on his gloves.

"Shall I saddle a mare for Mademoiselle Erin?"

Gaharet thought about it for a moment. "No. Leave my saddle off. Erin will ride with me." He doubted the arrangement would please Erin, but that did not perturb him. He longed to have her in his arms, body pressed against his. If putting her on his horse with him achieved that end, he would do it.

"I will prepare your horse, Mon Seigneur." Henri grabbed the tack and headed into a stall with a bay stallion. He bridled him and led the horse out, handing Gaharet the reins.

"Enjoy your ride, Mon Seigneur."

"Thank you, Henri."

He swung a saddle bag containing food and a skin of wine across the horse's withers then led the big stallion out of the stables toward Erin. She paced the courtyard waiting for him, hair covered by her headscarf, the burgundy fabric of her dress outlining her body as she moved.

The color suited her, stirring a hunger in him he had tried ignoring for the past week and a half. *Merde.* He wanted her. With Erin, his body had but one thought and it slammed into him every time he set eyes on her. His darker half lurked perilously close to the surface, restless, keen to assert its place, to preen, to make her his. Soon, he placated it. Soon.

Since their visit to see baby Georges, something in Erin's demeanor toward him had shifted. Whether her conversation with Eleonore or seeing him holding the baby had elicited the change he could not be certain, but she no longer curtailed the time she spent with him. Now, every time he turned around, she was there. Listening to his exchanges with his people, studying him. Sometimes she looked thoughtful. At others, puzzled. Sometimes her surprise amused him. Did he not fit her expectations of a tenth-century chevalier? If only she knew.

He often found her in the library, looking for his ancestor's journal, no doubt. She would never find it. He had sequestered it away, uncertain of what its pages might reveal. She had read enough of it to keep her searching for it, though.

He took advantage of those moments to converse with her, asking her about life in her time — how people lived, the houses they built, the clothes they wore and the wars they fought. That a liquid could power a vehicle with no need of a horse to pull it intrigued him. That vehicles could float in the air carrying over four hundred people unnerved him. The reasoning for moving pictures of people behind a glass screen he could not even begin to fathom. She had laughed when he scoffed at such a ridiculous notion. He had warmed at the sound, pleased their conversations no longer held the combativeness of their first few days.

On occasion, she would broach the subject of the amulet and he would reiterate what he had already told her. Those two little lines would appear between her eyebrows, her lips would thin and she would end the discussion with a frustrated huff and an angry swish of her skirts, stalking away.

At times he would judge her relaxed and amenable enough and attempt to discuss her excavation of Langeais Keep. She would merely smile at him, eyes wide in feigned innocence, and profess a previous promise to help Anne, or to visit Eleonore, or to be somewhere in the keep other than with him. He would let her go, listening to her retreating footsteps, silently daring her to break into a run. She never did.

Talking to her had both eased and excited his desire in equal parts, but he had kept his inclinations under control in an effort to attract her with his words, as hard as that was. As hard as he was. Constantly. Many a time they met within the confines of a corridor, and the temptation to gather her in his arms and carry her off to his chamber had sorely tested his restraint.

She desired him as much as he did her. He could see it in all her small gestures, her body language. He could smell the sweet scent of her arousal every time she walked into the room. Knowing she pleasured herself in her bedchamber every night threatened to rip away any semblance of control he had. The compulsion to burst through her door and sink himself into her soft, wet heat grew stronger by the day. Yet still she resisted it. So he waited, he watched and he talked.

The time for talking was done. Lothair had summoned him to Langeais Keep and now Gaharet needed answers as much as he needed her. He could not afford to wait any longer on both counts. Her avoidance of disclosing information about the excavation site, and about his death, ended today. And the time had come for him to make her his.

He swung up onto his horse, adjusted his sword to the side, and nudged the animal to stand beside her. His horse, used to a master who was not entirely human, stood quietly. Leaning over, he grasped the startled Erin around the waist and lifted her onto the horse in front of him, her legs dangling on one side. Her hip fit nicely against his groin, her shoulder against his chest, and the top of her head just below his chin. Perfect. They had half a day's ride to reach Langeais. There would be plenty of time to talk. Among other things.

"Nobody said anything about *me* going riding," she muttered, holding her body stiff in his arms, anxiety rolling off her in waves.

"Comte Lothair has summoned me to Langeais Keep. As you predicted he would."

Her face paled, the bitter scent of her fear spiking the air. "There's no need for me to go. Perhaps it's best I stay here." She squirmed against him, attempting to slide from his horse.

He tightened his arms around her, keeping her firmly in place. "Do you not want to see Langeais Keep, meet Comte Lothair? I would have thought an archaeologist would be eager for such a chance." He resisted his need to comfort her, assure her all would be well. He suspected she would not welcome his touch. Taking up the reins, he nudged his horse forward, her fingers clutching at his surcoat.

"Sure, ride us both to our deaths with a little sightseeing on the side and lunch with the devil himself."

He chuckled. "Perhaps, perhaps not. I have you, do I not? Your knowledge of Lothair, of this century, gives us an advantage that no one could anticipate." His words were meant to reassure her, but she merely grunted in reply. He urged his horse into a trot, the motion making her cling to him.

"We could have gone in a carriage or a cart. Walked even. Walking is good. Or, here's an idea. We don't go at all."

Her voice gave a telltale quiver. Had she not ridden a horse before? Had he known she would cling to him like this, he would have taken her riding days ago.

"I cannot ignore a summons from the comte, and we will make better time on horseback. Relax, Erin. I will keep you safe. I will not let you fall."

He pushed his horse into a canter, forcing her back into the protection of his arms and against his chest. She only gripped him harder. He suppressed a smile. He would delight in it while he could, inhaling her intoxicating scent, her body pressed against his. They would be in Langeais soon enough, and he would not be able to focus his attention on her so much. He would need his wits about him then.

Lothair and Renaud were making plans and, while defying the comte and secluding himself away on his own lands might seem a safer option, it blinded him to their scheming. He had no wish to die, had no foolhardy desire to sacrifice himself like some glory-bound chevalier's squire. Trouble and betrayal had found them, and he would face it, not hide in his stone keep cowering. He would need to exercise caution, but Erin's information could give him the upper hand over their enemies if she shared her knowledge. By bringing her along, he had given her little choice.

Ensuring they would not be without allies at Langeais Keep, he had sent messages to all his men of his summons. They would be there when he arrived. Safety in numbers. Of the six, only five he could trust. But which five?

Cantering down the hill, they rode under the portcullis and beyond the walls, heading for the dark, cool expanse of the trees.

"We're going through the forest?" Her voice pitched high, and her hand gripped him tighter. "Isn't there a road, villages to pass through? I'd like to see the villages."

L'enfer. He had made an error in judgment the night she'd followed him into the forest. He had meant only to track her, keep her safe and observe how far she would be willing to go. Watching her pick her way through the trees in those tight-fitting clothes of hers, his need to scent her, to show her his true nature, had overwhelmed him. Drawing too close, he had frightened her.

"Do not worry about wolves, Erin. They will not bother us. I will make sure of it." He relaxed into the rhythm of his horse's gait as they slipped beneath the whispering canopy of birch and beech, chestnut and pine, the thud of his stallion's hooves a steady beat along the worn trail.

Cresting a rise a good number of leagues into their journey, Gaharet reined his horse to a walk. He nudged him down an embankment and across a trickling brook, following its course, allowing his stallion to pick and choose his way along the water's edge. At this slower pace, Erin loosened her grip on his arm, and began taking in their surroundings. He gave her a few minutes reprieve before breaking the silence. What he wished to talk about would not make her happy.

"When we arrive at Langeais," he began, "I have an interest in your impressions of it. I imagine it will have changed much over the years."

"You have no idea."

"I have many ideas about Langeais based on the things I have learned about your time, though I could not attest to their accuracy." Changes in language over the centuries had resulted in some very unusual phrases. He had come to understand many of them were not meant to be taken in a literal sense, but he could never be certain which ones. "Tell me of some of these changes?"

"Well," she said, "for starters, there's a substantial bridge crossing the Loire River, and there's the fifteenth-century château. It's huge, in a way that you couldn't possibly comprehend. The ruins of Langeais Keep are a pimple on a pumpkin by comparison."

He frowned. "A pimple on a pumpkin?" What an absurd expression. He waited for her explanation.

"It means tiny, hardly noticeable."

Langeais Keep towered over the village of Langeais. How it could be *hardly noticeable* beside this château, he struggled to imagine. Perhaps he did have 'no idea'. "I see. What else?"

"It's a town full of really old buildings — houses, churches, the château — still standing after all those centuries. Being there, it's easy to imagine you're back in the past. Not as far back as this, but it's like a slice of history preserved, and yet amongst it all is evidence of modern living. Houses with pitched roofs and gable windows lining streets where cars and trucks — those liquid powered vehicles I told you about — drive past their front doors. People exploring rooms of the château with its fifteenth-century furniture, wearing clothes like the ones I wore when I came here. Every morning, walking from my hotel to the keep, I would take a different path, exploring the streets. Where I come from, we have nothing quite like it. It's a history lover's dream." She chuckled. "At least for me, anyway."

"Each day you would leave this '*hotel*' and go to Langeais Keep and dig in the dirt looking for things from the past to study?"

"Mmm-hmm."

"You enjoy this work?"

Her face took on a wistful cast. "Yeah, I do. Finding something, an artifact, a piece of history preserved, puzzling out what it means, how it fits into the lives of the people who owned it, I love it. It's a snapshot of how they lived. For a brief moment, I'm transported back to their time, able to see, feel, touch their lives."

She didn't look at him as she spoke, staring out at the trees. He kept quiet, not willing to break the spell, lest she stop talking, stop sharing.

"I once thought I'd study art, but one day I skipped school and ended up at the museum. They had this visiting exhibition of medieval warfare, and I walked in there and saw swords, crossbows, chain mail all from the fourteenth, fifteenth and sixteenth centuries. It astonished me that something from so long ago had survived and had stood the test of time, as real and as solid as they were back then. I spent hours in there that day, totally absorbed in it, forgetting everything else, learning all I could about the pieces in the exhibit. I went back the next few days, too. The rest, as they say, is history."

"And now you dig up pieces to go into collections such as these."

"Exactly. Of course, I had to study a lot before I could do that, but I've worked on quite a few excavations since I graduated."

"None of them quite like this one."

She gave a rueful laugh. "No. No artifact has ever transported me back in time before. If I'd have known that would happen, I might've left the amulet where I found it."

"Then you would never have experienced what you have." And he would never have met her.

"No, I wouldn't have."

They rode along in companionable silence—the brook leading them out into a grassy meadow.

"Where did you find the amulet again?"

She rolled her eyes at him. "Nice try, Gaharet. If I tell you everything you want to know, what reason would you have to disclose the information I need?"

"Mmm." Intelligent woman. "Very well. Ask a question and I will answer it." And he would, within reason.

The little line appeared between her eyebrows as she thought about it, chewing on her thumbnail. Would she ask about the amulet or something else? If she had read any of his ancestor's journal, even those first few lines, she might have other questions. She could have made connections he was not ready for her to make. He wouldn't lie to her, but he may need to be a little creative with the truth.

"What do you do with the amulet when you go out into the forest every night? Is there some ritual? Are you part of a sect, or a coven of witches? Do you follow the old religion?"

He suppressed a smile. She certainly had persistence. "I do nothing with the amulet. It has no ritual attached to it, save for the inscription that brought you here. I do not worship any of the old gods, nor do I belong to a coven."

"You don't deny that you go out into the forest every night?"

"Not at all. I do go into the forest every night. I like to go for a run. It's peaceful at night and it helps me clear my mind."

"Really? Naked?" She glanced up at him, color creeping up her neck to her cheeks. Giving in to her demand for reciprocal information was a small price to pay to see her like this. Her face was flushed and her green eyes glazed, that she recalled their first encounter written clear across her face.

He arched his eyebrows. "Have you ever tried running in armor?"

"No." She laughed. "But one would assume you would at least wear clothes."

He shrugged. "It's very freeing, pitting oneself against nature in our natural form. You should try it sometime."

He looked down at her, bottom lip caught between his teeth, his gaze fixed on her mouth. With a little gasp, she turned away from him. He almost laughed. *Mon Dieu, he could spend a lifetime teasing this woman.*

"I don't believe you. If you don't want to tell me, that's fine, but don't expect me to share anymore, either."

"It's *your* choice not to believe me, Erin. I have told you the truth. I go for a run in the forest every night. You can ask Anne, or any of the servants. They will confirm it. You cannot in good conscience refuse to answer my question simply because you doubt the veracity of my words."

Her frown was back. "But what of the amulet?"

"What of it? I have already told you what the amulet is for, what it does."

She raised her eyebrows at him. "You really think I'm stupid enough to believe you would have a spell crafted to protect a piece of jewelry? A very bland, simple disc, hung on a chain with your family crest stamped on it?"

"You know exactly what the amulet does. You have experienced it. Beyond that, there is little I can tell you. I do not know who created them, or where the language came from. I would like the answers to those questions as much as you."

She studied his face, her dissatisfaction evident.

"Now, will you tell me where you found the amulet? Please."

She looked out over the meadow, squinting in the sun. "Given the state of the ruins, it would be very hard to pinpoint the exact location."

An absolute certainty settled over him. Of all the places in Langeais Keep he would wish for it not to be found, one place, one room, he dreaded more than all others. "You found it in the underground cell."

Her startled gasp confirmed it. *L'enfer.* The underground cell. Lothair's version of an oubliette. Newly built, Gaharet had overseen the construction of it himself at the comte's request. Where Lothair had come up with the notion he had never ascertained, but the idea of having somewhere particularly unpleasant to hold prisoners had appealed to the comte. A place with no light, no fresh air and no hope. His hand clenched around the reins. Lothair had confined one of his kind in that godforsaken hole.

"I..." She sighed, her shoulders slumping. "Yes. I found it in the underground cell. It surprised us all, really."

He forced himself to relax. She was talking, telling him what he wanted to know. His anger he would save for Lothair, Renaud and the one who betrayed the pack. "It surprised you to find the amulet in the cell?"

"Finding the cell surprised us. Langeais Keep had long been a sightseeing attraction, much like the château. Any excavations ceased there many, many decades ago. Until our team came along."

"Something convinced you to start a new excavation?" He shifted the reins into one hand, placing his free hand on her thigh, giving it a squeeze of encouragement.

"In researching you, we found a document."

Her focus shifted from the meadow to his hand. Would she permit him this intimate touch? She made no attempt to brush him off, and he allowed himself a small, triumphant smile.

"You have mentioned my chaplain's journal."

"Not that document. Another one."

Now he was getting somewhere. "And what did this other document disclose?"

"It was a ledger, severely damaged. No one had managed to decipher it. When we applied updated techniques, we were able to get clear images of construction records for the keep. One line recorded a construction signed off by you."

He nodded. "The construction of the cell. I remember signing it." Had he known one of his men would die in it, he would have resisted Lothair's desire to build it more vehemently.

"There was another entry added after yours. Written by someone else, dated August 999. It recorded the cell's first prisoner. No matter how hard we searched, we could find no other reference to the cell, the prisoner, or your death."

"And you assumed I was the prisoner of that cell. That I died there."

She placed a hand on top of his, giving it a little squeeze, offering him comfort. Gaharet kept his expression neutral, but he rejoiced at her unconscious gesture.

"It's a theory we were exploring. Then I found the amulet."

He nodded. Her conclusions were a natural presumption, even if they were wrong. "And what of the other artifacts you found?"

"Oh no. You want more information, start talking. Tell me about the bloodstone, or the secret that's mentioned in the inscription. Or perhaps you'd like to explain the purpose of the room on the top floor with the bolts on both sides of the door. Who did you lock in there? And why?"

His nostrils flared. The training room. He *had* given her free rein of the keep. Of course she had left no corner unexplored. And she'd been on the top floor, taken a blade from his armory even. With her gift for keen observation, she would not have missed the broken straps or the gouges on the door. In time, she would need to know the purpose of that room, need to make use of it herself to aid in the training of her wolf. Once he'd turned her. Not yet, though. He could answer none of her questions, but he needed his answered.

"You found bones in the underground cell, did you not?"

She expelled a loud sigh. "I guess you don't really want to hear what I have to say, then?"

His horse plodded on, reaching the edge of the meadow and plunging them back into the coolness of the trees. He did not want to force her into answering, but unless he was prepared to lie to her about the training room—and he wasn't—he had no other choice.

"Think about where we are, Erin, where we are going. For the moment, you are in my care, under my protection. If something were to happen to me, as you have suggested it will, where does that leave you?"

"I know." She swiveled to face him, almost unseating herself from the horse, grabbing his arm to steady herself. "Why do you think I keep asking about the amulet? Something is going to happen to you, and soon, and I need to get home before it does. Before I get caught up in it."

"It is too late for that, Erin. By this afternoon we will be at Langeais Keep. Help me. Tell me what you know. I will do everything in my power to keep you safe, to prevent my chaplain ever needing to write those two words in his journal."

"Give me the amulet, tell me how to reverse the spell and you won't need to worry about keeping me safe. I'll be gone."

"I do not have an amulet with me." At least not one with an inscription. Not that it would do her any good, even if he did. The amulet had but a single purpose — to hide their existence. Never meant as a means to transverse time, no reverse spell existed. Not one he knew of. He could not send her home. Not even if he wanted to. If she knew the position she was in, would she help him? He suspected she would take such news badly, so he kept the knowledge to himself. For now.

She glared at him. "You did this deliberately, didn't you? You've brought me along so I would have to tell you everything I know. If I don't, I'm risking my life along with yours." She turned her back on him, staring off into the forest, her body rigid against him. "Yes, to answer your question, we did find a skeleton in the underground cell. It belonged to a tall male, whose age I had yet to determine, but I found the amulet with his bones."

Gaharet frowned at her vehement response. Was it fear that had her reacting so? Or because he had outmaneuvered her? She glared down at his hand still resting on her thigh and shoved it away. *Merde.* His little filly was a complicated creature. Regardless, he pressed on.

"What else can you tell me about the bones?"

"Not much," she said, her tone little more than a growl. "We have no way of telling how long the man was in the cell for, but we do know they'd chained him to the wall."

"And?"

"And at some point, the chains snapped. Whether this happened prior to his death or after, we can't be sure."

"Anything else?"

She gave him a look that promised retribution at her earliest possible convenience.

"Given the damage on the bones, I suspect the cause of death was decapitation."

He hesitated. He had to know for certain. "Was there anything unusual about the skeleton or the shackles?"

Her eyes met his before skittering away. "What makes you ask that?"

Foreboding tightened his chest. "What did you find, Erin?"

She shook her head. "It's nothing, really." But her frown told a different story.

"It caught your attention. What did you find?" For a moment, he thought she would not answer. He did not wish to push her any harder, but he must know.

"They made the shackles of silver, not iron."

There could be no doubt. One of his kind had died in that cell. Worse, Lothair had known he had a werewolf imprisoned. There was no point in using silver shackles on a human. But a werewolf... It was the only thing that could bind them. Which of his men had Lothair captured? Lance, Aimon, one of the twins? Had they given Lothair what he wanted or had they died because they refused?

"I hope you have a plan that will keep us from being thrown into that cell. Or better still, we turn this beast around and head back to the safety of your keep. Dying in the tenth century doesn't hold a lot of appeal for me."

He turned her to face him, cupping her chin. "Look at me, Erin."

She raised her gaze to meet his.

"Do you really think I would allow any harm to come to you, *ma petite pouliche*? I told you that night in the forest that I would protect you, and I will."

A look of uncertainty flashed across her face.

"Knowing what you have told me, I am better prepared for what we will face. Thank you."

He leaned closer, her lips so close, so tempting. She pushed at his chest, struggling to get out of his grip, and he let her go. With a startled squeal she lost her balance, overcorrected, and before Gaharet could catch her, she slid feet first off the horse and landed on her bottom on the ground.

"Erin, are you hurt?"

He pulled his horse to a halt—his foot out of the stirrup, ready to dismount, to go to her aid—but the scowl on her face stopped him. Staring at her, sprawled on the ground unhurt, indignation burning bright in her eyes, he stifled a chuckle. Laughing now would not endear her to him at all. Her scowl deepened, her lip curled up in a snarl, and he gave into the impulse and threw back his head and laughed.

She gaped at him, then her features softened and a smirk tugged at the corners of her mouth. She looked down at herself sitting in the grass and started laughing, too.

"Yes, all right. I guess it is pretty funny."

"I am sorry, Erin," he said, still chuckling. "I should have caught you. You are testing my commitment to keeping you safe already. Come." He reached his hand out to her. "I will not let you fall again."

She got to her feet and dusted herself off. He moved the horse in close, intending to pick her up, but she dodged away from him.

"Erin, we still have a long way to go," he said, bemused. "Come, let me reseat you."

She crossed her arms over her chest and thrust her chin out at him. Was she still angry with him? He sat on his horse, willing to wait her out. She could not possibly think to walk back to his keep. Could she? They had come too far.

"Clearly I can't ride like that," she said.

"Like what?"

"With my legs on one side. I'll fall off again."

"Not unless you struggle against me. You were doing fine until then."

She remained silent, arms across her chest, refusing to budge, a direct challenge in her green eyes. She looked adorable.

"How do you want to ride?" At least she planned to continue the journey with him, but how *did* she want to sit on the horse?

"Like you."

Startled, he stared at her. "You want to ride astride?"

"Yes. Is that so bad? It's the way it's done in my century, and it'll be much easier for me to balance. Besides," she said, emphasizing her point by placing her hands on her hips, the pert thrust of her breasts nearly unseating *him* from the horse. "I'm sure it's much more comfortable for a woman to ride astride than a man. I've never understood the logic behind forcing women to ride side saddle while men could ride astride. It's not like we have any" — she gestured to her groin area —"dangly bits to get in the way."

Dangly bits? He grinned. *L'enfer, his little filly is a bold one.*

Said dangly bits approved, and they sat up and took notice. He moved his horse closer for another attempt at reseating her on his horse, but again she stepped out of his reach. He reined in his horse, staring down at her.

"Erin, you cannot ride astride with a long dress." Aside from that, he did not think they would make it very far with the sweet curves of her behind pressed against his bits that were in immediate danger of no longer being dangly.

She arched an eyebrow at him. Reaching down, she tucked her dress up. This action brought the hem of her dress up to above her knees. Gaharet stared at the pale expanse of skin such a move revealed. What was worse — tight-fitting men's breeches or bare skin?

She held her arms up. "Now lift me up."

Mesmerized by her calves, he obeyed. Placing her in front of him, she swung one of her legs across the horse's neck until she sat astride, the hem of her dress inching higher, to mid-thigh. She leaned back against him, the backs of her knees resting against his kneecaps, his thighs snug against her near naked ones, and suddenly the aforementioned dangly bits were downright hard. All thoughts of skeletons, excavations and silver shackles evaporated, and he could only think of her. Their journey to Langeais would be a long ride indeed.

Chapter Nineteen

Erin groaned, relieved beyond all measure, when Gaharet reined in the horse beneath a small stand of trees on the edge of a clearing. A gently flowing stream meandered over mossy rocks. Remnants of summer wildflowers poked up through the grass, and the fronds of weeping willows swayed in the afternoon breeze. An idyllic spot for a break, but all Erin cared about was getting her two feet back on the ground. Her butt ached and her legs were dirty, sweaty and covered with horsehair. If she never rode another horse again, it would be too soon. She also had to answer the call of nature rather urgently.

They'd cantered across the countryside in silence, skirting around villages, passing through postcard worthy meadows, and cool, peaceful forests. Their bodies forced together by the motion of the horse, every thought, every emotion burned away, but one. Her mind full of the way his knees pressed into the back of hers, his chest flush against her shoulder blades, and her bottom fit snug against his groin, her desire for him eclipsed everything. She hadn't thought it through when she'd insisted on riding astride. The intimacy of it took her breath away.

Gaharet dismounted and secured the horse to a tree. Lifting her from the horse, he slid her body down his before placing her feet on the ground. Her nipples hardened to painful points. Catching the same heat mirrored in his eyes, she broke away, stumbling past him.

"I have to pee," she mumbled, heading along the stream to find a convenient tree behind which to relieve herself.

Having taken care of the discomfort in her bladder, she returned to the water's edge, pulling up the hem of her dress, and rinsing off her legs in the cool water. He stood behind her, silent, watching. She didn't need to look to know his gaze was on her. Awareness fluttered over her skin. She wanted him. Oh Lord, how she wanted him, but... She needed to find a way home. Getting involved wouldn't be a smart thing to do.

Standing, she turned to face him. "Gaharet, I—"

"Shh." He lifted a finger to her lips. Planting a kiss on her forehead, he wrapped his arms around her and pulled her against him. Held in his arms, staring into the dark, swirling depths of his eyes, her words stalled in her throat and slipped away. He leaned in, his warm breath fanning across her cheek, his beard brushing against her skin, stirring nerve endings into a frenzy.

"Are you ready to admit you want this, *ma petite pouliche*? That you crave it as much as I?" he whispered into her ear.

Her eyelids fluttered closed, her body no longer a solid mass, but liquid heat coalescing before him and in danger of pooling at his feet.

No, I can't, I shouldn't.

"Yes."

"Truly?" He placed soft, open-mouthed kisses along her jaw, nipping, tasting. Erin tipped her head back, giving him greater access, and he abandoned her jaw to press a kiss on the sensitive patch of skin below her ear. Her knees went weak, and she clung to him. "You will let me take you? Here, in this meadow?"

All hope of intelligent thought vanished, moving her beyond resistance and well into the territory of mindless desire.

"I will have your answer, *ma petite pouliche*." He sucked on her earlobe, a gentle nibbling at tender flesh with his teeth.

She moaned. She should stop him now, push him away. "Yes."

"Tell me what you want. Tell me what you need."

His voice was a husky whisper against her throat, his mouth trailing kisses down to its hollow, his tongue flicking against her heated flesh. He was ice to her sunburn, cold water to her burning thirst. Her whole body strained to get closer, to feel every inch of him, to slake this fire that burned. She'd beg if she had to.

"Kiss me. Take me, Gaharet. Please."

With a growl, his hand slipped beneath her veil, grasping a fist full of her hair, angling her head, taking her mouth in his with a deep open-mouthed kiss that possessed, that spoke of a hunger unleashed.

Oh yes.

He picked her up as her knees buckled under his onslaught, carrying her to a grassy spot on the bank and laying her down. He knelt beside her, devouring every inch of her, staring at her from under hooded lids. His dark gaze lingered first on her lips, her breasts and the vee at her thighs, his breathing heavy and ragged. Erin extended her arms and reached for him. She'd have him before she changed her damn mind.

He needed no more encouragement, and he cast aside his sword, shucked his surcoat, armor and gambeson and placed his hands on her, sliding them up across her stomach. Erin arched her body into his caress, her need to have him pressed against her an imperative.

He groaned and, supporting his weight on his elbows, he positioned himself over her, his knee nudging apart her thighs. Her desperate fingers sought skin, pushing under his tunic, running up his back, hips arching against him. The evidence of his arousal pressed against her, rock-hard and large. She shivered, a soft moan escaping. He caught the sound with his mouth, allowing her no reprieve. His tongue plundered, tangling with hers, demanding she respond in kind. With his large hand, he cupped her breast, teasing her pert nipple through the layers of fabric with his thumb and forefinger. It wasn't enough. She wanted more. Nothing less than skin on skin would satisfy her now.

Touch me, Gaharet.

As if hearing her unspoken request, his hand skimmed down her side, past her hip, pulling at the material of her dress, the slide of his fingers featherlight on her trembling thigh. Cool air replaced body heat, his fingers leaving her thigh as he pulled away from her. Erin's eyes flickered open. He closed his eyes, his breathing heavy and his face a mask of rigid control.

No. Don't hold back, Gaharet.

She yearned for him to lose control, craved the tenth-century warrior, his aggressive dominance. It's what had drawn her to him in the first place, no matter how much she'd denied it. She let out a murmur of discontent, thrusting her hips against his hard cock, reaching up to run her hands under his shirt. His stomach quivered beneath her touch.

"Stop," he growled, barely above a whisper, nostrils flaring, a strong, musky scent filling the air. "Close your eyes."

She mewled in protest.

He leaned down, resting his forehead against hers. "Close your eyes. Please."

Dark eyes stared into hers, the shadows shifting within their depths more pronounced than she'd ever seen before. She reached up to touch his face, and he flinched.

"Please."

"Okay." Her eyelids fluttered closed. The gentle touch of his lips pressed first on one eyelid, then the other.

"Thank you," he murmured against her cheek.

Then he claimed her mouth, demanding and *hungry*. He'd relaxed his control. He'd let the beast loose.

Oh God, YES!

His hands resumed their discovery of her body, and she lost herself in his touch, his kisses. She moaned, his hand slipping to the inside of her thigh, her muscles clenching in anticipation. Her pussy throbbed, wet and begging for his touch, his large hands teasingly close, but not close enough.

He grabbed her firmly about the waist, rolling over, taking her with him, draping her body over his. His hands slipped beneath her dress, cupping her bottom, pulling her hard against his erection.

"Erin." He nuzzled against her neck. "You do not know how much I want you." His voice, rough and husky, scraped over heightened nerve endings, sending shivers through her whole body. "I have wanted you since the first night I saw you."

Erin pushed at his black tunic and straddled his hips to give her better access. Her hands slipped beneath the fabric, reveling in the play of muscles across his abdomen, his bare skin hot beneath her hands. She ran her fingers over his chest, hair tickling her palms. She flicked her fingernails across his taut nipples. He let out a hiss, shifting her, pressing the thick bar of his erection against her. He held her hips firm and thrust hard, grinding against her. Mouthing a silent moan, head dropping back, her hips responded, rocking along his hardened length.

She opened her eyes to look at him and froze.

"Gaharet." Her mouth went dry. "Gaharet. Stop." Her desire vanished — all her attention fixed at the edge of the meadow.

His hands stilled, his body tensing beneath her.

Up on the rise, unmoving, watching them, stood a big, sandy-colored wolf.

Gaharet growled, low and menacing. Erin glanced at him, alarmed. Did he *want* the beast to attack them? More angry than apprehensive, Gaharet angled his head up the rise, glaring at the beast. She returned her stare to the wolf, afraid to let it out of her sight for even a minute. She squealed as Gaharet rolled her off him and got to his feet, wrenching his armor back on, thrusting his arms into his surcoat.

"What are you doing?" she ground out through gritted teeth, getting slowly to her knees, afraid to make any sudden movements. "You'll just make it angry."

The wolf had barely twitched an ear.

"All is well, Erin," he said, pulling her to her feet and placing her behind him. "He is no threat to us."

Gaharet's lip curled in a snarl, and he stared at the wolf, as though challenging it to defy him.

"Are you crazy? It's a wolf. A big wolf. As big as that one I saw that night I followed you from the keep."

She peered around his arm at it. Like that night, the wolf didn't snarl or bare its teeth. It merely regarded them.

"Wait a minute. Look." She pointed at its neck. "It has a gold chain around its neck. That black one in the forest had one, too. I wonder if they're someone's pets."

The wolf's hackles rose, its ears flattened against its head, and it growled low in its throat. Erin clutched the back of Gaharet's surcoat. *Oh God, now what?* Would Gaharet draw his sword? Could he fight the wolf off?

Gaharet didn't reach for his weapon.

"What are you doing here?" He snarled at the sandy wolf.

Erin gaped at him.

Has he lost his mind?

To her astonishment, the wolf didn't respond to Gaharet's challenge. Instead, it inclined its big, sandy head up stream, raised its nose, and sniffed the air, its ears pricked forward. She glanced up at Gaharet. His eyes narrowed, and he stared in the same direction, tilting his head to the side in the same manner as the wolf.

Her attention flicked between the two of them. What the hell was going on? Some form of silent communication?

Gaharet nodded at the wolf. "I owe you." He gave an abrupt flick of his hand, shooing the wolf away. And the wolf obeyed, trotting off into the trees. Erin stared after it. What the hell just happened?

"Why did that wolf just leave when you asked it to?" It had to be someone's pet. She could think of no other rational explanation.

"Not now, Erin." Gaharet buckled on his scabbard and sword.

Erin flinched at his brusque tone. She stepped away from him, turning toward the horse. Gaharet blocked her path, brushing the back of his hand against her cheek, tilting her chin, forcing her to look at him.

"We will talk, Erin, about many things, but we have more pressing matters at this very moment." He dropped a lingering kiss on her lips, making her toes curl. He stepped away from her. "We have company." He pointed to the five mounted and armed men cantering toward them.

How did he...? Had the wolf warned Gaharet? She shook her head. Those were questions for another time.

She stepped closer to him as the five men approached. "Should we be worried?"

"That depends."

"On what?"

"On what type of mood he is in."

"Who?"

"Erin, the man on the lead horse is Lothair, Comte de Anjou."

213

Chapter Twenty

"Gaharet." Lothair brought his horse to a halt before them. "I received word you were on your way, so I came to meet you and give you company." His gaze slid to Erin. "But I see you already have company." He winked at Gaharet. "You sly dog. You have not told me of this woman, Gaharet. Keeping secrets from me now, are you?"

Lothair's gaze lingered on Erin, and Gaharet pulled her closer within the protective embrace of his arm.

Lothair riding out to meet him was unexpected. He had Ulrik to thank for the warning. It did not excuse his vassal from following them, of spying on them. He and Ulrik would have a long talk when they got to Langeais. A discussion he had put off for far too long.

"Mon Seigneur Comte." Gaharet drew Erin to stand in front of him, his arms clasped around her waist. "May I present Erin of the family Richardson?" He assessed the situation — the desirous looks from Lothair, the sly grins of Lothair's men. "My betrothed."

Erin spluttered, tensing in his arms, but wisely said nothing.

"Gaharet, my friend. You gave no indication you wished to be married. Why did you not say? I could have found you a most suitable wife, one with a good title, money and land."

"I have more than enough of those."

"She *is* lovely. A bit old, but" — his gaze raked over Erin, taking in her disheveled dress and the bits of grass sticking to her head veil — "perhaps she makes up for it in other ways."

Gaharet's hackles rose. A throaty growl rumbled not from him, but from Erin. He turned her away toward his horse before she could respond to Lothair's insult. They could not risk her giving voice to her displeasure, as justified as it may be. She muttered a whispered retort beneath her breath. Foul words. Words he had never expected to hear slip from her delectable mouth, calling Lothair unflattering names that would make a battle-hardened chevalier blush.

Gaharet made a show of coughing to cover her voice. Lothair did not have the acute hearing of his kind, but he would not take kindly to her insults should he hear them. Over his horse's back, he caught sight of the big, sandy wolf hiding downwind among the trees. Ulrik. His tongue hung out, uncontrolled mirth shaking his whole body. Ulrik collapsed to the ground and rolled around on the grass, laughing so hard he could no longer stand on all fours. Unlike Lothair, Ulrik had heard Erin's curses. Gaharet's lip curled in a snarl, glaring at the wolf, and Ulrik's amusement died. Getting to his paws, he slunk away into the trees, his tail between his legs.

Gaharet mounted his horse and pulled Erin up in front of him, side saddle. They had no choice but to ride with Lothair and his men all the way to Langeais. There would be no time to talk and no time to finish what they had started by the creek. *L'enfer*.

About to give herself to him freely, at last surrendering to the heat between them, she had reached for him, rocked her core against his straining cock. Gaharet grunted as she shifted on the horse, his unsated desire flaring anew as her hip brushed against his groin. He was so hard it hurt.

"Sorry."

She tried shifting away, but he held her close.

"I'll survive," he whispered back. "For now."

She flushed, and the scent of her arousal spiked. Good. He had plans to pick up where they left off as soon as the opportunity presented itself. Unfortunately, that would not be for some time. If he must be uncomfortable, filled with anticipation of having his cock buried in her to the hilt, he would have her thinking about it, too.

"Why did you tell him I am your betrothed?" she murmured into his neck.

Gaharet hesitated, the words on the tip of his tongue. Taking her as his wife had been his intention almost from the beginning, but as cautious as his little filly had proven to be, he could not be sure of her reaction to such an admission. Not yet.

"Lothair and his men knew what we were doing when they rode up. Did you see the looks they were giving you?"

She nodded.

"Unless you are content to fend off unwanted advances, it is best this way. As my betrothed, you are under my protection. No one will dare proposition you for fear of my reaction."

"Oh."

He stilled, her disappointment ringing loud in that one word. Gaharet touched a soft kiss to her hairline, more confident in her feelings than he had been a moment ago. He caught Lothair's smirk at their whispered conversation, the urge to visit violence on the comte difficult to resist.

Gaharet forced his grip on the reins to relax. He reached into the saddlebag, tearing off a chunk of bread and handing it to Erin. They had a decent ride ahead of them, and she would be hungry by the time they reached Langeais Keep. Having her mouth busy for at least part of the journey would make it difficult for her to respond to anything Lothair said. Lothair had plenty of time for pretty women, but neither their conversation nor their opinions interested him. If Erin attempted to control the conversation as she had with him that first morning in his hall, unlike Gaharet, Lothair would not find it amusing.

Her body pressed against his, they set off for Langeais. The keep guard surrounded them, whether guarding them or preventing escape, Gaharet could not be entirely sure.

Lothair pulled his horse alongside them. "You caught me by surprise with your little announcement back there, Gaharet."

"It was not my intention, Lothair, I assure you."

"You did not think to mention her when we last met?"

Gaharet glanced at his comte. "If you recall, we had other pressing issues to discuss."

Lothair inclined his head. "True. Still, had I known you were in the market for a wife, I would have provided you with a few excellent choices."

"As grateful as I would be for your efforts, I would have refused them all."

"What? You would refuse what I have to offer — connections, wealth, youth and titles over this one. My, my Gaharet, her charms *must* be exceptional."

He ogled Erin, running his gaze up and down her body. Erin choked, and it took all Gaharet's self-control to not knock Lothair from his saddle.

Gaharet rested his hand on top of Erin's, rubbing his thumb across her knuckles. A gesture meant to reassure and restrain. She placed her other hand on top of his and she squeezed. He relaxed a little, turning his attention back to Lothair.

"I find her very charming," he said, aware of two pairs of ears hanging off his every word. "And there is a small matter of…of an obligation." In his peripheral vision, he caught Erin's sidelong look, and he winced. He could find no other way of describing the situation to satisfy Lothair.

"The d'Louncrais family is indebted to another family? This Richardson family? This is the first I have heard of it."

"It happened in another place, another time, far removed from my family's current circumstances." Gaharet shrugged. "I have put off taking a wife for too long and I find myself looking forward to such an agreeable situation."

"Mmm. She widowed? She is too old for this to be her first marriage. Does she have children? Is she fertile?"

Erin snorted and Gaharet coughed to cover it.

"Nasty cough you have there, Gaharet. You want to get that looked at."

Gaharet made a show of clearing his throat. "This is her first marriage and as for her fertility — she is healthy. I am sure there will be no problems."

Once he made Erin one of them, short of having her head separated from her body or being burned at the stake, there were very few things that would not heal with werewolf blood. It was werewolf blood that had saved Aimon's life.

"Gaharet. Is a family obligation more important than heirs? She is at least a score and some years old. Can she even bear children at that age? And one has to wonder why she has not been married before. Is she tainted? Is her family forcing you into this marriage? You only have to say the word, Gaharet, and I will deal with this Richardson family."

Gaharet grimaced. Lothair would not let this rest. Chances were Lothair had a cousin he would have liked to see Gaharet marry, strengthening his allegiance through a familial connection. He had no desire to cement his family's fortunes to those of Lothair. He would no sooner marry into the comte's family than he would create Lothair his army of werewolves.

"There are no other Richardsons for you to concern yourself about, Lothair. When she arrived at my keep, she was alone in this world."

"An orphan? You have taken her in? If you wish to provide for her, then give her a position in your household. In the kitchen or as a chambermaid. You can still bed her, but you need not marry her."

"I could do that," said Gaharet, "but I have chosen not to. She will make me a good wife. I have made my decision, and I will not be changing it."

"Hmpf. Very well, Gaharet. You seemed determined."

Lothair would still send out messengers the moment they reached Langeais Keep, searching for information regarding Erin and her family. It would all be in vain.

"Have you given any more thought to our last conversation, Gaharet?"

"I have."

"And?"

Gaharet speared Lothair with a cautionary look. "That is a conversation best kept private, do you not think?"

"You are right. We will converse as soon as time permits. I am rather eager to begin this new project. I will see the destruction of Blois and all who stand in my way."

Gaharet clenched his jaw. Lothair would never get his werewolf army. Gaharet would make certain of it.

Chapter Twenty-One

They arrived at Langeais by mid-afternoon, the sun angling across the landscape, Erin's weary mind rousing at the sight of the village wall. They entered the gate, waved through by the gatehouse guard. Erin craned her neck from side-to-side, marveling at all she saw. Of the Langeais she knew, there was no sign. Its modern streets, stone buildings, cafes spilling their latte sipping clientele onto sidewalks and the majestic château were absent. In their place, a sprawl of wattle and daub buildings smothered in a smoky haze. Children played alongside the dirt road, horses stomped inside a stable, a blacksmith pounded away beside a hot forge and, rising out of the hill above it all, imposing and formidable, the square stone keep jutting out of the landscape.

Now there's a phallic symbol if ever I've seen one.

Erin glanced at Comte Lothair.

Compensating for something?

Erin covered her mouth, swallowing a laugh. Instinct told her Comte Lothair would not appreciate her observation.

Villagers scurried out of the way as they plodded through the streets, the comte's guard flanking them. Shoulders hunched, eyes wary, children gathered to their mothers were shuffled out of sight. From the corner of her eye, Erin scrutinized the comte, careful not to stare or draw his attention. If he was aware of the villager's reactions, he didn't show it. Deep in conversation with Gaharet about a neighboring comte's army, he paid them no attention. Erin drew her arms about herself, suddenly chilled.

Written accounts of Comte Lothair were few, but what she'd gleaned from them painted a disturbing picture. Skillful in battlefield tactics, he'd steadily expanded his county. Territory he had claimed by force. Several historical documents mentioned his unpredictable temper, his fearsome reputation, his infidelity throughout his first marriage and his questionable grip on sanity. Some accounts were a little more eloquent, professing to be able to see the crazy in his eyes 'glowing like a demonic fire had settled in his soul'.

Rivals and detractors often penned unflattering details, so Erin and her colleagues had viewed these accounts with a healthy amount of skepticism. Observing the reaction of the villagers, listening to Gaharet's guarded responses, glowing demonic eyes aside, Erin could no longer question the truth of these accounts. *Le Diable* indeed. Comte Lothair was a man to be feared.

Erin turned away, her hands clenching in her lap. What had Gaharet done in proclaiming her his betrothed? Had protecting her hastened his own demise? A large hand covered her clenched fingers, giving them a gentle squeeze. She had to trust Gaharet knew what he was doing.

They passed through the square — no sign of the fate soon to befall the comtesse. Shouts rang out as they approached the keep gatehouse, and guards hurried to open the gate. They rode through, entering the bailey and dismounting. Gaharet handed the reins to a waiting stable hand. His sword, he relinquished to the gate guard. Gathering her close to his side, he led her up the hill toward the keep, his presence a reassuring comfort.

The bailey bustled with activity. Peasants and servants scurried about. Chevaliers in varying-colored surcoats entered the gate under the watchful eyes of the guards. Stable hands lead horses away with a clop of their hooves and clinking harnesses. A few noblemen in fine robes of deep reds and dark blues lingered, talking to one another, their wives standing dutifully beside them. Living history flowed around her and it took her breath away. The sights, the sounds, the smell of wood smoke hanging in the air.

Gaharet leaned toward her. "So, what do you think of Langeais Keep?"

Halting, Erin tilted her head up, following the wall of the keep to the very top. "Impressive."

The understatement of the century.

The solid, square tower loomed above them. Far more dramatic in its entirety than the crumbling ruins so familiar to Erin, its forbidding presence dominated the landscape. Never again would she look at the ruins of the keep and not remember this moment, seeing it how it once stood guarding the crossing of the Loire River.

"Gaharet," called Lothair. "When you have your betrothed settled, we have things to discuss." He turned on his heel and stalked away, his guards trailing behind him.

Gaharet steered her across the grounds, through a small, protected entrance, and into the keep hall. A low buzz of conversation echoed about the enormous room, a fire flickered in a pit in the center, and men in chain mail mingled, the scent of meadowsweet hanging thick in the air. Here, unlike in Gaharet's keep, there were other odors the sweet rushes on the floor could not conceal. Odors of sweat, dampness and something she couldn't, and didn't want to name.

A flash of gray fur and a long tail scurried across in front of her, disappearing into the throng of people. She stifled a squeal.

Gaharet shrugged. "Welcome to Langeais Keep." Placing his hand at the small of her back, he guided her forward into the crowd of men.

Armored chevaliers parted, conversation paused, faces turned to follow their progress across the room. As they passed, whispers pursued them and Erin faltered, her throat constricting. A sea of bearded faces turned in their direction. One young man nodded at them, another smiled, and still more stared at her with open curiosity.

They made their way through the men to the far side of the hall, Gaharet unfazed by the obvious interest of so many, while every stare, every muttered word, prickled up Erin's spine. She never could stand being the center of attention. Not like this. Not since...

Thomas Mathiesen.

Erin rolled her shoulders back, straightening her spine. She could do this. She wasn't a fifteen-year-old kid anymore. She licked her dry lips and gave a tentative smile as she passed chevalier after chevalier. She hastened her steps until they reached a doorway on the other side of the hall.

"I will settle you in with the women, for I must attend Lothair," said Gaharet. "Stay there until I come fetch you."

She nodded, ascending the stairs with Gaharet. The rumble of conversation returned to the hall, the quiet of the stairwell a blessed relief.

"Be careful, Gaharet. I don't know why Comte Lothair confined you in that cell," she murmured, keeping her voice low, "but it seems we've already antagonized him with your announcement of our betrothal."

"Do not worry about Lothair. He will want to discuss it further, I have no doubt, but I will handle him."

She scrunched up her nose. "Going to discuss the state of my virginity in more depth, are you?"

Erin couldn't imagine Comte Lothair being any more restrained in private than he was on their journey.

She yelped as Gaharet pulled her into his arms, the curve of the stairwell blocking them from curious eyes in the hall below. He ducked his head, nuzzling at her neck, and Erin melted against him, tipping her head back, giving him better access.

"I do not care if you are a virgin or not." His whispered words were hot against her skin. "But if you are one," he murmured, running his hand down her back to her hip, pulling her in tight against him, "that will change tonight."

Desire exploded in a rush of sparks and heat. "Don't end up in Lothair's underground cell because of me, Gaharet." Her words were little more than a breathy whisper, her mind struggling to stay on track. "You can revoke our betrothal. Tell Lothair I'm barren. Blame me. I'll be back in my world soon and he won't be able to touch me."

An emotion flickered across his face, gone so fast she barely had time to register it. Regret? Sorrow?

A door opened down the corridor, feminine laughter cascading down the stairs. Heavy footsteps approached, and he released her.

"Our betrothal stands. I have no intention of rescinding it. Let me worry about Lothair. Come."

He held his hand out to her. It hung there between them, her heart pounding in her chest as she stared at it. She reached out, slipping her hand in his. His nostrils flared, his eyes darkened and with a smile curling up the corner of his mouth, he led her up the stairs.

He swung open a door to a room, revealing a dozen giggling, gossiping women seated in a semi-circle, hands busy with needles and thread. With a gentle brush of the back of his hand against her cheek, he promised to return, and left her standing in the entryway alone, facing unfamiliar women and an afternoon of embroidery.

Oh boy.

Playing the part of a well-bred tenth-century lady might be a little more difficult than she'd expected. With all attention focused on her, she could only hope Gaharet wouldn't leave her here for too long.

* * * *

Gaharet took the stairs back down to the hall, a spring in his step and a smile on his face, as he sought out his men. He had things to discuss with them before Lothair monopolized his time. Weaving through his fellow chevaliers, smiling, nodding, accepting congratulations on his betrothal as he went, he searched the crowded room for his vassals. He found Ulrik and Aimon on the far side of the hall, talking, heads close, mugs of mead in their hands. They beamed at him as he approached. He joined them, and they patted him on the back, congratulating him.

He shook his head at their exuberance. "Do not get too excited yet."

Aimon held out his hands. "Are the rumors false? Are you not betrothed to the woman you found wandering around your keep?"

Ulrik smirked. "You looked damn betrothed to me before Lothair arrived."

Gaharet clenched his jaw, itching to erase the smug expression off Ulrik's face. Not here, not now. Not in the hall.

"You and I need to talk." Gaharet pinned Ulrik with a glare, his words little more than a growl, and Ulrik stiffened, a snarl curling on his lip. Aimon shook his head and turned away. Ulrik would get no support from him. "This is not open for debate, Ulrik, and is long overdue."

Ulrik sighed, his shoulders slumping. "Very well, we will talk, but for now, tell us why we should not find your betrothal reason to celebrate?"

Casting a furtive glance over his shoulder, Gaharet leaned in, lowering his voice. "She does not yet know what we are, and I am uncertain how she will view such information."

"From what *I* observed, she is strong, feisty and bold enough to make demands of you. Perhaps she will accept it better than you think." Ulrik took a sip of mead, a glint of mirth in his eyes.

How long had Ulrik been following them?

"You are satisfied she has no connection to Lothair or Archeveque Renaud?" Aimon's words cut through the tension.

"There is no possibility of her having any connection with either."

Ulrik's eyebrows rose. "Truly? Where *is* she from?"

Two pairs of eyes regarded him with open curiosity.

Gaharet shook his head, rubbing the back of his neck. "You would not believe me if I told you."

"Congratulations, Gaharet." Edmond clapped him on the back, his voice booming as he and his twin joined them. "Today is a day of good news." He raised his mug in salute and drank it down, grinning. "We also have something to share."

Gaharet raised an eyebrow. Had one of the twins found a mate also?

"Not as good as your announcement, but something that might be helpful." Edmond leaned in closer. "We found something, Gaharet."

Aubert produced a pouch from within his surcoat, tipping some of its contents into his palm, holding it out for them to see.

Gaharet sniffed. Some kind of herb.

"Got it from a woman deep in the forest." Edmond snarled over his shoulder at a chevalier approaching them and the young man quailed, beating a hasty retreat. He turned back to Gaharet. "The woman is a healer. Rumor has it she has certain...abilities." His deep voice dropped lower, barely above a whisper. "Casts spells."

"What is it?" Gaharet pinched some of the herb between his fingers, raising it to his nose, taking in its scent. It had a musty, pungent aroma that brought to mind mice infestations in grain stores.

"Hemlock."

"Hemlock?"

Edmond nodded. "We sought the woman out, went to see if she knew of something for pain, something to take it away and make you sleep. Allowing the body to heal pain free—if you catch my meaning."

Gaharet kept a tight rein on his emotions, possibilities burning within him. "Is it dangerous?"

"Minute amounts will render a person unconscious and control muscle spasms. Larger doses can be toxic to humans."

"But we are not human," murmured Ulrik.

"Where did you find her?" Gaharet would pay this woman a visit as soon as circumstances allowed. As a witch, with a knowledge of spells… His hand moved to the amulet resting close to his heart. Would she also have knowledge of them?

"Not far. Due east of our clearing beyond the walls, no more than five leagues. Do you think we will be needing stock of this in the near future, Gaharet? Now you have a betrothed?" Edmond's face lit up with an eagerness barely contained.

Gaharet nodded, a slow smile forming. "I think yes, Edmond. It would be best to acquire some, for I will have need of it in the days to come."

The men grinned. For the first time in a long time, they had hope. Even Ulrik seemed buoyed by the news. If Erin would have him, now they had a means to temper the pain, he would turn her. He would wait no longer. Tonight he would make her his, then he would make her one of them.

Chapter Twenty-Two

Archeveque Renaud glanced over his shoulder as he slipped into the forest, the sun dipping low behind the walls of Langeais Keep. Cool air stole beneath his robes, and he cursed the necessity for him to be away from the comfort of his chambers. Soon he would have no need to be skulking about in the wilds, meeting with the likes of the man—no, the monster—he forced himself to collude with.

Things were moving along nicely. Comte Lothair had fallen for their ploy. His lip curled up in a sneer. *Fool.* So hungry for power, it had taken very little to get Lothair's attention. A few well-placed hints, a request for an audience without d'Louncrais, the suggestion he could boost his army with a supernatural force more than enough to pique Lothair's curiosity. To contemplate working with an animal, a hellish beast more nightmarish than human, imagining he could tame it, perhaps wishing to become one... The man was insane, a menace and a means to an end. Renaud had no qualms about sacrificing the comte, or anyone else, to get where he wanted.

Through the gloom of the trees, he picked out a patch of color, a glint of steel. He stiffened. The likelihood of him encountering someone other than his accomplice out here, beyond the watchful eyes of the keep, was small, but he could not be too cautious. Unlike the beast in the clearing, he could not tell by smell alone who awaited him.

Renaud surveyed the forest, searching for anything out of place, an ambush, a trap. Not that this man needed such ploys. He caught no sign of any other presence, so he pressed on. A lifetime of twisting others' desires to his own use told him he still had the upper hand. This man-monster, this chevalier, needed him, would not have approached him otherwise. For now, the chevalier posed no threat to him, but that could change. He would take more precautions next time.

"I know you are there, Renaud. Stop wasting my time. I do not have all day."

Renaud smirked at the impatient summons. He stepped into the clearing, skirting the grazing horse and approached the lone chevalier. His sword drawn and held loosely at his side, the man scowled. The chevalier found their collusion as distasteful as he did.

Renaud was not a small man. As the second son, his family had once assumed he would make an excellent chevalier, but the man before him loomed larger, broader, more *everything*. All his kind were. Until now, no one had noticed this anomaly. To be fair, when there were more of them, it had helped them blend in. With so few left, the differences between the other chevaliers were stark.

"You endanger us both by insisting on this meeting." The chevalier snarled, stepping closer, using his size to intimidate. "Be careful summoning me on a whim. I might withdraw my assistance. Without me, you have no hope of entrapping Lothair."

Renaud stood his ground, met his stare. "Without me, you lose the opportunity to destroy d'Louncrais. Need I remind you, over half of your kind are dead by my hand?"

With a flick of a wrist, the chevalier pressed the tip of his sword up under his chin, an inhuman growl reverberating in his chest. "Are you threatening me, old man? You are here on your own, and I could easily cut your throat."

They stared at each other, shapes shifting behind the chevalier's irises, a strong musky scent surrounding him. The beast pressed close, wanting to take over. Renaud had experienced it often enough to recognize it. The time would come when he would force this confrontation, but for now, he still needed the information this man provided.

He stepped back, pushing the sword away with the palm of his hand. "I will be more considerate of your time in future." He let a conciliatory note leak into his voice. He would play whatever role necessary to achieve his goal. The chevalier lowered his sword.

"We are here now and we have much to discuss. If my plan is to be successful—"

The chevalier snorted. "Your plan?"

Renaud tilted his head to the side, assessing his accomplice. "Our plan," he said, conceding the chevalier his point. Separating Lothair from d'Louncrais' influence was essential to his plan. Using d'Louncrais to enact his own, and the comte's, downfall—that was ingenious, and he had the chevalier to thank for that.

"How did d'Louncrais react to my meeting with Comte Lothair?"

He had gone to great lengths to set their trap, while leaving enough of a trail for d'Louncrais' young minion to follow.

The chevalier shrugged. "Predictably."

"I assume Lothair gave him full disclosure after I left?"

"Of course. I told you he would."

Renaud arched an eyebrow. "And?" he asked, careful to keep his face a mask of mild interest. It would not do for the chevalier to suspect how much he needed his information, his assistance. He refused to give away such an advantage.

"D'Louncrais is certain Lothair believes you. He is concerned, very concerned."

Renaud released a chuckle he could not contain. "He should be."

The chevalier looked down his nose at him, a sneer curling at the corner of his mouth. "Your overconfidence will get you killed. Lothair does not trust your motives. Neither does d'Louncrais."

Renaud grunted. Comte Lothair was not an easy man to outmaneuver. D'Louncrais even less so. "But does he still trust d'Louncrais? That is the real question."

"Lothair made the connection." The chevalier tugged at his beard. "He suspects d'Louncrais."

"Excellent."

The chevalier shook his head. "D'Louncrais will not sit idle. He still has more influence over Lothair than anyone else."

"That may be, but perhaps d'Louncrais himself has given us a way. I wonder what he would do if we threatened his woman."

A flicker of confusion crossed the chevalier's face, and Renaud nearly chortled his delight. The chevalier did not know.

"You have not heard of d'Louncrais announcement of his betrothal?"

The slight widening of the chevalier's eyes told him he had read the situation correctly. D'Louncrais had yet to inform his vassals of his bride to be. *How interesting.*

For a moment, neither man spoke, but whatever thoughts rolled through the chevalier's mind, they were not pleasant. His knuckles turned white around the grip of his sword, and he glared at the forest beyond the clearing, his expression sour as though tasting something unpalatable. *Well, well, well.* The chevalier's loathing of d'Louncrais ran deeper than he thought. He resisted rubbing his hands together, reveling in the possibilities.

"Yes, word is all over the keep," he said, observing the chevalier's reactions. "D'Louncrais is rather enamored with her charms, or so the gossip goes." Renaud had not counted on d'Louncrais bringing a woman with him to the keep. Far from disrupting their plans, it worked in rather well. He could use this woman. His mouth twitched. D'Louncrais had made a serious miscalculation, bringing her to Langeais.

The chevalier took a step toward him, eyes narrowed. "Did you have something to do with this woman, Renaud? Did *you* send her to d'Louncrais?"

The question surprised him, and Renaud's mind raced at its implications. Who *was* this Erin of the family Richardson? Did she, too, have ulterior motives? He gave the chevalier an enigmatic smile and a nonchalant shrug of his shoulder, neither confirming nor denying the accusation. He had it on good authority Lothair had sent messengers to find out all he could about the woman. Renaud would send his own men. He would not allow an unknown entity to ruin his plans. Not when they were so close to coming to fruition.

The chevalier rubbed his chin, silent for a moment, lost in thought. "This new turn of events could work in our favor."

"Mmm?" Renaud already had a few ideas, but it would not hurt to listen.

"There was an incident—"

Renaud stepped closer, licking his lips.

"The particulars are of no concern to you, but d'Louncrais will fight for her. He has already proven that."

Has he, indeed? "We threaten her, force him to make a choice."

The chevalier tapped his finger against his lips. "It could work." He took a few steps away before turning and pinning Renaud with his stare. "Once this is over, once you've dealt with d'Louncrais and you have Lothair, what are your plans for the woman?"

"The woman?"

The question seemed innocent enough, but... Understanding dawned and he hid his disgust behind a mask of indifference. Finding a woman prepared to lie with a beast such as them, to bear their devil's spawn, could not be easy. It would stand to reason then why d'Louncrais would fight for her.

"You want the woman for yourself, I take it?"

"Yes," he said, a slow nodding of his head. "Yes, I would. I, too, am in need of wife and"—his eyes flashed, his lips paring back to reveal extended canines—"it will give me great satisfaction every day, for the rest of my long life, knowing what once was d'Louncrais' will belong to me."

Renaud studied his accomplice. The chevalier's thirst for vengeance ran deep, whatever the cause, and it would cloud his mind and make him blind to all else.

He held up his hands as a sign of acquiescence. "I have no use for the woman. I will not stand in your way."

There would be no need. What happened to the woman was of little consequence to him, but this man, his accomplice... He knew too much. He could not let him walk away.

Chapter Twenty-Three

Erin stood, her lips forming a tight, polite smile, gaze darting from face to face as the women stared back at her with open curiosity. She licked her lips and inhaled a deep breath through her nose, steadying herself. She'd chant an ohm if she thought it would help.

Custom dictated she greet Comtesse Marguerite first, but... Her gaze slid around the circle of women, searching for a clue, a suggestion of rank amongst the women, a feature she might recognize from documented descriptions. Nothing. Only a sea of indistinguishable high necklines and long dresses with embroidered trim and matching headscarves.

"Come, my dear." An older woman gestured to a spare stool. "I am Dame Adeline. Welcome."

Erin moved with studied calm, resisting the urge to sprint across the room, sliding onto the vacant seat.

"Comtesse Marguerite is indisposed today," said Dame Adeline. "She will not be joining us."

Sniggers tittered around the circle.

"Indisposed? Is that what they call it?" muttered someone.

A stern look from Dame Adeline and eleven pairs of female eyes focused on their needlework with conscientious concentration.

"Here." The woman to her left offered her a friendly smile, handing her a piece of cloth and a needle, pointing to her basket of thread. "You can use some of mine. Nothing I create will have any use in the near future. Needlework is not my finest skill."

"Thank you." Erin took the proffered items, grimacing at the needle and cloth.

This should be interesting.

Give her a trowel, a string line, a brush or even a pencil and paper and she would be in her element. Embroidery, any form of sewing really, had always confounded her.

"I am Kathryn," the woman offered, leaning toward her. "Kathryn of the family Beauchene."

"Erin of the family Richardson."

Erin glanced from the blank cloth in her hands to Kathryn's piece, dainty purple violets and green leaves weaving across the cloth. Somehow, she would have to create something similar.

Oh boy.

She selected cotton from Kathryn's basket. First step—thread the needle. That she could do.

"Mademoiselle Erin, is it?" A sharp voice cracked across the hum of conversation, chatter fading to silence.

Erin dropped her hands into her lap, seeking the owner. An imperious face stared at her from across the room, eyes skimming over Erin from head to toe, distaste twitching her lips and marring her brow. Erin shifted on her stool. Gaharet thought she'd be safe here. He didn't have a clue.

"Yes, I'm Erin."

Most of the women had their eyes down, hands busy with their stitches, but the conversation didn't resume. Two women on either side of the speaker made no pretense at embroidery, openly staring at her.

Here we go.

"I am curious, Mademoiselle Erin," said the woman again, the clear ringleader of her little posse. "How *did* you snare a man like Seigneur Gaharet d'Louncrais? Do tell."

"Manette." Dame Adeline's glare cut across the room, resting on the woman. "Manners."

"Ma Dame Adeline. With all due respect, we are all dying to know. The most eligible man in this county, Seigneur Gaharet could have his pick of wealthy, titled women. He has shown no interest in any of several desirable matches available in this court." She indicated herself and the other women in the room. "Now he brings to Langeais Keep his betrothed. A woman none of us have ever heard of."

"Manette," whispered Kathryn, leaning close. "Married to Monsieur Robert, a man twice her age. Terrible bore, grossly overweight, but very wealthy and influential. A fantastic match considering Manette's family had a title, but no money. Not as good a prospect as Seigneur Gaharet — wealthy, titled *and* handsome." Kathryn smirked. "Rumor has it she fixed her sights on Seigneur Gaharet, but he showed no inclination toward her. She would kill to change places with you."

Erin snapped her gaze to Kathryn. *She means kill figuratively, right?* Erin clenched her fingers around the cloth in her lap. She raised her chin, focusing her attention on Manette.

"It is a matter of an obligation," she said by way of explanation, echoing the words Gaharet had spoken to Comte Lothair.

All eyes focused on her — needlework forgotten.

"From a long time ago when the d'Louncrais family circumstances were different."

"How very fortunate to have the d'Louncrais family indebted to you. Would that we all could have a man like Seigneur Gaharet as our betrothed."

Erin shifted her attention to the woman on Manette's right.

"Odila," whispered Kathryn. "Married to Monsieur Jean-Luc — young enough, not unattractive, but mean, with a foul temper and little patience. I have heard he punishes her for the smallest infringement."

"A man as wealthy as Seigneur Gaharet could easily dissolve a debt with coin. I wonder why he did not?" This from the woman on Manette's left.

"Ladies, enough." Dame Adeline's authoritarian stare moved around the circle of women, lingering on Manette and her cronies. With flushed faces, all eyes snapped back to embroidery. Except for Manette. She tapped her chin, smiling. She'd made her point.

Erin bristled, repressing the urge to cross the room and slap the woman.

"I am very fortunate. Seigneur Gaharet is a very honorable man. He could've turned me away when I arrived at his keep with no family to speak of. He could've chosen not to marry me, and I would've been content with sanctuary in his home." She gave a nonchalant shrug of her shoulder. "Gaharet made the decision, not I."

Manette's eyes widened, and another woman stifled a gasp. Erin pursed her lips to prevent smiling. They'd caught her deliberate dropping of Gaharet's title. Wouldn't it shock them to hear the things Gaharet had said to her in the corridor?

"Welcome to Langeais Keep, Erin," said Dame Adeline. "Come now, ladies. Less gossip, more embroidery."

The women returned to their needles and thread, and Erin let her shoulders relax, turning to Kathryn. "What about you? Were you able to make a good match?"

Kathryn's hands paused mid-stitch. "Not yet. I am fortunate that my father is consulting me on the choice of my husband. He found happiness with my mother, and I think he would very much like for me to find that, too, but…"

Strange shapes shifted behind Kathryn's eyes, swirls of darkness flitting in their depths. Erin's eyes widened, and she peered closer. She shook her head. Looked again. Nothing. Only pretty hazel eyes. A trick of the light.

"But?" Erin prompted.

"It is difficult finding a suitable match." Kathryn pressed her lips together in a thin line. "And people are beginning to talk. Most women are married and have children at my age." Leaning over, Kathryn demonstrated how to insert the needle to create a leaf pattern. "Perhaps you can help me?"

"Me?" Erin focused on making a leaf pattern of her own, stabbing the needle through the cloth, grimacing as she pricked her finger on the other side. "How can I be of any help?"

She completed a few more stitches, eyeing her woeful attempt at a leaf. As long as she didn't have to exhibit her work at the end, it didn't matter what they looked like, only that she participated.

"Seigneur Gaharet is not the only good marriage prospect. His vassal, Monsieur Aimon..." Kathryn caught her bottom lip between her teeth, her cheeks flushing pink. "All of his vassals are suitable marriage prospects, but the likelihood of me ever being considered as a potential wife for them is negligible. Unfortunately, being accomplished at embroidery is not the only thing I lack."

She leaned over, showing Erin how to make a violet. "Despite Seigneur Gaharet being family, I do not move in the same society as the d'Louncrais."

Kathryn and Gaharet are related? Erin stared at her blob of purple stitches masquerading as a violet. "I thought Gaharet was the last of his line?"

"Oh, he is. We are only related by marriage. He is my cousin. His immediate family are all gone. His mother, my aunt, was killed — attacked in the woods. Gruesome thing. Her death shocked us all."

There, again, those dark swirls dancing within the depths of Kathryn's irises. And why, as Gaharet's cousin, did she not move in the same social circles as him? Some scandal, perhaps?

"His father died in battle not long after. Some say he lost his will to live after his wife died. And then his brother died soon after, also in battle."

Anne had said much the same, without all the detail, but Erin's focus was on Kathryn's unusual eyes. Gaharet's eyes did the same thing. What did it mean, those shadows that came and went? Could Kathryn be the key to understanding Gaharet's secrets? Would Kathryn confide in her something Gaharet would not? She stabbed the needle through the cloth again, completing another blob of purple stitches, showing no resemblance to any flower she'd ever seen. Maybe roses would be easier.

"So, Aimon?"

Kathryn flushed.

"White-blond hair, wounded in the battle of Montsoreau?"

Kathryn nodded, her gaze flicking across the room. Erin followed her gaze to Manette, who made no attempt to conceal her interest in their conversation.

"You can certainly do better than some others, and if I can help in any way, I will."

Hope shone in Kathryn's eyes. "Thank you. You do not know…" She dropped her voice to a whisper. "Manette and Odila are not the only ones with distasteful husbands." She cast her gaze to a small, childlike woman across the room. "Therese's betrothed is a big brute of a man. If I do not choose soon, my father will be forced to make an arrangement, and my options are no more favorable than hers."

Erin smiled at Kathryn. Perhaps she had an ally here. She didn't know how much longer she'd be stuck in this era, but she'd take any help she could get. She dropped her gaze to her needlework and frowned, comparing her efforts to Kathryn's. If Jackson Pollock did embroidery, it would probably look something like hers. Thankfully, spending the rest of her days sewing and gossiping didn't feature in her future. Once she had the reverse spell… Her hands stilled. There had to be a reverse spell. *Right?*

Of course there was. She just needed Gaharet to tell her, then she'd be back in the twenty-first century wearing jeans and T-shirts, working on a dig site and all this would be a thing of the past. Literally. No more long dresses and restrictive head veils. No more horseback riding. She'd have instant hot water at the turn of a tap, flushing toilets, breakfast and coffee. Her mouth salivated at the thought of coffee and those amazing croissants from the Langeais bakery. But no more Gaharet.

Erin paused in her attempts at needlework, frowning. That thought hurt way more than it should have. Purple thread disappeared as she speared the needle through again. She yanked it back, completing another violet. She couldn't deny she wanted him, and had the wolf and Comte Lothair not interrupted them, she would've had sex with him in that meadow.

She snapped the cotton, re-threaded the needle with green cotton, and attacked the cloth again. *Maybe tonight.* Her body thrummed at the thought. She poked the needle through, another stitch in the leaf completed and reefed it back through. If, with her knowledge, they circumvented his fate, she would leave here knowing she'd helped save a good man. And, if tonight went as Gaharet planned, with one hell of a memory. Warmth spread through her body, her panties dampening. But was that enough?

Erin dropped her hands in her lap, staring at the material and her woeful attempts at embroidery. How many of these stupid violets did she have to do? She wrenched at the cloth, but it snagged on her dress. Flipping it over, she gaped at it. She'd sewn the bloody thing to her dress.

"Shit."

She clapped her hand over her mouth, the room shocked into silence. Kathryn muffled a giggle. Across the room Manette gloated, Dame Adeline frowned and the priest in the flowing black cassock standing in the doorway stared at her, eyes boring through her. She paled.

Damn it.

"Mademoiselle Richardson I presume?"

Erin eyed the pectoral cross around his neck and the magenta skullcap. Not any priest—an archbishop, an archeveque. Great. Just what she needed right now—more attention. High-ranking attention. She pasted a bright smile on her face. "Votre Excellence."

"Come, my dear. Let me take you for a tour of Mon Seigneur Comte's keep. And while we walk, you and I can have a little chat and become acquainted."

One look at Kathryn's startled expression told her being afforded such an esteemed guide wasn't an everyday occurrence.

"Thank you, Votre Excellence. How very kind of you."

Erin snapped the cotton tethering the needle to her embroidery, handing it to Kathryn. With a false smile she concealed her distaste, and her concerns over hygiene, and knelt and briefly kissed the ring on the archeveque's outstretched hand. Shoulders back, head held high, ignoring the embroidered cloth attached to her skirt, she cast one last look at a bewildered Kathryn and allowed the archeveque to lead her from the room.

* * * *

As the door closed behind them, he slipped his arm through hers, walking her past the stairwell, down to the hall and along another corridor. A tall man, large of bone rather than muscle, he matched his large stride to suit hers, his heavy robes swishing as he moved.

"Congratulations, Mademoiselle, on your recent betrothal. Seigneur d'Louncrais is a fine match." He patted her arm, smiling at her, guiding her down a set of stairs. "Many a young lady will be most disappointed to hear he is no longer available." He chuckled, but there was no real humor or warmth in it.

"Thank you, Votre Excellence."

"Wealthy and well connected, a most trusted vassal of Mon Seigneur Comte. If I may be so bold to say, you have done remarkably well for yourself considering your circumstances."

Gaharet's betrothal sure had garnered a lot of interest and a lot of speculation.

"A woman without family," he continued, leading her along another corridor, nodding at a passing servant girl, ignoring open doorways, "and no obvious connections. I am not familiar with the Richardson family." He frowned, pausing at the top of another stairwell. "You must have traveled far." He started down the stairs, and Erin had little option but to do the same. "What county are you from?"

"I'm... I'm not from Frankia, Votre Excellence."

"Mmm, I thought as much. Your manner of speaking is a little odd. Bretaigne then?"

Erin hesitated, then took a risk he would not have connections across the sea. "Yes, I'm from Bretaigne." She could only hope Gaharet didn't give Comte Lothair a conflicting answer.

He pursed his lips. "Rather convenient."

"Pardon?"

"Sorry, my dear." He patted her arm again. "Only muttering away to myself. You are such an unusual choice for someone such as d'Louncrais, that is all. I suspect he has his reasons for choosing an older woman with no known connections, wealth or family."

She opened her mouth to answer him, but he cut her off with an indulgent smile.

"Reasons beyond this debt I am hearing talk of. The comte would dissolve this obligation if d'Louncrais asked it of him. Or d'Louncrais could ensure your financial security in other ways. Find you a suitable husband, a widower perhaps. Yet he has chosen to wed you. I find that rather curious."

Wonderful. Neither the comte, nor the highest-ranking priest, found Gaharet's choice of a bride satisfactory. Or his explanation.

"Perhaps he likes me for my disposition, or my beauty." She struggled to keep an edge from creeping into her voice.

The archeveque smiled, all teeth, jutting cheekbones and cold eyes. "Mayhap it is as you say." His expression proclaimed he doubted it very much. "If my memory serves me, Gaharet's father married in much the same manner. Caused quite a stir. The d'Louncrais always did things their own way."

He led her down another corridor, this one darker, narrower. Before them, an open doorway leading to a darkened room. So much for a tour. After descending two flights of stairs, they should be on the lower level of the keep. Nothing down here but storerooms. Odd that he should bring her here.

"Would you hold this for me while I set to lighting this room?" Without waiting for her to answer, he withdrew a key from within his black robes and handed it to her, detached a lit oil lamp from the wall and disappeared into the room.

Erin frowned, tapping the key against her hand, pacing the corridor. She'd like to think as a member of the clergy she could trust he meant her no harm, but in this era men entered the priesthood for a variety of reasons, some of which had little to do with a calling from God. Should she take this opportunity to leave him, return to the room of women and their embroidery? She might make a few wrong turns finding her way back, but she'd manage.

She held the key against her chin. Upsetting an archeveque might not be wise, and she'd no real justification for thinking he had ulterior motives. Only a vague, unsettled feeling in her gut.

And what of this key he'd given her to hold? Chunky, lacking in the intricacy of more modern ones, it had all the hallmarks of a tenth-century key, except for one thing. It appeared to be made of silver. *Highly unusual.* More commonly they were made of copper alloy or iron. Not this one. It brought to mind the shackles she'd found in the underground cell.

Erin paused in her pacing and surveyed her surroundings, attempting to place herself amongst the layout of the ruins she knew so well. The lower level, a doorway at the end of a long corridor — it all looked disturbingly familiar. Could she be standing only meters from the grate to the underground cell? The cell Gaharet would die in? A tightness wrapped around her lungs and her throat. Had Comte Lothair already confined Gaharet in there? Could that be why the archeveque had brought her down here?

She stalked toward the room, intent on gaining access, but the archeveque appeared, blocking her entry.

"Ah, my dear, the key, if you do not mind?" He took it from her, as she angled to see past him into the now-lit room, his large shoulders impeding her view.

The archeveque grabbed her hands, rubbing his thumbs over her palms. She recoiled from his touch, but he held her hands fast, surprisingly strong for a man of his age.

"Hmm. Not a single mark. No burns, blisters, not even a reddening of the skin."

"Excuse me?"

"You are not one of them. At least not yet."

Erin wrenched her hands out of his grasp, pushing past the archeveque into the room. There. In the corner. Just as she suspected. A heavy iron grate covering a hole. If she went any closer, she'd see narrow, steep steps. Steps she'd trudged up and down a hundred times.

She spun back to the archeveque. She pointed at the offending grate. "Who have you put in there? Is it Gaharet? And what do you mean, I am not one of them? One of what?"

The archeveque remained in the doorway, impeding her exit. *Shit.* She'd trapped herself.

Bad move, Erin.

"Why would you think we would confine d'Louncrais? Do you know what he truly is?" The archeveque's stare bored into her. Erin swallowed. Whatever secret Gaharet protected, it was a secret no more. Perhaps he did still practice the old religion, or they suspected he did.

The archeveque tilted his head, running his gaze over her, assessing her. She shivered. With a priest involved, that was the most likely explanation. Had he thought she'd blister and burn at the touch of silver? Is that why he'd handed her the key?

"Perhaps he revealed himself to you, showed you his true form?"

True form? "Votre Excellence, I'm afraid I don't know what you speak of. Seigneur d'Louncrais is a good man, a fine match. You said so yourself. He has shown me nothing but kindness. In the time I've spent in his keep, I've seen nothing untoward. Nothing I would imagine would require his confinement."

If the archeveque ever got his hands on an amulet, her words would mean nothing. That didn't mean Gaharet deserved to die in that cell. Or that she wouldn't do whatever she could to prevent him from being imprisoned there. She'd take him to the twenty-first century with her if she had to. Because he was a good man. And he'd taken care of her when he didn't have to.

Yes, they are my reasons. My only reasons.

"You defend him. Interesting. I have it on good authority he would do more than defend you. He would fight for you."

Erin's mouth dropped open. Gaharet would fight for her? Her heart thumped in her chest. And this man would use that, use her to get to Gaharet. No. She could not be the reason he ended up in that cell.

Straightening her shoulders, giving him a haughty look worthy of Manette, she moved to push past him. "This is ridiculous. I'm returning to the women."

He grabbed hold of her elbow, his grip bruising. "Not so fast, Mademoiselle."

She struggled against him. "Let. Me. Go. Whatever it is you're accusing Gaharet of, you're wrong, and I assure you he will be furious to learn that you are treating me this way."

"My dear," he chuckled. "That is what I am counting on." He dragged her toward the grate.

"Mon Seigneur Comte will hear of this." She gritted her teeth, resisting her forward trajectory with all her strength.

He threw back his head and laughed. "When he has d'Louncrais in this cell, forced to do his bidding, he will *thank* me."

"Forced to… Gaharet already… The comte wants to use witchcraft?" She shook her head, grimacing as his fingers bit deeper into her arm and he pulled her another step closer to the grate.

"Witchcraft? Oh, you ignorant girl." He yanked her the last step. Leaning down, with his free hand he unlocked the grate with the silver key and hefted it open. "What a nasty surprise it would have been for you on your wedding night when d'Louncrais turned you into one of them. Into a werewolf."

Sudden clarity knocked the air from Erin's lungs. The midnight runs. Gaharet's uncanny sense of hearing and smell. The way his eyes swirled with something dark, something hidden. And the wildness about him, like a beast caged. The room on the top floor with gouges in the back of the door. The words of the amulet's spell—*those who favor moonlit night*. And the last line—*So no man of their secret learns.*

The archeveque's eyes lit up. "You have seen something?"

"No." She shook her head. Werewolves were a myth. No more real than... Her heart stuttered... Magic spells and time travel.

"No matter. You will see soon enough."

The archeveque pulled her to the lip of the narrow stairs. She stumbled, her limbs shaking. Not in the cell. She couldn't let him lock her in there. Time slowed, all sounds faded but for the thumping of her heart and her ragged breathing. The heel of her boots scraped for purchase on the first narrow step, the archeveque's forceful grip pushing her forward.

"If attacked, do what you can to get away. Go for the sensitive areas – the nose, the eyes, the groin." Advice given at a safety-for-women talk she'd attended at uni. She'd thought she'd never need it. Now she did.

Erin spun around, lashing out with her free arm, the heel of her palm connecting with the archeveque's nose. His head snapped back, blood spurting from his nostrils. She followed up with a solid kick to the groin. He howled, releasing her, dropping to the floor. Erin hitched up her dress, leaped over his body and, without a backward glance, fled the room, racing along the corridor and up a flight of stairs.

She turned left and raced along another corridor. Where should she go? Back to the women? To the hall to find Gaharet? She turned a corner. Where was she? She hesitated at the head of another long corridor, her chest heaving.

Just keep moving, Erin.

She heard voices, and headed in their direction, turning yet another corner and slamming into a wall of hard muscle.

"Erin?"

She looked up. A chevalier. She moved to push past him, but he grabbed her arm.

"What are you doing here?" His raspy voice sent shivers down her spine.

"Let me go." She glanced over her shoulder. No sign of the archeveque. Yet. "I must find Gaharet d'Louncrais."

"Erin." He held her firm by her shoulders. "You should not be here. You should be with the women."

She didn't have time for this. She darted another look over her shoulder. There would be reprisals for attacking the archeveque. As soon as he recovered, he would come for her. Or send guards after her. Her and Gaharet. She must warn him.

"I have to get to Gaharet d'Louncrais. It's important."

The chevalier's nostrils flared, and his eyes widened. He grabbed her hand, flipped it palm up and stared at the archeveque's blood.

"Yours?" His raspy voice deepened into a growl.

"I..."

She backed away from him, retreating down the corridor. She halted. No, she couldn't go that way. She had to get past this chevalier.

"Erin. Look at me."

He stepped closer, pulling her shoulders around so she faced him. "I am Ulrik, one of Gaharet's men. You are safe with me. Now tell me, who are you running from?"

"How do I know I can trust you any more than I can trust the archeveque? He just tried to shove me in an underground cell."

"Archeveque Renaud?" He snarled, and she shrunk away from him. He took a deep breath and let her go, holding up his hands, backing away from her. "Erin, I won't hurt you. You have my word."

He cast a glance around the deserted corridor, and reached beneath his chain mail, pulling out a small gold amulet. As it swung around on the chain, she caught alternate flashes of the familiar Theban script and the howling wolf's head.

She stared at it, mesmerized, until he tucked it away beneath his armor. One of Gaharet's men. Ulrik. Gaharet's childhood friend? He must be. Or another werewolf.

"Tell me what happened."

She steadied her breathing, licked her dry lips. "The archeveque was supposed to be taking me for a tour of the keep. Look, Ulrik, I can't stay here. I need to get to Gaharet. Once the archeveque recovers, he is bound to come after me."

"Recovers?" His eyebrows shot up.

She held up her hand with the blood on it. "I think I might have broken his nose. And then I kneed him in the" — she looked down at his groin area — "you know."

"You broke his — ?" He barked out a laugh, though Erin, for the life of her, couldn't imagine what he found so amusing. "Come. I will take you to Gaharet."

Shaking his head, still chuckling, he took her by the elbow and led her down the corridor. "Gaharet is in for an interesting time with you."

Chapter Twenty-Four

Seated beside his comte on a raised dais at the end of the hall, Gaharet observed the festivities before him — drinking, bawdy jokes, tall tales of bravery, the usual. He had Erin safe, ensconced with the women. His men mingled amongst the ranks of chevaliers below, and Lothair, his deadliest opponent of all, sat by his side. Of Archeveque Renaud he saw no sign.

Raucous laughter and the stench of unwashed bodies filtered up to them. Glad to be away from the crowd, the cloying smell of meadowsweet failing to conceal the rankness of the hall to his sensitive nose, Gaharet waited.

After a long and uncomfortable moment, Lothair broke the silence. "You are keeping secrets from me, Gaharet?"

Gaharet turned to his comte, his eyebrows raised. "My betrothed? I assure you, Lothair, you were the first to know. Ahh, I understand. It vexes you she is not of your choosing."

"Not my choice? Gaharet, I have never heard of the woman. Or her family. Nobody has."

Gaharet shrugged. "I told you. It is an old family connection. She is of no threat to you."

Lothair grunted. "We shall see." He took a long drink from his goblet. "There is also this thing with Renaud."

"You doubt me because of one of Renaud's schemes now?"

Temper flared in Lothair's eyes, but Gaharet refused to look away.

"I have served you faithfully for years, Lothair. I pledged allegiance to you and I have kept my vow." He had not broken his oath, not yet.

Lothair frowned. "So you have, my friend, but will you continue to do so?"

An emotion he had not seen directed at him before shone bright in his comte's eyes. Distrust. Curse you, Renaud. Gaharet looked away, his gaze flitting from one vassal to the next, picking them out of the crowd. He frowned. No Ulrik. More than likely, he entertained a young woman in some dark corner of the keep.

"There was a time I thought you would do anything I asked, Gaharet. Given me your all. Perhaps I was wrong. Perhaps you have deceived me all this time."

Gaharet hesitated, tugging on the end of his beard. "You have never asked for something beyond my capacity to give."

"There are things you would deny me? *Me*? Your comte?"

Gaharet sighed. Denying Lothair anything was a good way to start a battle, but Renaud had left him with little choice. "There are things it is best not to ask for," he said, after a moment's pause. "Things you should not, and would not, ask for if you knew the consequences. Beyond that, I will serve you as I always have. As will my men."

Gaharet matched Lothair's stare, concentrating on keeping his breathing even.

"You do not deny it, then? That you are one of…them?" Lothair's eyes lit up, a hunger dark and tainted, barely contained, shimmered in their depths.

Imprisonment, torture, death—the ever-present threat hanging over them should anyone uncover their existence. Gaharet had made his peace with that. Had lived with the possibility all his life. Not this, this *fascination*, this longing to subvert his kind for a darker purpose. How on God's dear earth would he keep them out of Lothair's clutches?

He squeezed the arm of his chair, keeping a tight rein on his inner beast. Patience. Calm. Renaud's time would come. He would make sure of it, Lothair be damned. "Is there any point?"

Lothair's eyes bored into him. "No, I suppose not. And your men? Your vassals?"

Gaharet inclined his head.

"Well, my friend." Lothair chuckled, though it held no mirth. "I am glad I am the one who owns you."

Lothair sipped at his wine, settling back in his chair, his limbs loose, purveying all that was his. "Now tell me, Gaharet, who must I speak to so I can achieve my end goal? Who do I need to have kneeling at my feet, submitting to my will? Please tell me your leader is not the Comte de Blois."

Gaharet remained silent.

"Will you not tell…?" Lothair's eyes widened, searching Gaharet's face. He sat up in his chair. "You. *You* are their leader? This… Alpha?" Lothair shook his head, incredulous. He pressed his lips together. "You know what I want, Gaharet. I *will* ask it of you. Perhaps you might want to rethink your position."

"Perhaps." Gaharet nodded. "And perhaps you may want to consider why the archeveque is so keen for you to ask for something his profession clearly defines as evil."

Lothair's eyes narrowed, and he rubbed his chin. Gaharet had bought time, not a reprieve, but he would take what he could. Lothair would ask and Gaharet would deny him. The battle lines were drawn. How much time he had he did not know. Lothair was notoriously unpredictable.

Gaharet pushed himself out of his chair, stepping down from the dais.

"Do not go too far, Gaharet. I am sure I will need you before long."

"The only place I plan to be," said Gaharet, allowing a hint of a smile to curl up at the corners of his mouth, "is finishing up what I started this morning with my betrothed. You know which chamber to find me in. Please do not interrupt me this time. I do plan to be busy for quite a while."

Lothair laughed, raising his goblet in Gaharet's direction. "Make sure you enjoy yourself, my friend. Tomorrow we get down to business. Tomorrow we begin this new project of mine."

Gaharet repressed a shudder, stepping into the sea of armored men. Lothair did not shift from his position, following him with his gaze as Gaharet moved among the assembled chevaliers. He needed to alert his men, tell them... Tell them what? Prepare to fight? Prepare to flee? He could not, would not, create an army of werewolves for Lothair. The consequences were too terrible.

Gaharet stopped to talk to a group of chevaliers, accepting a mug of ale, spending a few moments among them idly conversing. He congratulated a young lad on his new position in their ranks before slipping away from them. The hairs on the back of his neck continued to prickle, awareness of Lothair's gaze following him about the room.

Nodding and smiling his way around the hall, Gaharet did his best to appear relaxed. He came across Aubert, Edmond and Aimon and paused long enough to alert them. They had to make plans, prepare to leave Langeais and slip away in the early hours of the morning when the keep went quiet, when the servants and guests slept, using the cover of darkness that favored their kind over man. Even with their enhanced abilities, Gaharet and his men were no match for Lothair. The comte had an army, and the numbers were all in his favor.

After only a few moments, they separated, mingling amongst their fellow chevaliers, engaging in conversation and revelry. Stopping by Lance and Godfrey, Gaharet passed the word to them before moving off into the crowd again. Scanning the room, he searched for Ulrik. His vassal had a lot to answer for.

Ulrik appeared in a doorway. Cradled beneath his arm, Erin, her body pressed familiarly against his. Rage boiled up inside Gaharet. His hackles rose and his lip curled in a snarl. He bared his teeth, the need to shift and defend his claim over this woman, an overpowering urge. A hand rested on his shoulder, and Gaharet spun around, growling at the person who had taken such liberties.

"Easy, Gaharet." Lance cast his gaze to the end of the hall, to the dais where Lothair watched them, curiosity burning bright in the comte's eyes. Gaharet took a deep breath, forcing his wolf back under his control and tucked the hand already changing, out of sight. He turned his head away from Lothair, letting his jaw slide back into place.

"Changing in the middle of the hall? Not the smartest thing you have ever done."

"I am going to kill him." Gaharet snarled, his hands clenched by his sides in an effort to restrain himself.

"Who? Ulrik or Lothair? Both deserve it, I am sure."

Gaharet tried pushing past his friend, but Lance blocked him, gripping his arms. "Now is not the time, Gaharet. You know that."

"I know. I know." He ran a hand through his hair, ground his teeth together. He glanced at Lothair, but his comte had gone. His attention returned to Ulrik and Erin, and he growled deep in the back of his throat. Chevaliers turned to look at him.

"Stay calm, Gaharet. Give Ulrik a chance to explain. Perhaps there is reasonable justification for him to be with your woman."

"Perhaps."

Lance eased his hands away from Gaharet's arms. "If not..." His expression turned grim.

Gaharet nodded. This time, Ulrik would get no second chance.

Lance clapped Gaharet on the shoulder. "We will meet again beyond the walls, my friend." He turned to leave.

"Lance." Gaharet called him back. "If something were to happen to me..."

Lance frowned. "Is there something you are not telling me, Gaharet?"

Gaharet hesitated, the words to disclose Erin's discovery in the underground cell caught in his throat. He shook his head. "If something should happen to me"—his gaze sought Erin—"take care of her for me. Take care of Erin."

Lance's eyes widened. "My friend? Have you fallen in love with this woman? Gaharet, is she your mate?"

A warmth spread through his chest; his gaze fixed on Erin's face. "Yes, Lance. She is my match in all ways." He flicked his gaze to Lance. "Vow to me, you will see that she is safe if I am unable to." There was an urgent note to his voice he could not repress.

Lance nodded. "Of course, Gaharet. Of course."

Some of the tension eased from his shoulders. "Thank you. Stay safe, Lance." His wolf held in check, Gaharet made his way through the armored chevaliers to Erin and Ulrik.

Before Gaharet could demand answers, berate him, rip his throat out, Ulrik released Erin into his care. He pulled her in close, holding her within the circle of his arms, her touch a soothing balm easing some of his fury. At the sharp tang of blood, his nostrils flared.

Ulrik leaned close. "She has Renaud's blood on her hands, Gaharet."

"Renaud's?" What the hell was she doing with Renaud? He dragged her back into the shadows. Ulrik followed.

"You were with the archeveque? Why?"

She rolled her eyes at him. "He offered to take me for a tour of the keep. He's an archeveque. It's not like I could refuse him."

"Renaud tried to put her in some underground cell, but she got away," said Ulrik. "She hit him on the nose, then kicked him in the groin."

"You kicked — ?"

Merde! Of all people. If her aim was as true as the night she had used the same tactic on him, it would surprise him if Renaud could even walk right now.

Gaharet's eyes narrowed in on Ulrik. "Interesting it was you who encountered her. What were you doing lurking in the corridor?"

Ulrik straightened himself to his full height. "What are you suggesting? That I was following her? That I would be in collusion with *Renaud*?" He spat the name out as though something foul had settled on his tongue. "You are lucky I found her. Heaven knows what could have happened had she run out into the hall, blood all over her hands." His eyes widened and he took a step back. "That is what you think. That one of us has sold out to Renaud. That *I* have sold us out to Renaud."

Shock, disbelief, anger flitted across Ulrik's face.

Gaharet did not flinch. "This discussion is not over, but now is not the time. We need to leave. Quietly. I may need to go into hiding."

"And the rest of us?"

"Not if you do not defy Lothair as I plan to do, but if I were you, I would not wish to be around when that happens."

Ulrik nodded, retreating into the crowd, an angry set to his shoulders and a frown across his forehead. Gaharet did not care if he had ruffled Ulrik's sensibilities. Right now, he needed to get Erin hidden — keep her safe. Taking her hand in his, he led her into the darkened corridor away from the hall.

Chapter Twenty-Five

Erin's altercation with Renaud changed things. Gaharet wanted her out of the keep, away from Lothair and out of Archeveque Renaud's reach. Now.

"Where are we going?" asked Erin, running to keep up with him.

Slowing his pace, he matched her shorter stride. "Somewhere I can protect you. I cannot risk the time to explain right now, Erin. We will discuss it later."

"More secrets." She muttered the words beneath her breath, but he heard them.

He glanced over his shoulder at her. "Mmm?"

"Lothair isn't the only one you're keeping things from."

Gaharet halted so abruptly she ran into him. He spun around, placing a hand on each of her cheeks, forcing her to look at him, her face pale, her green eyes troubled. "I will explain everything, Erin. I promise. Right now, I need to get you hidden."

"Because I assaulted an archeveque?"

"Among other things."

"Among other things? What *exactly* does that mean? What other things?"

His breathing stalled. What had Renaud told her?

"Trust me Erin. *Please.*"

He would tell her, he must tell her, but not here, not now. He caught a scent, another presence hovering just out of sight. A keep guard sent to follow him? To report back to Lothair? *L'enfer.* Their chances of sneaking out of the keep were dwindling. With people coming and going along the corridors, a dead guard would draw attention.

Erin placed her hands over his, a hesitant, gentle touch drawing his focus back to her.

"I trust you Gaharet, but my life is on the line here, too, and you have some serious explaining to do. No more secrets."

He exhaled, closing his eyes for a moment. She trusted him. He could not have asked for more. Nodding his agreement, he leaned in, took her mouth in a brief, chaste kiss. "No more secrets."

Gaharet changed direction, leading her along the corridor and farther into the keep. He stopped in the kitchen, ignoring Lothair's man keeping his distance, and had the cooks prepare a plate of food for them. He wound his way through the keep to the upper levels and found the room he searched for. Another keep guard hovered amongst the shadows. Lothair was taking no chances. Gaharet had never resented Lothair's cunning intelligence more than he did right now. Leaving would be more difficult than he had thought but leave they would. He would bide his time.

He sent Erin through the doorway, following her, closing it and sliding the plank in place, barring the door. He had Erin with him, as secure as she could be for now. They had a few hours to fill before the keep went quiet for the night and Gaharet planned to use those hours well.

He placed the plate of food down and lit a candle from the brazier, moving about the room lighting the oil lamps.

"Are we safe here?" she asked. "I think I broke an archeveque's nose. Surely he won't allow that to go unpunished?"

Gaharet shook his head, giving her a reassuring smile. "I doubt Lothair will do anything about it. We have all wanted to hit Archeveque Renaud at one time or another. Considering his nefarious intentions," he said, lighting the last of the oil lamps, "I imagine Renaud will not mention the incident."

Despite his calming assurances, Gaharet was not so certain. Lothair had flogged men for lesser crimes than hitting a priest and would again if it suited his purpose. Renaud could prevail on Lothair to do what he had failed — confine Erin in the cell, attempt to force Gaharet to comply in exchange for Erin's life. His mouth went dry and his stomach churned. An unthinkable choice, one he hoped to never have to make.

"Are you sure?"

Gaharet came to stand before her. "You are safe here with me, Erin."

He cupped her cheek with his hand, brushing his lips over hers. His need for her roared to life, hitting him with a force that nearly sent him to his knees, an overwhelming imperative to make her his. *Well, almost safe.*

Perhaps she sensed it, felt the presence of his beast close to the surface, for she backed away from him, her breathing shallow. She wandered about the room, refusing to look at him, touching the jug of wine on the table, the goblets, running a hand along the wall and fingering the fabric of the bed covering. He moved to stand behind her, his hands resting on her shoulders, her body trembling beneath his hands.

"Did Renaud say anything to you, Erin?"

Her breathing hitched, and her heart rate increased. He turned her toward him, and her gaze skittered away from him, her face flushing. He reached out, taking hold of her hand, and turned it palm up to reveal the blood.

"Here, let us take care of this."

Gaharet led her to the table, sat on the stool, and moved her to stand between his thighs. He uncorked the wine and searched the room. "We need a cloth."

"Why don't you use this?" Erin held up her dress, revealing something stitched to it.

He frowned, peering at it, and threw back his head and laughed. "They would have to be the *worst* violets I have ever seen. They are violets, are they not?"

She giggled, the tension easing a little from her body. "They're supposed to be violets, yes. As you can see, embroidery is not a talent I possess. Just get the thing off so we can use it as a rag. It won't be much use for anything else."

Gaharet gripped the embroidered cloth and her dress and ripped them apart. He doused the rag in wine and, with gentle hands, he wiped the blood off her palm. "You really hit the archeveque de Tours?"

"And kneed him in the balls."

He winced, his own groin flinching. "I know what *that* feels like."

"You handled it much better than he did. It dropped him to the floor."

Gaharet chuckled. "I can imagine." He shook his head. "Oh, Erin." He brought her palm up to his lips, planting a soft kiss on it. "You are an amazing woman."

She gasped and bit her bottom lip. "I am?"

"Oh, yes." His lips trailed a line down the inside of her wrist. "I am so glad I was the one who found you."

She frowned. "And why is that?"

He slid the flared sleeve of her dress back, ignoring her question, nibbling at the sensitive skin on the inside of her elbow.

"Why would you be willing to fight for me?"

He paused, lips hovering over her soft skin. Only his men could know that. "Did Renaud tell you that?"

"Among other things," she said, borrowing his words.

Gaharet released her arm, unfolded himself from the stool and, placing a palm behind her neck, pulled her closer. She did not resist.

"Among other things?"

He leaned in, dragging in her heady scent, dropping soft, open-mouthed kisses on the curve of her throat, his tongue flicking out to taste her. He repressed a moan, every part of his body demanding he pick her up, throw her on the bed and touch her, taste her, have her writhing beneath him until she screamed out his name and begged for release.

"He said you'd turn me into a werewolf."

Gaharet stilled, the frantic beat of her pulse fluttering beneath his lips. "Do you believe him?"

"I... I don't know." Her voice quivered, but she did not pull away.

Gaharet lifted her chin, forcing her to look at him. "Are you afraid of me now, Erin?"

She stared at him, confusion, uncertainty and awareness flashing across her face. Nostrils flaring, he caught the scent of her arousal. Afraid or not, believer or nonbeliever, she wanted him.

Gaharet stepped away from her, unlaced his surcoat, removed it and laid it across the stool. She tracked his every move. She yearned for this. Her body told him everything he needed to know — the rapid beat of her heart, the glazed look in her eyes, the slight tilt of her head exposing her sensitive throat.

He shrugged out of his mail, dropping it to the floor, unlacing and divesting himself of his padded gambeson. His vambraces and greaves followed, cast aside. Her eyes never left him, devouring him, as hungry for him as he was for her.

Her breathing became shallower as he stepped closer, circling her, until she all but panted with her need for him. He stepped up behind her, leaning close to her ear, all thoughts of Renaud and Lothair gone, replaced by visions of her beneath him as he thrust into her.

"I would never hurt you," he whispered, nipping at her earlobe, the shiver coursing through her body, fanning his own desire. He ran his fingers down her spine, her body arching in response, and his own hunger burst forth, a deep, possessive growl escaping his throat and his hands shaking.

Be gentle.

Gaharet gritted his teeth. He would keep his word. He would not hurt her and he would *not* let the beast loose tonight.

She reached up, releasing the pins from the concealing headscarf, letting the material fall to the floor. Raising her hands above her head, she waited for him to remove her overdress. She was giving him her permission, coming to him willingly. His blood pounded in his veins. She knew, in the dark recesses of her mind, she knew — whether she admitted it or not — and she would still have him. Knowing this made his hands tremble and his cock throb. He had found his mate at long last.

Gaharet took a deep breath, lifting the heavy material over her head, letting it join her headscarf. He unlaced her under-dress, scarcely touching her, slipping the garment from her shoulders. It fell with a rustle of fabric. Her chemise followed.

His breath caught. His mouth went dry. "What manner of clothing is this?" He ran his fingers over the thin strip of material clinging to her body. He had imagined her bare beneath the garment, but this…this scrap of material slipping between the cleft of her cheeks inflamed him in a way his imaginings had not.

"It's called a —"

She broke off with a gasp as he gave in to temptation, kneeling down, dropping soft kisses and nibbles at the base of her spine, his fingers playing with the stretchy material. *Mon Dieu*, the woman tested his control. Had he known, while she explored his keep, sat across the table from him to dine and read his books in his library, she had been wearing *this* beneath her gown, he would never have been able to resist her until now.

* * * *

Erin let her head fall back, a soft moan escaping her lips. Her fingers itched to touch him, but two firm hands prevented her from turning around as he slipped her thong over her hips, down her legs to the floor, and she stepped out of it. His fingers slid up the backs of her legs, caressing the sensitive skin behind her knees. He palmed her cheeks before moving up her spine to the clasp of her bra.

"And this?" he asked, a hint of confusion in his voice. Fingers followed the strap of her bra over her shoulder. They paused, reaching the lacy cups encasing her breasts. His strangled groan had her nipples beading and her clit throbbing. His hands hovered over the wisps of lace, tracing the patterns in the fabric. Erin swayed against him, waves of desire pulsing through her. She longed for more—a squeeze, a suck, her nipples hard and ready for his attention. When she could bear it no longer, she reached behind her back and undid the clasp, slipping her bra to the floor.

She turned to face him, her vulnerable flesh quivering, needy and aching. His dark gaze burned, flitting over every naked inch of her, the force of his lust slamming into her. A growl rumbled in his chest, deep and throaty. Her skin prickled and her thighs clenched.

He touched his mouth to hers. A gentle caress, his tongue sliding across her bottom lip, teasing her mouth open, and she let him in, matching his desire and more. She plastered herself to him, searching for a way to get to his skin. The need to feel him, touch him, burned. She hungered—the strength of her need overpowering and a little frightening. No man had ever aroused her like this.

She whimpered under his tender touch. It wasn't enough. Where was the full-blooded male, the hard warrior, the man who commanded an army? The Gaharet who'd chased her when she ran, demanding his victory kiss? The man who had boldly stated his intentions, declaring she would be his? *He* was the one who captivated her, pushed at her boundaries, daring her to desire something she'd convinced herself she'd never, ever wanted. This gentle Gaharet, this...tenderness... It was...nice. She didn't *want* nice. Hard to believe she'd *ever* wanted nice. She craved the confident, powerful, overtly sexual Gaharet d'Louncrais, whose hungry gaze followed her everywhere.

"Please," she begged, her hands clutching at his tunic. He left her mouth, trailing delicate kisses down her jawline. "I need..."

She snaked her hand down his body, cupping his erection, rubbing her hand along his hardened length, articulating what she wanted with her actions far better than her words.

He groaned, his cock twitching beneath her hand. "I am trying to be gentle," he growled against her throat. "Stop making it so damn difficult."

She forced her fingers up under his tunic. They skidded across his toned abdomen. "To hell with gentle."

She pulled at the tie on his leggings, her desperate fingers fumbling with the laces.

"I am trying hard not to lose control, my little filly."

Soft kisses down her throat punctuated his words, the sweet endearment melting her heart.

She mewled in protest. "But I want you to."

A throaty chuckle against her neck spiked heat through her body. "No, you do not. Not yet," he rasped, his breathing heavy, the muscles of his stomach quivering beneath her hand.

"I could always run," she whispered into his ear.

Breath hissed from between his teeth. He shook his head at her. "No."

She pulled away from him, catching her bottom lip between her teeth. Whatever it took. His gaze fixated on her mouth. She let her tongue slip out and slowly, deliberately, she licked her lips. A guttural groan escaped his throat. She spun on her heel and raced around the bed.

In two steps, he'd bounded over it, trapping her within his arms, crushing her in his embrace. He took her mouth in a savage kiss, giving her no quarter, his tongue invading, a frenzied tangling with hers, leaving no space unexplored, unclaimed.

Yes!

Here, now, dark hair tousled and loose about his face, she could imagine him a werewolf. His strength, his power, his rawness barely contained, burned in the shifting shadows of his dark eyes. A shiver ran through her. It excited her, stoked the smoldering coals of her desire to a raging blaze, consuming her. There was only one way to put that fire out. Him.

"I need you naked," she whimpered into his mouth, tugging at his clothing.

He released her, stripping away the last of his clothing and his boots, and pulled her back into his embrace, smashing his mouth against hers.

Oh God.

His skin was against hers. She'd fantasized about this since they'd met, how it'd feel to have his body pressed together, with *both* of them naked. The reality took her breath away.

He groaned, spinning her around so fast it made her dizzy, pushing her back onto the bed, covering her body with his. The weight of something dropped on her chest, gold glinting in the flickering light of the oil lamps.

His amulet?

The thought was fleeting as greedy hands caressed her body—a slide down the underside of her breast, a touch at her waist, a caress on her inner thigh. Her legs parted. Wet and ready for his touch, all her brain functions ceased, lost in sensation.

"Erin," he murmured, a husky rumble against her collarbone.

Even the way he said her name affected her.

"I have wanted this," he said, his mouth dipping to her breast, nipping the underside, "waited for this," his tongue flicking her nipple, her hands clenching in his hair, "for so long." He sucked her nipple into his mouth, starting a violent clenching of her pelvic floor. She moaned.

Firm hands spread her legs wider, his fingers teasing, brushing against her inner thigh. He ignored the little thrusts she made with her hips, her soft protests. She growled at him. He chuckled against her breast, his breath warm on her moist nipple. She grabbed his hand, pushing it where she craved his touch. With a flick of his wrist, he reversed the move, claiming first one hand then the other and pinning them above her head. He slipped his leg between hers, pressing his thigh against her, rubbing against her needy core. Her eyelids fluttering closed, she ground against his leg.

"Open your eyes. Look at me, Erin."

The punch of command in his voice forced her eyes open, and she was drowning, lost in the swirling depths of his dark eyes.

He transferred her wrists to one hand, his free hand roaming over her body—a roll of a nipple wet from his tongue between his thumb and forefinger, a slide of his palm over her stomach and a squeeze of her inner thigh.

Shifting his leg, he cupped her mound. His fingers slid across her sensitized nub. She gasped, biting her lip to prevent crying out. He rubbed, pressing slippery circles around it, pinching and tapping. She struggled to free her hands. She wanted to touch, too, but his grip only tightened, holding her firmly in place.

Fingers sliding through her wet folds, he promised but did not deliver. She bucked against him. She needed. She *wanted*.

"Gaharet."

He slipped a finger inside her and she moaned, unable to hold back. His mouth captured the sound, his tongue thrusting in rhythm with his fingers in the age-old mimicry of sex. He slipped another finger in, scissoring them, pushing against her walls, owning her. She arched against him, her climax building, hips thrusting against his hand as she chased her release.

He growled, pulling his hand free. "No. Not on your own. Not until I am inside you."

He braced himself on his elbows, shifting between her legs, rubbing the head of his cock in her slickness. The feel of him, thick and long and hot against her, so close, started an ache deep inside her.

"Please. I need... Gaharet..." Her voice faded on a breathy moan, as his cock ground against her clit.

"What do you need, *ma petite pouliche*? Tell me."

"I need…you…now."

He shuddered against her. "Let me make you mine."

"Yes… Please." She whimpered, a drawn-out sigh to the slide of his cock through her slick folds.

He nudged his cock at her entrance and thrust hard, filling her, seating himself deep. She cried out, clenching around him. He groaned. A strong, musky odor filled her nostrils, heightening her arousal. It faded as quickly as the strange cracking and popping sounds she could hear over his ragged breathing.

Or was it hers?

He began a slow grind, and she threw her legs around his hips, clasping her ankles together. She matched him, straining against him, taking him all, hips rising to meet him.

"Harder. Faster."

He shifted the angle, thrusting into her, rubbing against her clit with each stroke, playing her body like a master musician. Never had she lost herself so completely to a man's kiss, his caresses. She'd known it would be good, had feared its sublime power, but now she was here, with him deep inside her, she couldn't imagine not wanting this again. He'd forever spoiled her for other men.

She tossed her head from side to side, her walls fluttering about him. So close. She was *so* close. Their sweat-slicked skin slapped together, her body tightening. She was so full of him in every way. She arched her back, crying out as her orgasm ripped through her. He released her hands, and she flung them around his neck, her fingernails digging into his shoulders, her body shuddering. He stiffened, thrust deep, roaring as he came, spilling inside her. She clamped her teeth on his shoulder and bit down, muffling her cries as he pulsed deep inside her.

He collapsed beside her, pulling her with him, her body sprawled on top of him, still buried inside her. She trembled, residual spikes of pleasure shooting through her.

"You bit me," he grumbled, his voice reverberating through her body.

Erin snuggled closer, wiggling against him, still breathing hard. He groaned, and she raised her head to look at him, questioning. Could he possibly want to do it again? Already?

His arms thrown back, resting under his head, he regarded her through hooded lids.

"Sorry," she mumbled.

"What for — the biting or for wiggling?"

She chuckled. "Both."

Erin rested her cheek on his chest, listening to the beat of his heart and his breathing as it slowed. Her gaze caught on something nestled in the dark hair of his chest. An amulet with the familiar howling wolf's head. She picked it up and turned it over.

"Oh. It's different."

In place of the inscription, a large, dark red stone gleamed.

To bloodstone shall they return, so no man of their secret learns.

"This is the bloodstone."

Chapter Twenty-Six

Gaharet remained silent as Erin studied the amulet, those two little lines of concentration appearing between her eyebrows.

"Ask."

When she looked up, he saw all her doubts, her fears, reflected in her eyes.

"Ask your questions and I will answer them."

She considered him for a moment. Would she confront her suspicions? Demand to know his secret? Or would she shy away from it? Reject Renaud's words as superstitious nonsense?

She worried her bottom lip with her teeth and his cock, still inside her, twitched. She gasped — her perfect, rosy nipples stiffening. He swallowed a groan, resisting the urge to rise up and take one in his mouth.

"This is not like the amulet I found at the dig site."

He gave a slow shake of his head. "No."

He held himself still, all too aware of their nakedness and the way she lay straddled across him, the twin globes of her breasts brushing against his chest. This conversation would end right now if he could not get his body under control.

She tapped the amulet against her palm, a smile tugging at the corners of her mouth.

"That means it can't be your bones I found in that cell. They belong to someone else."

"Yes."

She fingered the gold disc with a light touch, almost a caress. He gritted his teeth, imagining her fingers on him, caressing him. *Mon Dieu.* She tempted him beyond all measure.

"Ulrik had an amulet like the one I found. He showed it to me in the hall so I would trust him."

Her pink tongue flicked out, licking her lip and all he could do was stare and nod, words eluding him.

"Who else has them? You said only family had these, but Ulrik is not a d'Louncrais, is he?"

"No."

He growled, whether at the thought of Ulrik being family or at the way she kept touching his amulet, he could not be sure, but it felt good releasing it, seeing her cheeks turn a dusky pink in response.

"Ulrik is not a d'Louncrais, but he is one of my vassals. He is family of a kind."

"Uh-huh. And who else is in this 'family of a kind'?"

Hands itching to touch her, he clenched them together behind his head, claws biting into his palms.

"Ulrik, Aimon, Godfrey, Lance, Edmond and Aubert—all my men, my vassals."

"So the amulet that brought me here belongs to one of your men?"

"Yes."

She pursed her lips, dropping the amulet on his chest. "You knew. All along you knew, and you didn't tell me. Even when I told you I'd a theory that you'd died in that cell." She frowned. "What else did you lie to me about, Gaharet?"

He reached out, cupping her cheek. "I did not lie to you, Erin. Not once."

She sat up, pulling away from his hand, the movement and the change of angle thrusting him deeper in her. He swallowed. Her eyes went a little unfocused and her mouth parted. Erin was not entirely unaffected by the motion either.

"You didn't tell me the whole truth. Lying by omission is still lying."

She gave a startled yelp as he reached up, pulling her against him, and rolled her beneath him, his legs wedging between her thighs. She opened her mouth to protest, and he captured it, silencing her with a kiss.

He released her mouth with a final suck on her bottom lip. "You are right. I omitted certain facts."

"And here I was, trying to save you." She sniffed. "I even thought of taking you with me into the future, so you didn't end up in that cell."

"You—"

His heart leapt at her words and a warmth spread through his chest. She cared. For him. For his life. And yet there was still so much about him she did not know. Things that may easily destroy this fragile intimacy between them.

"I am sorry for what happened today, for not anticipating the archeveque's actions. I thought you would be safe with the women."

She snorted, squirming beneath him.

L'enfer. If she moved like that again, he would lose all semblance of control.

"Have you ever met Manette?"

Licking his lips, his mouth only inches from hers, he forced himself to focus on her words.

"Manette?"

"Married to a man named Monsieur Robert."

"Mmm, I know Chapet."

He gave in to temptation, dropping kisses on her cheek, her ear, her jaw. Open-mouthed, featherlight kisses gentling his way across her skin. She tilted her head back, giving him access, a soft sigh escaping her lips. Gaharet nipped at her jaw, her sigh louder this time. He continued down her neck, stopping at the hollow of her throat to suck at her sensitive skin. He wanted to taste her. Everywhere. Elicit those little sounds of pleasure, telling him exactly what she liked.

"She—"

He gave a gentle thrust of his hips and she let out a soft moan—his cock hard, ready and willing all over again. It would never get enough of her. He cupped her breast, reveling in the way it filled his hand, plump and soft. He teased the nipple taut as he lavished attention on her neck, nipping at the top of her collarbone. His control over his body diminished with each stroke of his tongue, with every insistent thrust of his hips. She moved with him, grinding her hips against his, and he struggled to continue talking when his mouth yearned to do other things.

"Yes?" he prompted, in between open-mouthed kisses.

Her hands wandered down his back to his cheeks, clasping them, kneading them, urging him on, and he moaned against her shoulder.

"I don't... I can't..."

He moved inside her, a slow circular motion of his hips keeping him buried deep within.

"Gaharet!" she cried out, and he nearly lost his mind.

"Manette?"

"What?"

He had lost her to a haze of desire that threatened to engulf him, too.

"What were you saying about Manette?"

That he remembered the conversation when he would be hard pressed to recall his own name astounded him.

"Oh," she murmured, but that one syllable quickly turned to a long, drawn-out moan as he slipped a hand beneath her hips to pull her closer, to take him deeper.

"She wanted to be your wife."

He paused. He had not considered that Erin might not be familiar with the scheming of court women. "Erin—"

"If you stop now, I'm going to hit you like I hit the archbishop," she said, lapsing into her native tongue, and he chuckled.

"You actually hit the archeveque. I've wanted to do that for years."

She arched her back, grinding her hips against his, and he thought he'd never seen a more delightful sight—her beneath him, tousled blonde hair framing her face in a halo of gold, her lips parted in a silent moan and her face expressive with her need. Her need for him. *Merde,* she was beautiful. He resumed his circular motion with his hips.

"Gaharet."

Her voice, husky and thick, tore through him, a bolt of heat shooting straight to his testicles. Manette forgotten, his breath coming in sharp gasps, he continued his patient onslaught. With his slow, purposeful love making he was laying claim to his territory, branding her as his. This time he would take it slow — watch her beautiful face as she came clenched around him. He continued to move inside her, deep thrusts allowing her not a moment to think, only to feel.

Her soft cries spurred him on. She arched against him, her face flushed with passion, mouth open and her head flung back. Her body shuddered, her walls clamping around him, his name bursting from her lips. His own release burned through him, hot, hard and laying waste to the shreds of his control. He threw back his head, a howl rising in the back of his throat. She was his, and he wanted to proclaim it to the world in the most primitive and primal way he knew how. With gritted teeth, he restrained it, breathlessly whispering her name over and over again.

He rolled off her, pulling her against his chest, cradling her in his arms. Soon he would have to tell her all else he had yet to disclose. His other lies by omission. He dropped a kiss on her forehead, and she snuggled closer. For now, though, while she was content to not question him any further, he would enjoy this time, this moment that he had longed for since he had first set eyes on her.

Chapter Twenty-Seven

Cold night air swirled about, whispers of fog followed the river, and the distant glimmer of the moon cast a pale light over Langeais. The sounds of revelry, faint and muffled, floated through the still air as he stood on the parapet. A wolf howled close by, a mournful sound, filled with longing, echoing across the village, and he turned toward it. Another, deep in the forest's gloom, answered the call, its long, drawn-out howl fading into eerie silence.

"Do you think it is them?" He kept his voice low. His keep guards stood a respectful distance away, but he had no desire for them to be privy to this conversation.

"I believe so, Mon Seigneur Comte," said Archeveque Renaud. "The night calls to them. They are unable to resist it."

"Right under my nose and I didn't even know. Gaharet, Gaharet, Gaharet." Lothair sighed. "What am I going to do with you?"

"You know? That d'Louncrais is —"

"Of course I know, Renaud. You were not subtle. You told me a tale of a beast raised from childhood, able to hunt as wolves and fight as men. The intelligence of man wrapped up in the body of a predator with excellent hearing, perfect eyesight, an extraordinary sense of smell, along with strength, speed and agility. And damned difficult to kill. You forget I have fought many a battle with my men. There are very few who fit the description you gave me."

Very few indeed. Seven of them, and six of those had vowed investiture to the seventh — Gaharet. How many times had he seen Gaharet and his men in action on the battleground? Superior chevaliers, all of them. Stronger, larger and fearless. Coordinating their attacks, surviving injuries that should have killed them. He had dragged Gaharet off the field himself on one occasion, fearing him mortally wounded, and yet he had survived. *How was I so blind?* Now knowing of their existence, Gaharet's family crest — the howling black wolf — worn proudly, taunted him.

He peered closer at the archeveque, frowning. "Renaud, what is wrong with your nose?"

Archeveque Renaud raised his hand to his face, touching it gingerly. "The wench hit me."

"What wench? And why did she hit you?"

"D'Louncrais' betrothed, Mademoiselle Richardson. D'Louncrais has a strong attachment to her, and I believed he would make any attempt to secure her safety. I thought to confine her in your little underground cell —"

He rounded on the archeveque. "You *what*?"

"Your cell is a rather useful addition to the keep, I must say. Quite diabolical. I had hoped to get the woman into it. Force d'Louncrais to trade his life for hers."

Lothair closed the distance between them, his jaw clenched so tight his teeth might crack. "You attempted to confine the betrothed of one of *my* vassals in *my* cell without *my* permission?"

Renaud shrugged, standing his ground, a look of smug superiority flashing across his face. "You required proof. I was merely providing it."

Lothair snarled, and Renaud dropped his gaze, bowing his head. "My apologies, Mon Seigneur Comte. I thought only in furtherance of our plans."

Renaud's sudden obsequiousness did not fool Lothair. The man thought he could play him? He had made a serious miscalculation.

"I no longer need your proof, Renaud. Gaharet himself has confirmed your tale."

"He has?"

Renaud's whole body radiated shock, and Lothair derived gleeful satisfaction from it.

"You underestimated him."

They both had. He turned away, stalking back and forth along the outer wall, hands gripping the pommel of his sword, itching to use it. He could make Renaud's nose the least of his problems.

Lothair paused in the act of drawing his weapon. Logic prevailed, and he shoved it back into its scabbard, dropping his hand to his side should the temptation prove too great. He did not need swarms of churchmen descending on his county because he had disemboweled an archeveque. Not right now.

"You think d'Louncrais will give you what you want if you ask him?"

Lothair clutched his fist at his side, resisting his bloody impulses. "Not now, you *imbecile!*"

He spun away, focusing on the darkened buildings of Langeais, the forest beyond, anything other than Renaud, and the pleasure he would derive from gutting the archeveque. He leaned his forearms on the wall. Below him, the keep guard changed watch.

Gaharet had yet to defy him, but how far would he go to protect the woman? He had thought her important enough to wed despite her ignominious circumstances. Would he betray his comte for her? Betray him?

He cursed the curiosity that had prompted him to allow Renaud's petition for a private audience. The archeveque's plans only ever benefited the archeveque. He knew that. Gaharet had long tempered Renaud's influence, thwarting his many schemes. He had become complacent, relying on Gaharet. But in this, he could not trust Gaharet to stand by his side.

He glanced at Renaud. He would get what he wanted, one way or another, and if Gaharet opposed him, then so be it.

"Gaharet has locked himself in a bedchamber. He is having a pleasurable time with his betrothed. His vassals are out there somewhere, presumably," he said, gesturing out into the forest. "I have men standing guard in the hall outside Gaharet's room, and the guards at the gate are under my orders not to let him pass. As yet, Gaharet has made no effort to leave." He glared at Renaud. "It is your stupidity that is forcing my hand."

He called to his men, hovering behind him. "Assemble the guard." He faced Renaud. "I will take the chamber and its occupants."

He turned to Renaud, tapping his chin. "Do you think the woman is one of them?"

"Definitely not. She would have killed me if she was. Why?"

"I am curious to know what Gaharet finds so special about this woman. Once we have him in my underground cell, he will have no need of her." He readjusted himself in his breeches. "I think I might keep her. Taste her wares myself."

Renaud grunted, turned on his heel and stalked away, muttering something about base intentions and the work of the devil.

Lothair's smirk twisted into a scowl as he stared after the retreating archeveque. What game was Renaud playing? As Gaharet had pointed out, an archeveque had no business suggesting he work with an unholy creature. His hand rested on the pommel of his sword. One day, he would lose all patience with Renaud and his schemes, and with every interaction with the conniving weasel, that day drew closer and closer.

* * * *

Below the parapet, pressed up against the keep and hidden in shadows, Aimon stood, listening to the comte's footfalls fade away. Determination flashing in his bright blue eyes, he peeled himself away from the wall. He must warn Gaharet. He owed his life to him and would sacrifice it to protect him without a second thought.

Chapter Twenty-Eight

Erin lay beneath the covers, curled against Gaharet, his arm draped over her, her emotions unsettled. He'd burrowed under her skin. This man, this tenth-century chevalier. It had started with their first kiss, but with each day that passed, with each act of generosity, each revelation of the man beneath the warrior, he'd broken down her defenses. She hadn't wanted it to happen, had resisted its insistent pull, but the intimacy they'd shared had let him slip into her heart and take up residence.

She closed her eyes, trying to ignore the feel of his body against hers. She'd fallen for him. Fallen for the wrong man. Wrong not because he was an arrogant womanizer, all looks, charm and no substance as she'd once thought him to be. Nor because he was the type of man to bail the moment things became too hard, too much or when a better offer presented itself. Not Gaharet. The man defined responsible—unfailing and steady in his duties to those who trusted him and depended on him. He was everything she could ask for and more, with depths to him she'd barely begun to understand. And she desired him with an unexpected fierceness that took her breath away. Perversely, Gaharet was the right man in all ways but one.

He lives in the wrong damn century.

He dropped a light kiss on her bare shoulder, and she opened her eyes.

"You are frowning," he said, his voice rumbling against her skin, sending a shiver up her spine. "What is troubling you?"

You. How I feel about you. Knowing they could never be anything more than what they'd just shared. Because she'd be leaving soon. If she wasn't, could they become something more? He desired her, told her she was amazing, vowed to protect her, but would that be enough? Who was she to him? And where would she fit on his long list of responsibilities? First or somewhere further down the line? Questions she hadn't asked because she wasn't staying. There wasn't any point in knowing the answers. She'd not even asked him about the archeveque's accusation.

"Nothing. Just—"

Gaharet pressed a finger to her lips. "Shh. Someone is coming."

He flung back the covers and was on his feet, reaching for his breeches. Her eyes skimmed over his nakedness, watching the play of muscles across his chest. His dark hair fell in disarray about his shoulders, and an ache settled in her chest. He caught her staring, and his gaze softened. She looked away, her throat squeezing tight.

A scuffling of feet and a muffled groan from beyond the door reached her ears, and she bolted from the bed, hurriedly dressing. Had the archeveque come for her? The comte? Now was not the time to get all doe-eyed and emotional.

"Gaharet?" A whisper. Urgent. A soft knock on the door.

Gaharet pulled on his tunic, gambeson and armor and removed the plank of wood barricading the door. A chevalier with white-blond hair slipped into the room. Aimon? The injured vassal from the wall hanging? The man Kathryn wanted for a husband? An icy, Nordic warrior against Gaharet's enigmatic darkness, Erin could see why Kathryn favored him. Bright blue eyes shifted beyond Gaharet to the disheveled bed, to her, and a smile broke out on his face. She flushed, as embarrassed as any teenager caught canoodling behind the school stadium.

He returned his attention to Gaharet. "The keep guard is coming for you. Lothair will no longer wait till morning. He will not risk you leaving, not after what Renaud tried with your betrothed. Here. Take my sword." He handed the weapon to Gaharet. "You will not be able to retrieve yours. Lothair has ordered the gate guard to prevent your departure. He believes the rest of us are already beyond the walls."

"Oh, God."

Both Gaharet and Aimon turned to her.

"All will be well, Erin. I have another way of leaving the keep, but we need to move fast. Aimon, can you get us a horse? From the village?"

"Of course, but…" His eyes flicked to her. "It will be difficult to find one that will allow — "

Gaharet shook his head. "Not for me. For Erin."

What? Was he sending her back to his keep?

Aimon nodded. "I will meet you beyond the walls. Be safe, Gaharet."

Opening the door, Aimon peered into the corridor. With a final nod to them both, he slipped from the room.

"Come, Erin." Gaharet attached his greaves, slipped on his surcoat and buckled on his vambraces. "We must leave. Do not worry about your headscarf."

He took her hand and led them from the chamber. Two steps into the corridor, she encountered a body sprawled on the floor, his mouth open and eyes unseeing. Gaharet barely gave it a second glance. Another lay around the bend, a dark pool of blood spreading beneath his head. A chill ran through her body. Aimon had done this? She focused on keeping up with Gaharet, on his broad shoulders and the comforting feel of his large hand wrapped around hers. If she thought too much about the bodies, she'd lose her nerve.

They rounded a corner, coming to a set of stairs, voices echoing up from below, and Gaharet whisked her past them. Another long corridor, another set of stairs and more swift footsteps coming in their direction. Gaharet pulled her into the stairwell, hastening her down and out of sight. They continued on to the next floor, weaving along corridors, around corners and down more stairs. She hoped Gaharet knew where he was going.

"Halt!"

A man stood below them, blocking their way.

"By order of the Comte de Anjou, I must detain you."

Gaharet released her hand, taking purposeful strides toward him. The guard's eyes widened, and he attempted to draw his sword. Gaharet was too fast. He raised the sword and swung it at the guard's head.

Erin recoiled.

Don't look. Don't look.

But she couldn't look away as the man's head separated from his shoulders. The head, eyes agape, hit the floor with a sickening thud. It rolled toward her, the body collapsing at Gaharet's feet. A whimper escaped her, and she clasped her hand over her mouth, bile rising in her throat. His bloodied sword in his hand, Gaharet propelled her past the grisly scene.

He hadn't even flinched.

Her stomach roiled, the urge to vomit strong. She fought against it.

If, even for one moment, she'd had any doubts that Gaharet was first, and foremost, a tenth-century chevalier, they were gone. The trail of blood dripping from Gaharet's sword as they wound their way through Langeais Keep drove that point home.

Keep yourself together, Erin. Be thankful he is capable of such brutality. Lothair le Diable certainly will be.

They encountered no one else, and after several more corridors, with a cautious look in both directions, Gaharet pulled her into a darkened storeroom. He released her hand and the sound of something heavy being dragged across the floor reached her ears. A hinge creaked, and she breathed in stale air. Gaharet found her hand again.

"Duck." He placed a gentle hand on her head, forcing her to hunch over, steering her forward. Again, the sound of something heavy sliding along the floor. Disoriented by the darkness, Erin swayed a little and her shoulder brushed against a wall. She reached out to steady herself, her fingers settling on mossy rocks. She couldn't see a thing. Were they in a tunnel? How on earth could he see two feet in front of his face?

Erin crouched low, trailing along behind him as he led her first to the left, then to the right. The creak of another hinge, a slight breeze and they were outside the keep, under the moonlit sky, hidden from view by a prickly bush.

"Does Lothair know of this secret exit?"

Gaharet shrugged. "I do not know. It is possible. It is his keep, but Aimon's warning bought us some time."

"Right. Now, how do we get beyond the walls? Without anyone noticing?" She didn't think she could handle another severed head.

"Do you know what a postern gate is?"

Erin nodded. Guards manned the main gate. A smaller alternative concealed at the back of the keep was perfect for an escape attempt. "Would Lothair have it guarded?"

"It is doubtful. We are not under siege, and he believes us to be secure within. Come. The gate is not far from here. Stay close to the wall. We should be able to reach it unseen."

"All right. Let's do this. I think I've seen about enough of Langeais Keep to last me a lifetime."

Gaharet leaned in, cupping her neck in his large hand. "I am sorry, Erin. I should never have brought you here. But I cannot say that I regret all that has occurred here this night."

His lips captured hers, and she clung to him. For all that heartache loomed large on her horizon, she didn't regret it either.

He released her and they set off, staying close to the keep wall, Gaharet leading her to the postern gate. Luck was on their side when they reached it. The guards above caught up in an argument over a pretty servant girl. They slunk across the bailey, through the gate and into the trees beyond undetected.

"I never thought I'd say this, but I'm glad we're in the forest," she said, glancing back at the dark, looming mass of the keep. "Even if there are wolves in it."

Gaharet paused, shooting a glance at her over his shoulder. In the wan light of the moon, his expression was unreadable. With a sigh, he started out again, moving them deeper into the trees.

They trudged through the darkened forest, Erin sticking close on Gaharet's heels. The man had a truly uncanny ability to see in the dark. Given their current circumstances, the reasoning for that did not bear thinking about. A snort, a frightened squeal and the thud of hooves halted her in her tracks.

"There is no cause for alarm, Erin. It is only Aimon with the horse I asked him to find for us."

A few muttered oaths emerged from the gloom of the trees, and a horse and rider approached. The horse, eyes rolling, shivered and snorted, shying its way toward them as the rider struggled with the reins.

She kept her distance, sheltering behind Gaharet. 'You're not going to make me ride that thing on my own, are you?"

He cupped her jaw and brushed his thumb across her cheek. "All will be well, Erin. The horse will settle. Can you take the reins, please?"

She eyed the unhappy animal. Would she even be able to find her way back to his keep without him?

"I... I'm not good with horses, Gaharet." She scuttled backward as the horse lurched in her direction. "And I'll get lost on my own."

"You are not going alone, and the horse will be fine once Aimon dismounts."

"Are you sure?"

He gave her a brief nod. "I am sure."

Edging toward the horse, one reluctant step at a time, she reached out and took the reins from Aimon as he dismounted. The horse snorted, tossing its head and stamping its feet, pulling back on the reins. She cringed, shrinking away as far as the reins would allow. The horse could trample her or drag her along the ground if it bolted. Both appeared imminent, but the moment Aimon and Gaharet stepped away, the horse settled. Its nostrils still flared, its body trembled and its ears pointed toward the two men, but it ceased fighting against the reins, edging closer to her.

After a few words with Gaharet, Aimon slipped away, and they were once again alone.

"Why's he leaving?"

"Aimon is going to stay behind and make sure no one follows us. He will catch up with us later. He can travel much faster than we will be."

Erin frowned. Aimon would be faster? They had a horse.

Gaharet gestured to the horse. "He is calm now. Tie him to a tree for a moment. We need to talk."

She raised her eyebrows. "You want to talk? Now?"

"I promised you no more secrets, that I would tell you everything."

Everything? Her heart skipped a beat. But now? When half the keep were searching for them? "Gaharet—"

"Please, tie the horse up and come over here," he said. "I wish there was another way. I really do. I did not plan to tell you like this, but I have little choice. Come, Erin, we have no time to waste."

Was she ready to hear his secret? The true purpose behind the bloodstone? To hear confirmation of the archeveque's accusation and her suspicions? From the determined set to his jaw, they were going nowhere until they'd had this conversation. With a sigh and a shrug of her shoulders, she tied the now quieter horse to a tree. Taking a moment to steady herself, she turned to face him.

She blinked. *What the hell?*

"You're... You're *naked!*" She swallowed a small moan. Even now, with the threat of the comte finding them, she longed to run her hands over those perfect abs. She shook her head, pushing such thoughts from her mind. "*Why* are you naked?"

"Erin, come here."

He held his hands out to her. Her feet, of their own volition, obeyed. Her hands slid into his, seeking something solid, something human to hold on to. She raised her eyes to meet his.

"There is no easy way to say this."

He swallowed, his Adam's apple jerking up and down. For the first time since she'd met him, Gaharet d'Louncrais looked unsure of himself.

"I cannot travel on horseback with you because the horse will not tolerate my presence. I have not trained him to accept me as I have with my horse. You saw him with Aimon. It would be the same for me." He licked his slips. "The reason is —" He closed his eyes, exhaled, opened his eyes. "The reason is... Archeveque Renaud spoke the truth. I am a werewolf."

Erin stared at him. He thought he was a werewolf. A mythological beast.

She searched his eyes for any hint of confusion, deception, or doubt, but his gaze never wavered. Centuries of scientific knowledge, and her common sense, warred with all those little things she'd noticed about him that were different, unnatural. Little things that on their own amounted to nothing more than an unusually skilled chevalier, an experienced woodsman or a genetic anomaly. Collectively they pointed to a darker truth. She glanced over at the horse some yards away by the tree, its wide, wary eyes fixed on Gaharet. The horse sensed something. Something she could not.

"Erin, please say something."

There was only one way to know for sure. "Show me."

He nodded. "Watch closely. I will take it slow."

Uncertain about what she expected, perhaps nothing at all, at first, she could detect no difference. Then, beneath her palms, his hands changed. Coarse, dark hairs sprouted, his nails changed to claws and his bones shifted under his skin, making strange popping sounds and grinding noises as they reshaped. She gaped as his jaw shifted, elongated, his incisors growing longer.

Holy shit! He really was a werewolf. A *freaking* werewolf!

She jerked out of his hands — *no, paws* — and took a step away from him. Unable to look away, her heart pounded in her chest, as the Gaharet she knew changed. His body contorted, bones rippling beneath the surface of what was once skin but was now fur. He dropped to all fours, and she stood rooted to the spot as he completed his transformation. Gone was the tenth-century chevalier, the man, the human. In his place a big, black wolf. *The* black wolf.

How had science got it so wrong? And the myths of a half-man, half-wolf monstrosity? They, too, had missed the mark. This was something else entirely.

The wolf—Gaharet— sat down, regarding her. With the transformation, had he become all beast, his mind solely that of a predator? Or did some of the man linger? Awareness and intelligence shone in his eyes. Familiar shadows flitted behind his dark irises. Could it be that he was both man *and* wolf, regardless of what form he took?

She reached her hand toward him, fingers trembling, palm out. One slow step at a time, he moved closer, placing his big, furry head against her palm. She ruffled his fur with her fingers, and he pressed into her hand. Letting out an explosive breath, she stepped back and Gaharet reverted to human form. He reached for her, unsure and she paused, her insides quivering, her scientific, rational mind incapable of theorizing this away with a single logical explanation other than the obvious.

Gaharet d'Louncrais is a werewolf.

She touched the back of his hand—his skin, human skin, warm to the touch. He was still Gaharet. He wouldn't hurt her. He hadn't hurt her yet, and clearly he could have. She slipped her hand into his and he pulled her to him, enfolding her in his arms, kissing the top of her head.

"Thank you," he murmured against her hair. "Thank you."

He held her tight, pressed against him, as though unwilling to let her go. This confident, self-assured chevalier had feared her rejection. She'd seen it in his eyes. She pulled away from him. Returning home was going to hurt them both.

"Well, that explains why I found a wolf's skull, not a human one with remains in the underground cell."

He frowned. "It would. You did not tell me of that."

She ignored his jibe. "I have..." She bit her bottom lip. "I have a lot of questions."

She couldn't help but be curious. She paced in front of him. What did it feel like, his bones changing like that? Was he born this way? Or, as according to the myths, was he bitten?

A pleased smile tilted the corner of his mouth. "I will answer all your questions, but right now, we need to move. You will ride the horse, and I will travel on foot. Keep far enough behind me so my presence does not cause the horse to bolt but keep your eyes on me."

He reached for her, halting her pacing and slanted his mouth across hers, and for a moment Erin forgot where she was, forgot where this was all going.

Releasing her, he stepped away. "Let us move from here before Lothair discovers we are no longer in his keep."

They slung Gaharet's armor and clothes over the saddle and strapped his sword in place. Untying the horse, Erin hoisted herself into the saddle, sitting astride — decorum be damned. With a white-knuckled grip on the reins, she turned the horse and they set off into the forest. Gaharet in the lead, a mythological beast, a supposed monster, and yet a good man. Leaving him would not be easy.

Chapter Twenty-Nine

Lothair's lip curled back in a snarl as he glared around the chamber. He took in the ruffled bed, the half-empty pitcher of wine, the untouched plate of food and the woman's headscarf discarded on the floor. Gaharet *had* been here, but was long gone now, two of the keep guards dead in the corridor, evidence of his departure.

"Argh!"

He kicked a stool across the room, his men shrinking away from him. Nobody defied him. *Nobody.* Not even Gaharet. He paced the room, his sword arm twitching with his need to strike something, his rage building inside of him.

"Mon Seigneur Comte." The capitaine of his guard stepped into the room. "We have searched the keep. Apart from a decapitated guard at the bottom of a stairwell, there is no sign of Seigneur d'Louncrais."

"How is that *possible*?" He paused in his pacing, fixing his eyes on the now trembling capitaine. "You have guards at the gate and on the walls. The corridors are teaming with them. And yet somehow you let Gaharet d'Louncrais and his woman slip past you. You *imbêcile*."

"Mon Seigneur, perhaps he used the postern—"

Lothair drew his sword and plunged it through the capitaine's throat. Blood spurted from the man's neck, spilled from his lips and ran down his chin. The flames in the oil lamps fluttered and distant sounds of movement in the keep echoed up the stairwell, but in the room, in the corridor, no one made a sound. Silence bounced off the keep walls.

Lothair pulled his sword free with a wet, sucking noise and the guard collapsed to the floor, convulsing, his heels beating against the floor and a wretched gurgling coming from his ruined windpipe. Guards stepped back, their faces pale and their eyes averted. Lothair rolled his shoulders, cracked his neck. Now he felt better. Calmer.

"You." He pointed at another guard quivering in his boots. "Capitaine." The guard's eyes bulged. "Take twenty men and search this keep, the bailey and check the postern gate. I. Want. Him. Found."

"Yes, Mon Seigneur."

The man scuttled off to do his bidding.

Merde. There had to be someone in this keep who was not incompetent? Gaharet was but one man. He was the comte. He had an entire army at his command. It was inconceivable Gaharet could evade them for too long.

He rubbed his hand across his face. What a disastrous turn of events. Gaharet knew everything— his tactics, his battle strategies, his plans for expanding his county, the capabilities of his troops. Being at odds with Gaharet, having him in chains, would have cost him his advisor, a very competent commander of his army, and his friend. Having him at large, as his adversary, was truly troubling.

Lothair snarled as Archeveque Renaud entered the chamber. Renaud stepped over the body in the doorway, lifting his robes above the blood pooling on the floor.

"No d'Louncrais. He has outsmarted your keep guard, I see. Not much of an accomplishment, but terribly inconvenient all the same."

"You are not redeeming yourself here, Renaud." Lothair had no patience for dealing with the archeveque right now, not with his temper barely held in check.

"But I have a solution that will solve the problem of d'Louncrais, Mon Seigneur Comte."

"I hope it is better than your last plan. If not for your ill-considered attempt to confine Gaharet's betrothed, we would not be in this damnable situation."

"I have it on good authority —"

"Yes, yes. Your mysterious informant. What does he tell you *this* time?"

"They have a designated meeting point, beyond the keep walls. I have taken the liberty of having a few men set a trap for him."

"A few men? A *few* men? Do you really think a few men are going to best him? Gaharet alone is a match for half my army. And beyond these walls, his vassals are there to come to his aid."

"With your indulgence." Renaud motioned for Lothair to follow him to a quieter corner of the room, away from the ears of the remaining guards standing beyond the doorway, too terrified to move.

With a roll of his eyes, Lothair followed him. "This had better be worth my time, Renaud."

"There is an herb — wolfsbane — that has a powerful effect on his kind. It dulls their enhanced senses, taking away much of their advantage. It renders them almost human and makes it difficult for them to control their form. I have tested its potency myself, seen with my own eyes how it works. They are easily subdued, and even killed, when under its effects. We need only then bind him in silver."

"You have trapped and killed them?"

"Yes."

Lothair frowned. Over the past several months, reports of his vassals dying in random skirmishes had reached his ears. It had particularly troubled Gaharet.

"These men, these *werewolves*, you've killed... They were in my county?"

Renaud shrugged.

Lothair eyed Renaud through slitted lids. "When this is all over and Gaharet is in my cell, you and I are going to have a long discussion, Renaud. A very long, and possibly *pointed*, discussion." He raised the tip of his bloodied sword, tapping it against Renaud's chest. "I am not happy you have taken it upon yourself to kill some of my men for your own purposes. I will expect a detailed explanation of your actions."

Renaud smiled, all teeth and jutting cheekbones, pushing the tip of the sword away with his fingers. "As you wish, Mon Seigneur Comte, but perhaps we should apprehend d'Louncrais first."

Lothair grunted, striding past Renaud. "You." He pointed to a guard. "Saddle my horse and assemble two score of mounted men in the bailey."

"At once, Mon Seigneur."

"Come, Renaud. Show me this trap of yours." He swept from the room.

Renaud was most definitely scheming, but what was his end game? Now more than ever he needed Gaharet's support, his council, and he cursed his lack of it. His step faltered.

Oh, I see. Divide and conquer. He almost laughed. *Well played, Renaud. Well played.*

He continued down the corridor, a smile curling at the corners of his mouth.

I have your measure now, Renaud, and you will not win.

Chapter Thirty

Erin guided the reluctant horse after the black wolf, heading farther into the forest and away from Langeais Keep. She kept her distance, Gaharet's shadowy form barely visible amongst the moonlit trees. If she got too close to him, the horse balked, refusing to move. She wasn't an experienced enough rider to compel it against its will. Still, she kept the horse at a steady trot or canter for most of the journey. By the time Gaharet stopped at the edge of a small clearing, her legs were quivering with fatigue and her fingers had gone numb from gripping the saddle and the reins so tight.

She slid from the horse, stretching her limbs, and turned to see the last vestiges of Gaharet's wolf disappearing with a shake of his head. The threads of desire stirred at the sight of him standing tall, proud and naked. She sighed, turning back to the horse, hitching the reins to a tree and grabbing an armful of his garments.

"I think you should put these on."

She handed him his clothes. She wouldn't be able to resist temptation if he stood around naked for too long. His nostrils flared and his gaze burned hot, and she backed away before she took him up on the promise in his eyes. After retrieving the sword and his hauberk, she turned, startled to find Ulrik standing beside him.

Erin approached the men, placing Gaharet's armor and weapon on the ground. "Is he…? You know… Like you?" She couldn't bring herself to utter the word werewolf.

Gaharet nodded. Of course. He had an amulet. So, too, did Gaharet's other vassals. All his men then — Aimon, Godfrey, Lance, Edmond and Aubert were all…like him. He'd all but told her about Aimon when he'd explained about the horse.

"Ulrik was the wolf we encountered by the creek."

"Oh." Erin studied Ulrik. Sandy hair, sandy wolf. Hair color matches wolf color. *Interesting.* "Can I see?"

Ulrik looked to Gaharet.

Gaharet frowned, then shrugged. "Go ahead, but partial only," he said, a note of warning in his voice.

Partial?

"Very well."

Ulrik held out his hand, keeping an anxious eye on her. Slow and steady, his hand changed. Just his hand. Erin reached out with hesitant fingers and touched the paw. Moments ago, it had been human fingers. It felt… It felt real. Running her hand along the paw, she touched her fingertip to one of his sharp claws, jerking her hand away in an instant.

"I do not frighten you?" asked Ulrik, his face registering his surprise.

Erin swallowed, keeping her breathing steady. "A little," she said, "but not because I think you will hurt me. It's just..." She shook her head. "I can't believe this is possible. It's all supposed to be a myth, superstitious nonsense, and yet I'm seeing you change before my eyes, touching *fur* that should be skin." She ran her hand over his paw again, turning it over, brushing her fingers over the soft pads, marveling at it.

Gaharet growled, stepping in closer to her. Ulrik snapped his hand away, returning it to human form. She raised her brows at Gaharet.

He shrugged his shoulders. "It is a wolf thing."

"A wolf thing?" She glanced between Gaharet and Ulrik. It seemed more a primitive display of proprietorial male behavior to her, but as much as the modern woman in her rebelled at his chest thumping, a part of her heart thrilled at it. *The tenth century must be rubbing off on me.*

"You have not told her much, have you?" asked Ulrik.

"I know he's a werewolf. What else is there for me to know?"

"I have not had the time, and it is complicated," said Gaharet.

Ulrik turned to her. "In wolf speak, he is claiming you. Making sure I know you are his. Betrothals are the human equivalent. You and Gaharet have both."

Erin's eyebrows hitched, and she turned to Gaharet. "You told Lothair I was your betrothed to protect me, right? Right?"

Gaharet didn't answer her.

"Look, I..." She glanced at Ulrik, then back at Gaharet, her palms going sweaty. "I know we... We were..." She thought she had more time before she had to face this conversation. Would've liked some place more private. "In the keep when we... You know, but…" She wrung her hands together. He understood she couldn't stay here, right? "I don't belong here, Gaharet." God, it hurt to say those words, and the flash of pain in his eyes told her it hurt him, too. It made what she had to say all that much harder. "I have to go home."

Ulrik stared at her, his mouth agape.

Gaharet took her hands, moving her away from Ulrik, rubbing his thumbs across her knuckles.

"Erin, I have not told you everything about…about the amulet."

He had *more* secrets? A sense of foreboding slithered in her stomach. "What haven't you told me?"

He raised his eyes to the night sky, sighing, before settling his gaze on her. "Why did the amulet bring you to me?"

"You said it was because you were the head of the family."

"Think about the inscription, Erin. *To bloodstone shall they return.*"

She shook her head, not wanting to let his words to sink in.

"I have the amulet with the bloodstone. It is the binding amulet. You recited the inscription, activating the bloodstone, and it drew you in."

"What are you saying?"

A muscle ticked in his jaw. "The amulet only works one way. There is no reverse spell, Erin."

A shake started in her fingertips, working its way up her arms to her torso. "There's no… That can't…" She pulled her hands out of his grasp, the rub of his thumbs no longer soothing. "You mean I'm stuck? Here? In this century? In a world where people use swords to solve disputes? Where the highest ranked churchman wants to confine me in an underground cell, and my life is at the mercy of a comte they call The Devil." She began pacing in earnest, ringing her hands together.

He caught her shoulders, turning her to face him. "I will protect you, *ma petite pouliche*. Trust me to take care of you."

"I can't... I can't live here." In her distress, she'd reverted to English, unable to maintain her grasp on Old French. "I come from a world of modern conveniences, Gaharet. Where the life expectancy is greater than forty to fifty years, and people die of old age not in... *battle* or in childbirth. Where women get an education and have choices and freedoms that just don't exist here. Freedom to wear what they want, go where they please and have financial independence. I have a...a career. One I love and have worked damn hard for."

Ulrik moved closer. "What is she talking about, Gaharet? Why is she speaking in Anglo-Saxonne? And strangely at that?"

Gaharet snarled. Ulrik raised his hands, backing away.

"Erin, you may not have the same life as you had in your world, but as my wife, you will have more freedoms than most, I promise you." He cupped her face, his thumb brushing against her cheek. "I am wealthy enough to provide for you, to give you access to whatever tomes and manuscripts you wish. I can show you things, take you places, introduce you to people you have only ever had the chance to study or read about. You wish to wear clothes like those I found you in? Very well. I will arrange for some to be made for you. You may wear them within the keep any time you wish. I am not averse to seeing you in such garments."

He gave her a cheeky smile. She did not respond to it, and his smile slipped from his face.

"I will not curtail your freedoms, Erin. I may not be able to give you everything you are accustomed to, but I will give my all to make you happy."

Erin's bottom lip trembled.

"You should know, as werewolves, we view marriage differently to our human counterparts. I told you of my parents' marriage. You saw the wall hanging. You have heard the story of their love. This is how it is for all werewolves. If we find our mate. For years I longed for what my parents had, searched for it and despaired of ever finding it. I resigned myself to a match made of necessity rather than love." He stared into her eyes. "Since the moment I found you wandering beneath the full moon in naught but an undershirt and men's breeches, I have thought of little else. Once I held you in my arms, kissed you, I knew no other woman would do. You are the only one for me, Erin. You *are* my mate."

Her heart swelled even as it broke. The forest, Ulrik, the horse, receded. Her whole world narrowed down to this man standing before her, baring his soul. She blinked back tears and pulled away from him.

"There has to be some way to reverse the spell."

"I am truly sorry, Erin. If there is one, I do not know of it."

"Then we find the people who created it!"

With all her knowledge of the past, she would figure this out. "The script, the spell itself, all points to a witch. We track down any witches in the area, and we keep asking until we find the answers."

He shook his head. "We could search for years and not find anything. I have already spent many months looking—hours poring over tomes, scrolls and manuscripts, everything I could get my hands on. I am no closer to knowing who created the amulet."

"Then I'll keep looking."

Gaharet opened his mouth to say something then closed it, his expression shuttered.

"I am sorry, Gaharet, but… You're asking me to give up everything I know, everything I love. Would you do that? If I could find a reversal spell, would you come with me? Leave behind your keep, your wealth and your men? Would you turn your back on those that depend on you? On this life you have created? To be with me?"

He swallowed hard, his anguish visible in the downturn of his lips and the sagging of his shoulders. He cupped her face, dropping a kiss on the tip of her nose. "I would like nothing more than to follow you wherever you go, Erin, but I could not go with you to your time. I will not forsake my men, no matter how much it would pain me to see you leave."

And there it was. Erin backed away from him. For all he professed she was his one and only, she did not come first in his list of priorities. She knew what that felt like. Had experienced it many times over, playing second fiddle to her mother's boyfriends. No more than a shoulder to cry on for the woman who should've placed her in the center of her world. She couldn't, wouldn't, be that person again.

"I can't be your wife, Gaharet, or your mate. I have to go home."

He reared back as though she'd struck him. "Erin—"

She turned away from him, tears threatening to fall, her chest squeezing tight.

"There is a witch living close to here," he said, his voice toneless and flat. "In all likelihood, she knows nothing of us or the amulet, but if to leave here is what you truly wish, I will take you to her."

She met his eyes, jerking her head in a nod, not trusting herself to speak.

"The others will be here soon."

With a final anguished glance at her, he stalked past a stunned Ulrik. He pulled his hauberk over his head, grabbed his sword, and without another word, stepped into the clearing. Ulrik stared at her for a long moment, before following Gaharet.

Erin closed her eyes, a stray tear sliding down her face. Now more than ever, she needed to go home.

* * * *

Gaharet stepped out of the trees, a pain in his chest he had not felt since he had lost his brother. Did the intimacy they had shared count for nothing? Did *he* count for nothing? He was not some poor peasant farmer, offering her a life of poverty and hardship. Yet she would leave him? After he had offered her love? The one thing she professed she would wed for. She would reject his betrothal, refuse to be his mate?

His hand fisted around the grip of his sword so tight his knuckles were white. He had finally found the woman that could give him the love he so desired, and he was not enough for her. She would leave him, and he could not follow. Gaharet would give his heart, his soul, his everything to this woman to keep her by his side, but he could not, would not, abandon his people, his pack. He had watched his father do that very thing after his mother's death, retreating into his grief. Seen first-hand the havoc it wreaked and vowed never to do the same.

He wanted to rage at the unfairness of it all. Take up his sword and hurt someone. Rip into his enemies with teeth and claws. He tamped down a growl, his beast fighting for control, wanting to tell her she was his and she would not, could not, leave him. He would bite her, turn her. She would need him then. Need his help to accustom to her new nature, to help her train her wolf. She would have no choice but to stay.

He shook his head. No. He would not force his nature on her, on anyone. Not unless there were no other options. He would take her to the witch. There was no guarantee she would have the answer. They could search the whole county, find every witch that lived, and still not find what Erin sought. It would, however, give him time, and he would use it to do everything in his power to convince her to stay.

"Stop!"

Gaharet froze.

Ulrik came to stand beside him. "Can you smell that?"

Gaharet lifted his nose to the breeze. Pine, damp forest and earth and yet... He sniffed again. Faint, beneath the wet wood scent, a hint of a familiar and deadly floral note. He nodded, raising his sword.

"Erin, go into the trees. Stay out of sight."

Her face paled, and she retreated, hiding behind a large beech tree.

"Wolfsbane?" Ulrik drew his sword, eyes scanning from left to right.

Gaharet nodded. "Wolfsbane." The curse of his kind. No wonder those they had lost were half-shifted when they died.

He scanned the clearing. At first, he saw nothing. Then his eyes picked out a ring of disturbed grass. He edged closer. His knuckles rippled, coarse hair sprouted and his hand began changing without him willing it. He jerked back, and the shift halted, reversing until his hand returned to human.

L'enfer. He could not see the wolfsbane, but it was there. Hidden amongst the meadow grass and flowers, it formed a tight circle in the middle of the clearing. In high concentrations, too. Stepping into that circle would make him weak, unable to escape and unable to fight. Unable to solidify a form—human or wolf. Clever. Diabolical. Already heart sore, the betrayal cut deep. Wolfsbane. How could they?

"You were right to suspect betrayal. Someone has been talking," said Ulrik.

"Yes." Gaharet gritted his teeth. "Lothair and Renaud know about the amulets, too."

Ulrik gaped at him. "The amulets?"

"Yes," he said, his gaze never leaving Ulrik's face. "Renaud has an informant. For him to know of the amulets, and now wolfsbane, it has to be one of us."

Ulrik snarled. "How could one of our own do this? So many have died—children, women, family—for what?"

Gaharet did not answer him.

Ulrik stiffened. "You think it is me? That I have done...*this*?" He shook his head. "No, Gaharet. You and I have had our disagreements, but I would never betray the pack. *Never.* I know what it is like to lose my whole family. You know that. I would not wish that on anyone. This" — he pointed to the ring of wolfsbane — "I vow to you, is not of my doing."

Gaharet could detect no lie in Ulrik's words. If not Ulrik, then who?

A scream split the night air.

"Erin." He spun around, fear twisting his gut. A man in mismatched armor dragged her into the clearing.

"Get your hands off me! Let me go!"

Erin fought him, striking out with her feet and her hands, twisting in his grip.

"Be still, woman, or I will stick you with this."

The man wrapped an arm around her waist, pressing a dagger to her side. The blood drained from Erin's face, and she looked to him to help her.

A mercenary had his Erin, his mate. His blood boiled, his vision blurred and the urge to change, to tear the man apart, ripped through him.

"Keep calm, Gaharet." Ulrik's voice of reason punctured his fury, his fear. "We need to keep him out of that ring of wolfsbane."

The mercenary grinned, his mouth full of broken, yellow teeth, his gaze shifting a few feet beyond them. "Stop me if you can."

Gaharet risked a glance over his shoulder. More men were advancing from the cover of the trees — six, seven, eight of them, their armor poor, but their weapons still sharp. *Merde.*

His beast prowled within, clamoring to get out. It screeched for blood. He forced it down. Changing now would only leave him caught up in the constraints of his mail. He must stay in control. Keep his head. For her. He would not let his mate die.

Ulrik turned and faced the men. "It seems wolfsbane is more powerful than we realized. I did not smell or hear them at all."

Neither had he. He had not sensed their approach. No hint of their movements through the long grass had alerted him to their presence. He was as weak as any human, his senses more addled than he thought possible. Senses he had always relied on. That had never failed him in all his thirty-five years. Being caught off guard unnerved him. Even so, these mercenaries were no match for them. With their superior weaponry and experience, even with their abilities blunted, they out-classed these men. *If* he could keep a clear head. He would kill every one of them to save Erin.

He descended on the men, unleashing his fear for her, and his rage at being betrayed, upon the poorly trained and ill-equipped men. It was not a fight, but a slaughter. Gaharet felt no release as he cut down mercenary after mercenary, deflecting their blows with ease. In the periphery of his vision, he saw Ulrik killing as many of the rabble as he did, but he could not prevent the one mercenary from dragging Erin into the circle of that damned herb.

As he separated the last mercenary's head from his shoulders, blood spurting, the body dropping with a thud, Gaharet turned his focus to the single mercenary still standing. The man grinned, though his eyes darted about wildly, his grip on Erin tightening.

"Going to come and get her?" he said, taunting them, secure within the ring of herbs.

Gaharet snarled. "The only way you get to live is by sending her out to us while you remain safe inside your little circle of herbs."

"I suggest you bring her here," said Ulrik growling, flecks of blood, not his own, spattered across his face. "If we have to come in and get her, you are a dead man."

The mercenary chuckled. "I do not think so. I am getting well paid to deliver you up to Comte Lothair, and I have what you want. You either step into the circle" — he motioned at Gaharet — "or I kill her."

Gaharet growled, an inhuman sound coming from his very human throat.

"I might just kill her, anyway. Such a shame. Pretty little thing." He turned his head into her cheek and licked her face.

Erin recoiled. She whimpered, and the sound tore at him, his fear nearly driving him to his knees.

"Good girl. Show him how scared you are." The mercenary pressed the knife in harder, and Erin let out a sob. "Convince him to come and save you."

Ulrik placed a hand on his shoulder. "Gaharet, do not do it. Do not listen to him. There has to be another way. You are no good to us dead. Think of the pack."

Gaharet snarled. "Since when have you ever followed that creed?"

"I know. But you were right back then, and I was wrong. You stopped me from doing something that would have destroyed us all." Ulrik stepped in front of him, his chin raised, his face determined, blocking him from the mercenary. "And now I am going to stop you. I am sorry. I cannot let you do this."

"I do not have all night!" The mercenary tilted his head, listening, then threw back his head and laughed. "And neither do you."

A chill raced down Gaharet's spine. He heard it, too. The pounding of hooves heading their way. Close. Too close. They were running out of time.

He shifted his gaze to Ulrik. "I have lost my mother, my father, my brother and my closest friend. I will not lose her too."

"If you step into that circle, you will put yourself at Lothair's mercy. You know what he wants."

"I would never give Lothair what he wants."

"Then he will kill you."

Gaharet stared past Ulrik at Erin, her body trembling. How had he ever, even for a moment, thought he would not follow her? That he would put the pack before her? She was his mate and he would sacrifice *everything* for her.

"She is my mate, Ulrik." His gaze locked with Erin's. "I would die for her."

"No." Ulrik placed a palm against his chest. "We will find another way."

The mercenary sneered. "There is no other way. Not if you want to save her." He drew his arm back and plunged the knife into Erin's side.

Gaharet's world went still. Erin gasped, a tortured moan slipping from her lips. He roared, launching himself toward his mate, white hot rage burning through him. Ulrik slammed into him, knocking him to the ground. He howled, his pain and fury consuming him as Erin collapsed, gasping for breath, clutching her bloodstained side.

"Nooooo!"

Chapter Thirty-One

Held to the ground by Ulrik, Gaharet could only watch on as the mercenary dragged his knife free, holding the bloodied blade aloft, grinning in triumph.

"I am going to kill you this time." His voice cracked, and he fought against Ulrik's hold. His Erin lay dying.

"Despite what you think, you never lost me, Gaharet. I was always your friend."

The weight lifted from his body and Ulrik charged into the ring of wolfsbane, his sword raised. With a brutal overhand swing, he cleaved the man in two.

Ulrik dropped to his knees, his sword slipping from his fingers, coarse, sandy hair sprouting across his hands and his jaw extending. Shaking his head, his wolf disappeared, and he lifted Erin in his arms and attempted to rise. Stumbling, his head shifted to wolf, then back again. The wolfsbane had a hold of his body—his lack of control an unimaginable horror.

He struggled to his feet, then collapsed, dropping Erin. She moaned and Gaharet's heart squeezed.

Ulrik's spine, hips and legs shifted to wolf, held for a moment then changed back again. He pushed up to his knees, sweat beading on his forehead.

"Ulrik, roll her to me."

Ulrik's face contorted, his hauberk hanging loose about his shifting shoulders. He crawled to Erin and gave her a mighty shove. Erin tumbled through the grass, her arms landing beyond the herbs. Gaharet reached for her hand, coarse, dark hairs sprouting on the back of his arm, and he wrenched her to him, stepping clear of the danger.

He stared down at his mate's pale face, fear for her stealing all the breath from his lungs. He brushed the hair back from her brow with a gentle hand. "I am so sorry, Erin. There is no other choice. I cannot let you die."

Hovering over her, Gaharet called forth his wolf, dark hair sprouting across his face, his snout forming and his canines extending. Opening his jaw, he latched onto her wound. Erin screamed as his teeth bit in. He wanted to howl, to roar his pain, and hers, to the night sky, but he held on and kept his teeth sunk deep into her flesh.

As his saliva mixed with her blood, her body shuddered, a violent, uncontrolled spasm rippling through her. Releasing her, he pushed his wolf away, shifting back to human. It had begun. She would turn or she would die turning. A dull ache settled in his chest, and he dropped his head in his hands. This was not how he would have wished it to be, turning her like this, but there was no other way to save her. Picking her up, he cradled her in his arms, holding her shuddering body tight against his chest.

"Hold on, Erin."

"It hurts. It *burns*." She moaned, twitching in his arms.

Gaharet ached to take away her pain, her fear. "Stay with me, *ma petite pouliche*."

Unintelligible words spilled from her mouth. He must get her away from here, take her somewhere safe.

Ulrik uttered a guttural groan, collapsing onto his stomach, his breathing ragged and shallow, struggling to maintain one form or the other.

"Ulrik, can you crawl beyond the wolfsbane?"

Ulrik shook his shaggy wolf's head, his body shuddering as he partially shifted, his upper torso wolf, his lower half human. His body shifted to human again, and he dragged himself up onto his knees, reaching beneath his armor. He wrenched off his amulet, tossing it at Gaharet's feet.

"Throw me yours. If they think you are dead, they will stop hunting you."

He shifted again, his tunic ripping, his hauberk restricting his shoulders. His groan turned into a growl, his jaw shifting, his canine's extending before his bones slipped back into place and he was human again. He sagged to the ground, his chest heaving with the effort to maintain control.

"All the pack knows of our struggle. If I say I attacked you, they are likely to believe it. Take your mate, hide her and unearth this betrayer."

With care, Gaharet placed Erin's shuddering body against a tree and removed his amulet from around his neck. He held it in his hand, staring at the bloodstone. Ulrik had once challenged him for this, and now he was preparing to give it to him. He clutched it tight against his palm. The Ulrik he had once known would never betray them. The Ulrik he had called friend would leap to the aid of a woman without a second thought. Tonight, Ulrik had sacrificed himself for the good of the pack. For him. For Erin. He truly was his friend, as he had once been. Gaharet owed him everything.

He tossed the binding amulet at Ulrik.

Picking up Ulrik's, he stared at the plain gold piece. Where he once saw a dark red stone, now he saw script. Like the one Erin had found in the underground cell. She would be upset if she knew. He turned to her, slumped against the tree, her dress stained with her blood, her face flushed and tremors racking her body.

Coating his hand in the dead mercenary's blood, Ulrik smeared it across his mouth and down his throat. His body shifted to wolf and back again. He groaned, clutching at the ground.

"Go, Gaharet. Before it is too late. Take her to the witch in the woods."

Gaharet nodded. The horses were almost upon them. He doubted the one who betrayed them would be among the riders. No werewolf would willingly come this close to wolfsbane, but Gaharet did not want to take that risk. He wanted to be well down wind to avoid detection.

Slipping the amulet over his head, he scooped up Erin. With one last look at Ulrik collapsed on the ground, his body rippling beneath his mail with another shift, Gaharet left his friend behind and slipped into the trees.

* * * *

Lothair cantered into the clearing with two score of mounted guards at his back, their weapons drawn in expectation of conflict. Behind him rode Archeveque

Renaud, flanked by his own men—mercenaries. He reined in his horse and stared at the bloody clearing. He counted. Nine dead mercenaries. And Ulrik Voclain, on his knees, clutching his sword, his head hanging low.

"Well, Renaud," he said, swinging out of the saddle, striding toward the chevalier. "Your little herb seems to have caught us a werewolf. The wrong one."

Renaud barked orders and two of his men stepped past him, lifted Ulrik's head by the hair and kicked his sword out of his grasp as he attempted to swing it. As Lothair stared at the chevalier, contemplating his next move, Ulrik grimaced and his body contorted. Popping and cracking sounds accompanied the sudden appearance of sandy fur across his face. A muzzle formed and Ulrik's legs shrank, his breeches swamping him. Right before his eyes man became wolf. A very large wolf.

Lothair took a step back. "Now that is something I never thought I would see."

Renaud came to stand beside him. "Wait until his body is completely human again," he said to his men. "Then put the silver shackles on him quickly, before he can reach for the amulet."

No more than a moment passed, and the fur receded, the breeches filling out, and once again a human male knelt before him. One of Renaud's men snapped a silver manacle around Ulrik's neck. Ulrik howled and pulled at the shackle with his hands. He hissed as a mercenary clamped shackles around his wrists. They released his hair, and he slumped to the ground. Around the edge of the silver, a redness spread, blisters forming in its wake. Lothair leaned closer to get a better look. Interesting.

"Is silver going to be strong enough to hold him?"

Renaud smirked. "It does not need to be strong, Mon Seigneur Comte. It only needs to be silver. The metal itself will do all the work. He is helpless against it. Voclain could not break it if he tried. He cannot even shift into his wolf form now, even with the wolfsbane affecting him."

"That is comforting to know. I have never seen a wolf this big. He's enormous." He nudged Ulrik with his boot. "Where is Gaharet?"

"Dead."

Muffled, and muttered into the ground, the word was barely intelligible.

"Really? I see a lot of dead bodies here, but none of them are Gaharet's. This rabble would have been no challenge for him." He grasped Ulrik's hair, jerking him to his knees. "I will ask you again. Where is Gaharet?"

"He is dead."

Louder and clearer this time.

Ulrik chuckled. "I killed him. I finally bested him. It has only taken me a decade." Groaning, his shoulders slumped.

Renaud stepped closer. "I have been told Voclain once challenged d'Louncrais for the leadership of the pack. He failed the first time, but... D'Louncrais *was* vulnerable with the woman. I believe they fight in their other form, try to rip each other's throats out. Barbaric."

Leaning forward, Renaud pulled open Ulrik's torn tunic, pushing the shackle out of the way to reveal scars lacerated across his throat.

Ulrik hissed, silver touching a fresh patch of skin, then he spat at them, a mixture of blood and saliva.

"Charming." Lothair stepped back, studying the chevalier — the blood around his mouth and the scars on his throat. He snapped the amulet from around Ulrik's neck. Letting Ulrik go, he held it up. "I finally get to see one of these things."

Renaud's eyes lit up. "*That* is no ordinary amulet. Interesting. The inscription they recite mentions a bloodstone. This must be it." Renaud's eyes narrowed. "I imagine such an amulet would only be in the hands of the alpha. It appears Voclain is telling the truth. D'Louncrais *is* dead."

Lothair's gaze narrowed at Renaud's satisfied smirk.

"Very well, then. If we have the new alpha, let us get him back to the keep."

He beckoned two of his keep guard, who stepped in, lifting Ulrik up under his arms, dragging him away.

"You may return to the keep, Renaud. I will send for you when I return."

"Mon Seigneur Comte?"

"Leave, Renaud. I need a moment to think." He turned his back, dismissing the archeveque.

"Of course, Mon Seigneur." Renaud retreated. "I will await your summons upon your return."

Lothair paced within the circle of wolfsbane, staring at the ground until the jingle of harnesses and the pounding of hooves dwindled in the distance. He paused, and lifted his head, peering into the forest, searching for his vassal. Unlike Renaud, he was not so gullible as to believe the words of Ulrik Voclain. Not when the evidence in the clearing suggested otherwise.

"Gaharet," he called out, his voice carrying on the night air. "I know you are not dead, Gaharet. You may have fooled Renaud, but you have not fooled me." He swung the amulet about as he talked. "Ulrik is an impressive fighter, but he is no match for you. He is too impulsive and has too much of a temper."

He stared into the gloom between the trees, his gaze darting from shadow to shadow. Was it foolish to believe Gaharet was nearby? Watching. Listening.

"Either way, you have given up the pack. Now Ulrik can give me what I want."

Not a sound greeted his ears. Not the hooting of an owl, or the scratching of rodents. It unnerved him, and he settled his hand on the pommel of his sword. Should he draw it? Was he at risk of Gaharet attacking him? He did not think so. He stood in the middle of a ring of wolfsbane that had already taken down one werewolf tonight. That gave him all the protection he needed. And he was as good a swordsman as Gaharet. He dropped his hand from his sword, annoyed at his moment of weakness.

"You were right, Gaharet." He huffed. "You are always right. And I should have listened to you. Renaud is up to something, and he caught us…me…unprepared. Divide and conquer. That is his game. A good strategy. It could work. If we let it."

He peered into the gloom between the trees. Nothing. Damn it.

"You were always better at keeping Renaud in check. I think that is why he needed you out of the way." He chuckled. "He is after me, you know. Think of the notoriety, the advancement he will achieve for bringing me to my knees. The comte the church loves to hate."

A soft breeze rustled through the trees, but all else remained quiet.

"Well, it has been nice chatting with you again. You have proved you can get out of my keep without detection. I suspect you can as easily get into it unseen when you are ready to talk. Just talk. Do me a favor. Do not leave it too long."

He turned to leave, and a shadow shifted amongst the trees. He halted. Gaharet stepped out of the shadows and into his line of sight, cradling his betrothed in his arms. Lothair stood his ground, making no move toward his sword. He needed Gaharet and if tonight had shown him anything, Gaharet needed him, too. With a simple nod, Gaharet turned and disappeared into the forest.

Lothair smiled. Once again, they were a team thwarting that weasel Renaud. Gathering his reins, he mounted, turning his horse toward the keep. He glanced down at the amulet in his hand. He would have these werewolves under control. They would do his bidding. He was their comte, God damn it. They belonged to him.

* * * *

Unseen by all, a white, blue-eyed wolf lay hidden among the trees, belly to the ground. The news Gaharet was dead had sucked the wind from his lungs. He could not believe it. Did not want to believe it. Not Gaharet. He had wanted to howl his grief, force his way into the clearing and savage Ulrik for what he had done. Selfish, conniving wolf. How could he have sunk this low? But the bloodstone did not lie. And yet...

The clearing, rank with death, confused his senses. Or was it this wolfsbane they spoke of? From Ulrik's condition, he could well believe it possible. Gaharet had, at one point, been in the clearing, but had he died here? Lothair, it seemed, was no more convinced by Ulrik's confession than he.

Bewildered, uncertain, Aimon moved to slink away, go somewhere quiet and safe and try to make sense of it all, when a shadow moved amongst the trees. His relief, when Gaharet stepped forward, all but knocked his legs out from under him. As quick as he had appeared, Gaharet was gone, disappearing amongst the trees. Giving the clearing and the wolfsbane a wide berth, Aimon trotted after him.

Chapter Thirty-Two

When Gaharet stumbled upon the little, wooden cottage deep in the forest, he was near exhaustion. Carrying Erin in his arms for leagues had tested even his strength. He had stopped periodically, settling and soothing her as she slipped deeper into the turning. Her shuddering had increased, and her moaning had gotten louder. At one point she had struggled against him so much he had come close to dropping her. With some relief, but also trepidation, he approached the cottage.

He had found it, heading due east from the clearing, courtesy of his sensitive nose, the wolfsbane's impact lessening the more leagues he traveled. A curl of smoke puffed from the chimney, but the overall scent was one of herbs, some pleasant, some not so. That he remained in human form the closer he got convinced him of the absence of wolfsbane.

The door opened before he could knock, and a small woman stood in the doorway. Uncertain of what he had expected, this young, somewhat pretty woman with startling eyes—one blue, one green—did not fit with his idea of a healer or witch.

"I have been expecting you."

Her soft voice welcomed him, and she stepped aside so he could enter. Small, but warm and brightly lit, shelves laden with jars of powders, herbs, rocks, crystals and things he could not recognize lined the cottage walls. On the table, a large book lay open. The smell, more pungent in close quarters, came from a large pot over the fire, and he wrinkled his nose in distaste.

"Put her over there." The woman motioned to a small cot by a shuttered window, and Gaharet complied as she moved to stir the concoction in the pot.

"You were expecting me?"

She smiled, nodding, the hint of disappointment that flashed in her eyes gone before he had a chance to wonder at its cause.

"You know who I am? What I am?" He knelt beside Erin, brushing his hand across her forehead. She was burning up, and he was loath to leave her side. Gaharet had no sense they were in any danger, but he did not know this woman or what she might be capable of.

"You are d'Louncrais," she said. "The Black Wolf. We knew, in time, you would come back to us, that you would need us again. That is why my family has always stayed close to Langeais Keep." Ladling liquid from the pot into a bowl, she brought it over to him. "When members of your pack approached me for hemlock, I sensed you would soon seek me out." Reaching up, she touched the amulet that lay against his chest. "Centuries ago, your kind came to us for help, and we provided these."

"You have knowledge of the amulets?" He never expected to feel such conflicting emotions upon finding the ones he sought—elation that help was nigh, but dread that it could only hasten Erin's departure.

"Oh, yes." She frowned. "You did not know of our connection? Of your origins?"

Gaharet shook his head. "Our origins? You know this?"

She nodded. "You must have many questions, but first we must tend to her." Her smile softened, and she laid a gentle touch on his shoulder. "Fear not, Black Wolf. While her mind is in turmoil, her heart is not."

Erin moaned, a shudder rippling through her body.

The woman rested a hand on Erin's forehead. "The fever has started. It will not be easy, not with the added complication of this wound, but I sense she is strong. And she has you. Here." She handed him the bowl. "You will need to get her to take it. Just wet her lips with it. Anything you can get her to swallow will help."

"Hemlock?"

"Plus a few other herbs." She squeezed his arm. "I will make a poultice for the wound. She will have a scar, but it will heal."

Nodding, grateful, Gaharet returned his attention to Erin. Dipping the spoon in, he raised it to her lips, dribbling small amounts into her parted mouth. There was no going back now.

* * * *

Watching Gaharet enter the little cottage, Aimon sat down to wait, to watch and to guard. The door swung open and standing in the doorways was not Gaharet, but a young peasant woman. Could this be the witch that Aubert and Edmond spoke of? He had envisioned an old crone. She came toward him on quiet feet, and he slunk down low in the long grass.

Stopping a few yards away, she looked straight at him. "I know you are there, wolf," she called out. "There is no point hiding. I have come to tell you your alpha is well, as will his mate be in time."

Aimon popped his head up. How had she known he was even there? He sniffed the air. She was human, not wolf. Perhaps being a witch gave her extra abilities.

"Strange he has not the bloodstone amulet in his possession." She frowned, her eyes going unfocused. "Ah, the friend who was no longer is a friend again." Her gaze sharpened, boring into him. "Heed my words, wolf. That which was thought lost you will find. Hidden in plain sight, it is time for its presence to be felt. Guard it well and the reward shall be yours."

Aimon shook his furry white head. The woman spoke in riddles.

She smiled at him. "You are welcome to stay. Guard your alpha if it pleases you. He is caring for his mate. Her injury has forced the turning, but I will inform him of your presence."

She re-entered the cottage. The door closed behind her, and Aimon was once again alone. He scowled at the closed door. He planned on staying, whether he had her permission or not. He had no intention of leaving Gaharet unguarded.

Aimon rested his head on his paws, settling in for the long wait. His turning had taken three days — a blur of pain, heat, cold, thirst and hunger — but with the witch's help, perhaps Erin's transition would be easier. He hoped so. For Erin and for Gaharet.

Gaharet had saved his life, so Aimon would stay here, however long it took. Aimon owed Gaharet everything and he would stand by him until the end. Gaharet would always be his alpha, no matter who held the bloodstone amulet. Ulrik be damned.

Chapter Thirty-Three

Erin's eyelids flickered, but they didn't open. Her body burning, her muscles cramping, she slipped in and out of consciousness, lost in terrifying visions of a man with broken, yellow teeth, a dagger pressed against her side, of chevaliers, armor, blood and death. She cried out, but no one heard her, the sound echoing only in her mind. She fought to wake up, a moan slipping from her throat, but she could not surface, forced to replay the one scene over and over again. The stabbing pain in her side, rough arms releasing her, Gaharet's anguished cry as she fell. The torment on Gaharet's face as her eyes grew heavy, and her body cold. He'd said he would die for her, and she'd never even told him she loved him.

She broke the surface of her dreams briefly, as warm, bitter liquid dribbled into her parched mouth.

"Water," she croaked. None was forthcoming, only more of the same. She sank back under, a vision of a black wolf leaning over her, jaws clamping down on her wounded side. Erin opened her mouth to scream, but no sound came out and she watched, helpless to stop him, unable to break free of the wolf, the dream or the heaviness in her body. She burned, she froze, icy needles pierced her skin and her blood boiled in her veins.

She slipped away into blessed blackness, and when she surfaced again, slivers of something wet, juicy and raw slipped between her lips. She wanted to refuse it, spit it out, but when its metallic scent hit her nostrils, an alarming hunger consumed her and she swallowed it greedily, opening her mouth for more. Gentle hands fed her, dripped bitter liquid into her mouth and washed her face and neck with a cool, wet cloth.

She settled into a restless sleep. All the while, a comforting presence sat by her, holding her hand, talking to her, telling her she was strong, that she would make it through, that he loved her, that he could not lose her.

She'd no clue how long she'd been out when she finally awoke, the vestiges of nightmarish visions fading and her eyelids fluttering open. She lay on a cot, covered in blankets, wearing nothing but her bra and panties. Staring up at a smoke hole in a peaked, thatched roof, she tried to get her bearings. She rolled her head to the side and her heavy-lidded eyes took in her surroundings. A smoky hazed room, wattle and daub walls, a fire pit in the center and a familiar dark-headed figure sitting at the table, his back to her. Gaharet.

She closed her eyes. In the clearing, he'd fought to save her. Killed five men with brutal efficiency. And he'd been about to come for her, to take down the man who'd grabbed her from behind and dragged her into the clearing. She didn't understand why some herbs thrown about were so dangerous, but they were, and Gaharet had been willing to risk his freedom, his life, by stepping into the ring they had created. For her.

Somewhere, there was a witch who knew how to reverse the spell on the amulet. A spell that could take her back to her world, her life and her career. Take her away from this man and the possibility of a love so strong they'd make their own wall hanging as a testament to it. Could she walk away from that? Walk away from this intriguing, wonderful, sexy man and all they'd shared? A wave of emptiness washed over her. Would she ever recover from the loss? Or would she, as her mother was, doom herself to forever search for a replacement that would never fill that void?

She opened her eyes again, staring at his back, the low rumble of his voice sinking into her heart, her mind and her bones. With perfect clarity, she finally understood why her mother was so willing to throw everything away for the chance of such a love. She wanted that chance, hungered for it with every fiber of her being.

"Gaharet." With her mouth so dry and her throat parched, she barely made a sound, but his dark head turned.

"Erin, you are awake."

He rushed over, lowering himself to sit beside her on the cot. She rose, put her arms around his neck, and he pulled her into his embrace. She nestled against him, pressing her face into his shoulder. His strong musky scent filled her nostrils, the steady rhythm of his heartbeat loud in her ear. She did not need to go anywhere, to leave. This was home. *He* was home.

"I thought I had lost you." He brushed her hair from her face, planting a soft kiss on her forehead. "I have never felt such fear in my life." He put a gentle hand on her forehead. "Your fever has broken."

A woman, a gentle smile on her face, approached and handed her a mug. "Here, you will be thirsty."

Erin took the mug and drank, gulping it down.

"Steady now. Small sips." He took it from her. "How do you feel?"

She frowned. "I don't know." She put her hand to her side where the mercenary had stabbed her, feeling a wad of fabric, some type of dressing. "How long have I been unconscious?"

"Three days."

Three days! With a stab wound to the gut from a dagger of indeterminate cleanliness? And no antibiotics? She should be dead. With no analgesics, she should also be in pain. But she wasn't. She pulled away from him and peeked beneath the covers, peeling off some sort of poultice.

What the hell?

No wound, no stitches, not even a slight reddening of the skin. A thin line of scaring, flanked on either side by four smaller round scars, the only evidence of a wound at all. And just three days ago. It must be some miracle poultice.

She fingered the thin line of scarring. That was the knife wound. She touched the other scars, remembering. The black wolf.

"You bit me. Why? That man stabbed me, and you turned into a wolf and bit me."

"Erin," said Gaharet, his voice soft. "You were *dying*. I had no choice. I did the one thing that could save you."

He gave her a moment to let his words sink in.

"You bit me to..." Her voice trailed off, her eyes widening. "Am I...?" She rubbed her hands over her body. Did she feel different? No. Yes. Maybe. She looked around the room, at Gaharet, at her body. Everything seemed brighter, clearer. Scents seemed stronger—the smoke from the fire, the herbal stench coming from a large pot. She wrinkled her nose and focused elsewhere, further away. Damp earth from outside, the hint of moisture in the dew, and the pine of the forest—she could smell them all. And her hearing was sharper, picking up things she shouldn't be able to hear. The crawl of an insect on the floor across the room, the scratch of a rodent in the forest, and the rhythm of her own heart, beating a little faster than it should be. And hers wasn't the only heart she could hear. The woman's across the room, slow and measured, and Gaharet's too. Reaching out, she placed a hand on Gaharet's chest, the strong rhythm pounding against her palm even as she heard it with her ears.

He took her hands in his. "Believe me, Erin, in any other circumstances, I would have given you a choice. After..." His Adam's apple bobbed up and down. "After you declared your intention to return home... But you were dying."

She rested her hand over her scar. "Is that why I healed so fast? Why there is only a scar when I should still have a wound?"

He nodded, brushing his hand against her cheek. "All will be well, Erin. It will take some time for you to adjust, but I will help you. I will train you to use your wolf. When I am sure you have control—" he looked over to the woman, standing by the fire stirring a large pot—"we will discuss again your desire to leave." He dropped his hand to her shoulder and gave it a gentle squeeze.

She glanced at the woman disappearing out through the door, at the jars of herbs and powders and at the large pot bubbling over the fire. "You brought me to the witch?"

"It is her herbal concoction that helped you through the turning, and once you are strong enough —"

Erin pressed her lips against his, cutting him off. He went still, searching her face, a spark of hope flickering in his eyes.

"I thought I could leave you, but I can't." She drew in a deep breath. "I love you, Gaharet."

A tremor ran through his body. "Are you certain, Erin? You will not regret leaving your life, everything you know and love? Your job?"

"I shall miss it, and there will be times I will long for the things I can't have here, but I don't want to wonder what could've been. Regret a chance not taken. I want to *know*."

His lips curled into a smile, and he pulled her to him, taking her mouth in his, going deep. Erin moaned against his mouth, desire roaring to life, the heightened sensation of his lips on hers and his musky scent, all making her heart race. She growled deep in her throat.

Startled, she broke off their kiss, her hand going to her throat.

"Did I...? Was that me?"

Gaharet chuckled. "All of your senses are heightened now." He raised an eyebrow at her. "Care to test them?"

He slid his hand beneath the covers, his touch against her skin, his hand trailing up her stomach, sending waves of desire pulsing through her so strong she thought might faint from the intensity of it. She growled again.

"I will take that as a yes." His hand cupped her breast. "Welcome to the pack, Dame d'Louncrais. My mate, my love."

Then he claimed her mouth, and she surrendered to him, to her desire, and her new life. Whatever the future held in store for her, she would face it with him by her side. With her knowledge of the past and his understanding of the present, she would change his fate, just as he'd changed hers.

* * * *

Gaharet lay staring up at the thatched roof, worry for Ulrik and his men roiling in his gut. The coals in the fire had burned down, giving the room a soft glow. Beside him, snuggled into his side and sleeping soundly, her blonde hair splayed across his shoulder, lay Erin. He still had much to tell her. What had happened to Ulrik, how they had swapped the amulets and how he had revealed his presence to Lothair. He squeezed her closer, and she murmured, protesting in her sleep. He let his arm relax, and she settled. Tomorrow. He would tell her tomorrow. For now, he would enjoy holding his mate in his arms. She was his. She had chosen to stay and be his wife. He planned to have her by his side for the rest of his very long life. Lothair, Renaud and her history be damned.

**Want to see more from this author?
Here's a taster for you to enjoy!**

The Wolves of Langeais:
Wolf's Prize
K.E. Turner

Coming February 2024

Excerpt

If the scuff of her boots on the road matched the pace of her thundering heart, Kathryn Beauchene would complete the short walk to Langeais Keep in record time. Instead, she dragged her feet, her father beside her, his arm slipped through hers. Summoned by the Comte de Anjou! Nothing good could come of that.

"Are you tired, Kathryn? Did you not sleep well?" Her father's concerned gaze focused on her.

She smiled, patting him on the arm. "Just the usual nightmare, Father."

"Again? They seem to be increasing. You have not had so many in a row for several years now. Not since…" His jaw clenched. "Was it the same one?"

Kathryn avoided her father's eyes. "Always."

The scar on her arm burned, and she resisted the urge to rub it. It remained a constant reminder of the attack, of the darkness that now resided within her, finding release only in her sleep. For eleven years, the same nightmare had plagued her — a clearing, a pond, a woman with red hair and a man, but not a man. A man with no face, who morphed into a terrifying combination of man and wolf, fangs and fur. Snarling, snapping, it came for her, again and again and, without fail, her body would refuse to move.

Eleven years and it had never deviated. Not once. Until last night. With eyes the color of blue flame, chevalier Aimon Proulx, looking like one of God's warrior angels, had invaded her nightmare. Long, white-blond hair loose about his shoulders, his blue surcoat with its white dove insignia rustling in the breeze and his hand on the pommel of his sword — he'd drawn her to him, made her heart race and her body quiver.

She had awoken this morning feverish, with a desperate longing for Aimon Proulx. Her body thrummed with remembered heat. She blew out a breath. Aimon had occupied her waking thoughts a lot of late. She could only presume that to be the reason for his presence in her nightmare, but it unnerved her all the same. Most likely, she was one of many young women who dreamed of Aimon Proulx, but only *her* dreams contained monsters.

"Do you know why Comte Lothair has summoned us, Father?"

Farren Beauchene shrugged his shoulders. "I do not. They gave me no indication as to the nature of the comte's request. It is most likely a minor matter." His frown betrayed his true thoughts. Her father was worried.

"Perhaps it has something to do with Mademoiselle Erin Richardson."

They passed through the gate into the outer bailey, dodging a chevalier on horseback as they joined the crowd of people making their way to the keep hall. The comte would hear all public matters today, and the outer bailey had begun to fill with people—peasants, merchants, farmers, chevaliers and nobleman. Most would wait in line to petition the comte. Some, like Kathryn and her father, were responding to his summons. She spied Manette Chapet with her two friends, Odila and Lisette. She scowled. They had come for the spectacle, the chance to gossip and the opportunity to forge connections above their current station.

"Mademoiselle who?" Her father guided her around a group of farmers who had paused to discuss the likelihood of rain.

"Oh, Father, you must stay abreast of things. Mademoiselle Erin Richardson is all the talk in the keep."

He grunted. "I do not hold much for gossip. Too much trouble can come of it."

"I agree. You are lucky you do not have to endure hours of it like I must, but Erin Richardson is not gossip, Father. She is Gaharet d'Louncrais' newly betrothed."

"What? You say Gaharet d'Louncrais is taking a wife?"

They stepped aside for a Baron and his wife to pass.

"Yes, and a woman no one has ever heard of. Rumor has it, and it is purely rumor," she said, as they trudged up the hill towards the keep, "Comte Lothair is unimpressed. Gaharet did not consult him when choosing his bride to be."

Her father grunted again. "Gaharet is only *the* most powerful chevalier in this county. Lothair would want to be secure in Gaharet's allegiance. A bride not chosen by him, or at the very least vetted by him, would not have pleased the comte at all." He narrowed his eyes.

"His father did much the same when he wed your aunt, marrying a woman far beneath his station."

"He married her for love?"

Her father's gaze drifted away from her and over the people moving through the gate into the inner bailey. When he finally answered, his voice was soft and his eyes distant, caught up in his memories.

"Yes," he said. "I believe Jacques did marry Elise for love, God rest their souls. Much as I did with your mother. I guess some of us are born with that inclination."

Kathryn gave him a sad smile. Her father's stories, his memories, were the only things she had of her mother, and he infused his words with the depth of his love for his wife. He still missed her, even after all these years. Would that she could find a match such as her father, such as her aunt.

Her mind turned again to Aimon Proulx. She quashed the childish notion. She might fancy Aimon, but with a plethora of appealing options to choose from, would he even consider her? She had never fit society's expectations of a demure, proper lady. Less so since her attack. No self-respecting man would find those attributes appealing.

Still, Kathryn clung to her father's promise she could choose the man she wed. If she could not have love, then at the very least she would marry a man she did not despise. One she hoped would accept some of her wayward behavior.

"What would Gaharet's betrothed have to do with us?" her father asked, guiding her around a group of nervous young men waiting to be considered for training to become the comte's newest chevaliers.

"I met her in the keep this week past. She certainly brightened up the monotony of embroidering flowers and talking of the latest young man to pledge investiture." Kathryn rolled her eyes. She loathed those days. When she must behave as any well-bred daughter of a chevalier should. "I like her and I mentioned I would be very appreciative if she could put in a good word for me with Gaharet."

Her father jerked to a halt, pulling her out of the flow of people entering the keep. His brow furrowed as he rounded on her. "Why would you wish to do that?"

Kathryn raised her eyebrows at the gruffness in his voice. "Father, you may not have noticed, but I am not a little girl anymore. In a few months I will be a score and three years. I need to find a suitable match. People are beginning to talk."

"Yes, yes, I understand that. But how is it Gaharet can help with that? *Why* would you want Gaharet to help with that?"

"Apart from him being my cousin, and the most influential person in the county after the comte?"

Her father shook his head. "It is not wise to court attention from the d'Louncrais."

"Why ever not? Half the people in the court are vying for his attention. Why not us?" Her father would not meet her eyes. "Father, all Gaharet's men are unwed, and any of them would be a much better prospect than those who have indicated their interest in me. So far, most of my suitors are twice my age, fat, balding, mean, illiterate, unwashed or a combination of all the things I find abhorrent. Through Erin, I may have a chance to once again move in the same company as Gaharet and his vassals, perhaps secure the attention of one of them."

All Gaharet's vassals were a power unto themselves. No one questioned them or defied them. Would a wife of such a man be allowed certain liberties?

Her father's brow furrowed further. "It appears you have given this some thought, Kathryn. Have you set your sights on one of his vassals?"

Kathryn's cheeks heated. She had given the matter much consideration. Gaharet had six vassals — Lance, Ulrik, Godfrey, twins Aubert and Edmond, and Aimon Proulx. Lance was older than her father, despite looking no more than two score years, and he had a reputation for being stern and hard. He would want to discipline her and bring her under his rule. Definitely not an option.

Aubert and Edmond were huge with forbidding countenances. Not once had she witnessed a smile grace either of their faces, and they nary said a word that was not accompanied by a scowl. Kathryn found them rather intimidating. Ulrik had a reputation with the ladies, so Kathryn would steer clear of him, and Godfrey was a quiet, reserved, scholarly man. People often described her as willful and untamed. Not a good match. That left Aimon Proulx.

Like all Gaharet's men, he was as impressive physically as he was in his position in society. The second son of a Baron from an old, noble family, his reputation, unlike Ulrik's, was above reproach. Neither studious like Godfrey, stern like Lance, nor as unapproachable as the twins, he had an aversion to political intrigue and showed a fervent loyalty to Gaharet. If gossip were to be believed, Gaharet had saved his life.

Barely a few years older than her with bright blue eyes and a clean-shaven face, he set the hearts of many a young woman aflutter, including Kathryn's. That his presence made her thoughts jumble and her body tingle only added to his attraction. Whether his lack of a beard would signify better personal hygiene, Kathryn could not be certain, but it did appeal to her. Many of her would-be suitors had little familiarity with bathing. Sitting in the same room with them had been repugnant. Agreeing to wed them was out of the question. She could never marry a man she did not respect, and she could never respect a man whose stench made her stomach churn.

"I have to marry somebody, Father, despite my…" Kathryn cast her gaze around "…problem."

Problem? More a curse. The darkness within shifted, as if merely thinking of it roused it from its slumber. She forced it down.

Her father offered her a weak smile. "I know, but—"

"You wish to see me marry someone for love, like you and Mother." She gave him a wan smile. "Believe me, Father, I would like nothing more than to have what you and Mother had, but I must be realistic. The chances of that happening are not good. I must choose soon or risk the comte's attention." Her chest tightened. "Could this be why he has summoned us?"

Her father considered it. "It is possible, but unlikely. If, as you say, Gaharet has announced his betrothal to a woman the comte does not approve of, I think we would garner little attention by comparison."

"I hope you are right." Comte Lothair would not take her feelings into consideration when deciding who she should wed. Indeed, he would not care what she needed or wanted in a husband, nor would her father have any influence. "Marrying someone of Comte Lothair's choosing could prove disastrous."

Her father nodded, leading her into the hall. "Do not fear, Kathryn. We will find you a man you can trust and, with any luck, one you like."

A nervous flutter stirred in her stomach. She must marry, she had little other options, but she must also be careful. For should anyone find out her secret, should the church or the comte become aware of the beast she hid inside her, it would cost Kathryn her life.

About the Author

K.E Turner can't remember a time when she wasn't writing stories or reading books — as a teenager in class instead of doing math, in her lunch break at work, or at home when there's housework to be done. With a love of history, mystery, suspense, paranormal, and romance, she likes combining more than one element in her stories.

She writes spicy paranormal romances and romantic suspense, with strong but good hearted heroes, smart, sassy heroines and an often unexpected villain or two, to shake things up.

A Western Australian based author, she lives with her husband, two dogs, two cats and a menagerie of farm animals on their property in the southern region of the state. A hopeless romantic, she enjoys beach sunsets, sitting by the wood fire with a good book, and a nice shiraz.

K.E. Turner loves to hear from readers. You can find her contact information, website details and author profile page at https://www.totallybound.com

Home of Erotic Romance

Sign up for our newsletter and find out about all our romance book releases, eBook sales and promotions, sneak peeks and FREE romance books!